yolk

Other Books by Josip Novakovich

Apricots from Chernobyl
Fiction Writer's Workshop

yolk

short stories by

JOSIP NOVAKOVICH

GRAYWOLF PRESS

Saint Paul

Publication of this volume is made possible in part by a grant provided by the
Minnesota State Arts Board through an appropriation by the Minnesota State
Legislature, and by a grant from the National Endowment for the Arts. Signifi-
cant additional support has been provided by the Andrew W. Mellon Foundation, the Lila Wallace-Reader's Digest Fund, the McKnight Foundation, and
other generous contributions from foundations, corporations, and individuals.
Graywolf Press is a member agency of United Arts, Saint Paul. To these organi-
zations and individuals who make our work possible, we offer heartfelt thanks.

Published by Graywolf Press
2402 University Avenue, Suite 203
Saint Paul, Minnesota 55114
All rights reserved.

Printed in the United States of America.
ISBN 1-55597-229-2

2 4 6 8 9 7 5 3
First Graywolf Printing, 1995

Library of Congress Catalog Card Number 95-077951

Acknowledgments

The stories in this collection were originally published in the following:

American Way: "The Burning Clog," "Yahbo the Hawk," "Yolk"
Boulevard: "The Eye of God"
Chariton Review: "Petrol and Chocolate," "Raw Paper"
Chelsea: "The Address"
Epoch: "Dresden"
The European Magazine: "The Burning Clog"
Fiction: "A Drop of Cognac"
The Missouri Review: "Yolk"
New England Review: "Yahbo the Hawk"
New Virginia Review: "A Drop of Cognac"
Paris Review: "The Burning Clog," "Rust"
Ploughshares: "Apple" (Cohen Award)
Prairie Schooner: "Bricks"
The Pushcart Prize XV & XIX: "Rust," "Honey in the Carcase"
Southwest Review: "Hats and Veils"
The Sun: "Yahbo the Hawk," "Apple" (in a shortened version), "Hats and Veils"
The Threepenny Review: "Wool," "Darkened Vision," "Turkish Coffee," "Honey in the Carcase"

I would like to express my gratitude to the editors of the above journals with special thanks to Wendy Lesser, Richard Burgin, James Linville, and Bill Henderson.

And thanks to Gordon Thomas, Fiona McCrae, Janna Rademacher, Ian Morgan, and Anne Czarniecki, who helped me select and edit the stories; to Peter LaSalle and Bart Schneider, who identified my best themes; and to my wife, who read all my stories while they were in progress.

contents

For my son, Joseph Raphael
the great yolk-eater

The Burning Clog

My father's assistant Nenad used to tell me stories while hammering nails into the wood to pinch the leather so no water could leak into the clogs he was making. The hammer punctuated his stories like a gusle—the instrument of singers of tales—but more sharply, less melodiously.

Nenad told us about Prince Marko, who sucked his mother's breasts for seven years, and for seven more ate nothing but honey. Marko could squeeze water out of a log that had been dried for nine years. His horse could jump the length of nine lances and the height of three. On hot summer days, a hawk shaded him with its wings. Marko slew the giant Musa Kesejia, in whose breast, beneath three rib cages, were three hearts—the first working, the second dancing, and the third nesting a sleeping snake. When the snake awoke, the dead Musa leaped over the barren land.

Twenty years after Nenad had told his stories, I rushed to Weeping Willow, the village in Slavonia where he now worked by himself as a clog-maker. Where once horses ploughed the fields along a dirt road, now tractors oozed green oil in puddles along a paved highway. A cracked wooden shoe still hung from a pole on Nenad's whitewashed house to advertise his trade.

My entry startled Nenad. He quit working, and laughed for joy, then shook his head sadly. "Eh, my Yozzo, seven years have come and gone since we saw each other last."

After an hour of Nenad's talking, I interrupted him. "You are such a good talker. Do you mind if I record you?" From my shirt pocket, I pulled out a microcassette recorder I had bought in an electronics store in New York's Chinatown. Nenad's clear eyes looked at the cassette recorder as if it were a time bomb; his forehead showed its new creases, his graying eyebrows made tall arches, and he didn't talk until I turned off the machine.

"Nenad, where did you learn how to tell tales? At the hearth, on your grandfather's knee?"

"I went to the library to read stories, and then I told them from memory."

A myth fell apart right before my very ears.

"Of course," he said, "I added a thing here and there."

"But . . . I thought you were raised on oral tradition!"

"After every story you said, 'More! More!' So what could I do? I went to the library on lunch breaks to find more." He opened his calloused hands as if to show me that he hid no weapons in them.

I had thought that instead of attending a writing workshop back in the United States, I would simply listen to him for a couple of days and nights and find the formula for triggering a wellspring of storytelling in me, from our common ground. And now this.

"Still, who taught you how to tell stories? Grandmothers?"

"No. Why are you so stuck on this? It's easy to tell a story. You start right here, and lead the listener farther and farther away, or start from far away, and get us here."

"It's easy to say, but do it!" I said.

"Well, you have the beer mug in your hand. You give yourself a bit of time and go: A long time ago there was a beer mug, and it lived in a tavern. Of course, it was not the only mug living there. It lived with its twenty-three siblings. And many a dry lip . . . and off we go, see!"

"But how would you continue it?"

His wife nudged me to eat another walnut strudel with honey, though I must have had half a dozen already. I still wanted him to tell me a story, and I wouldn't let him give me a ride home until he did so, just as—though it's not worthy of such an archaic comparison—Jacob held fast to the Angel of God until obtaining a blessing.

"All right, I'll tell you as we drive," he said, and I followed him into his Fiat. We were silent while he cranked on the ignition. The forests and fields around the dark village breathed out damp and cool air straight into my nostrils.

"See that tall house? It rests on the foundations of our old house of baked clay."

I couldn't discern anything: it was so dark that all the sheep were black to me.

"At the beginning of the war, the Germans barged in there, seized my father and grandfather from the dinner table, and shot them to death against the barn.

"Several years later half a dozen Germans walked into our yard, and I had no time to run and hide in the woods, so I hid in bed and shivered under a thick goose-down cover. A pair of boots stamped over the floorboards toward me, louder and louder. The cover was pulled off and a huge soldier loomed over me. An 'Agkhh' broke out of my throat, my eyes bulged. The German lowered his hand, I thought to strangle me. Instead, he placed his cold palm on my forehead and held it there. Then he poured a glass of water from the bucket that was on the chair in the kitchen, put some white pills into the water, crushed them with a spoon, and pressed my lips with the edge of the glass against my teeth. I could hardly swallow. The liquid was shudderingly bitter—I thought it was poison, I would keel over and die. He took a paper sack out of his black leather bag—I guess he was a military doctor—and produced a honey cake. Where he'd got it I'll never know, but I am sure he hadn't baked it himself. He gave it to me, and I have never chewed anything sweeter before or since. He looked sternly at my mouth as if to make sure I was chewing. When I finished, he handed me another, and I chewed it slowly, savoring its honey. After swallowing the last of it, I wanted more, but didn't dare ask him with my voice or my hands. My eyes shifted in the direction of the paper sack.

"The German raised his forefinger and shook it sideways in front of my aching eyes, and said, 'Nein!' That was the only word spoken between us. He stood up and walked into the yard, his boots crunching gravel, less and less. He shouted something to the soldiers, and they all marched away, raising a screen of dust.

"Eh, my brother, you can't imagine how I felt right then. First he—for me it was the same German—kills my father, and then gives me the sweetest cakes I could ever have!"

"Hum" was all I could offer in the way of comment, and not through my mouth but through my nose.

When I visited Nenad a week later, he said, "I shouldn't have told you any war stories. Since then, almost every night I've been having nightmares. Would you like to help me gather our plums? Last night the wind shook them off the trees."

"Will you make plum brandy?" I asked, skeptical, since he was a pious Baptist.

"I'm afraid so—just to sell to taverns. The money's so short these days."

I put more plums into my mouth than into the basket because they tasted like pineapples. From nearby came a loud braying. I had never seen a donkey in the region, so I couldn't trust my ears and asked him what was making that noise.

"A donkey. Ten years ago a boy wanted a donkey and his father got him one from the coast. The boy grew up, his father and mother died, he went to the army and came back, and there he is, unmarried and living with his donkey. People say all sorts of things about him, but he is a good soul."

An old peasant walked by, galoshes flopping, on the way to Nenad's well. He turned the wheel and the rings of the chain crunched around the spindle. "By the way," the man shouted, noticing Nenad's mutt, who, with the courage of a fly, had just attacked a muffler-less truck on the road in front of us. "You should chain your dog."

"Why? The poor soul enjoys his freedom."

"Forget freedom. Yesterday he chased Petkovich's sheep into the creek—lucky thing he didn't drive them over the cliff. Hasn't Petkovich come over here to grumble yet?"

"No, Uncle Petar."

"Well, chain the bum if you don't want trouble."

As the old man carried his bucket away, tongues of water splashed left and right into the dust.

"He's been to America too," Nenad said. "You'd never be able to tell, looking at him."

"Well, can you tell such a thing? I'm sure you can't see any change in me."

"I can. You've got more of a swagger than before. You know, many people from Weeping Willow went to the States between the world wars." He counted them on his fingers, pointing to the houses obscured by trees, barns, and stacks of hay. He ran out of fingers, and started another round. "About half came back, not much better off than before. But Uncle Petar had won ten thousand dollars on horse races—at least that's what he said. I think he'd sold his lungs in Montana coal mines. Ten thousand dollars was a lot in the early fifties. Visiting home, here, he spent a thousand a day. If somebody wanted a bike, Uncle Petar bought him one. Radio sets, hats, ploughs, vodka, phonographs, sunglasses, guns—anything the peasants could think of, he bought them. People from other villages came and asked for presents. On Uncle's way out of the village a long procession accompanied him, longer than a doctor's funeral, longer than Tito's crew of Mercedes limos and military policemen on this road, paved just for Tito's visit. Two months later, Uncle Petar was back from America. He said he didn't want to work to buy presents. I think he feared those coal mines. Now he's one of the poorest people in the village."

The air was so clear—a powerful wind had blown the night before—that I could see to the south, over Nenad's wheat field, above the red roofs of a village on a hill, to a funeral procession with a horse-pulled hearse snaking its way up a dirt road, and beyond it, some fifty miles away, to the blue mountains of Bosnia, flattened like wet shirts on a drying line. To the east the approaching black clouds trapped the light from the setting sun, making the beech forest below radiant. We took baskets filled with blue plums into the workshop and placed them among wooden soles stacked in pillars near a round, wood-burning stove. "Does the stove look familiar?" he asked.

"Yes. It used to be in my father's workshop. In the winter the iron glowed red."

"I love that stove. But once in a while I look at it and get a fright. I see your dead father rubbing his hands above it. You know how strict your father was. One winter morning I heard his footsteps and just then I mis-hit a nail. The point of the nail poked through into the insole. I didn't want him to see my mistake, so I put the shoe into the stove.

"He comes in and says 'It's freezing!' He stamps the snow off his clogs on the dirt floor, rubs his blue hands, and dashes to the furnace. I freeze, my hand with the hammer up in the air, nails between my lips, like some worker's monument. He grabs a log, opens the furnace, and his arm stops. He leans his stubbly face almost all the way into the furnace, and he has something to see: flames dance on his wooden shoe in all the rainbow colors, wood crackles, the leather hisses.

"'So, Nenad, is that how you work for me?'

"'Agh, sorry . . . it was no good, a mistake.'

"'A mistake? Sabotage! Vandalism!'

"'But *Meister*'—we used German words in the trade—'the nail stuck out!'

"'So? You should hammer better. You could have pulled it out and rasped the crack.'

"'But the crack was a little too big.'

"'You could have waxed it!'

"'But that takes time. I heard you coming. I feared your strictness.'

"'Strictness? I'm so lenient! . . . You are fired!'

"'Agh, please, don't. What will Mother say? Where can I find another job this time of the year?'

"'You should have thought of that earlier. If you had at least spared the leather.'

"'I didn't have the time.'

"'You'll have enough time now. Out!'

"I begged him, but he again said, 'Out.' I kicked off my clogs and walked barefoot out into the snow. He caught up with me near the post office. I hastened my pace.

"'Hey, it's all forgiven and forgotten. I put myself in your shoes. It's all right.'

"I was ashamed. It was Saturday, a market day, and crowds of people stared at us—two sawdust-covered men, one pulling the other by the sleeve. When we were past the square, I said, 'You fired me. How can you go back on your word?'

"'I was too rash.'

"'But, *Meister,* we aren't Gypsies—ready to kill each other one minute and to kiss each other the next. If you say something, mean it, yes-yes, no-no.'

"'So, if in a fit of rage you say you'll kill a man, later when you're sober you'll kill him?'

"'Yes.'

"He laughed and put his arm on my shoulder and said, 'Eh, that's no good.'

"'I'd just be careful not to say something like that.'

"'When you're mad, you can say such a thing. Think about it. It's good to forgive quickly. If that's what Gypsies are like, let's learn from them. Come on, let's go back.'

"'No, I can't change my horses like that—so quickly! At least let me stew for a while!'

"'All right, you can come back to work tomorrow, but please take my shoes.'

"I refused, he insisted, and I accepted one of his clogs. To get my shoes, we hopped back to the workshop—he had the right shoe, I the left. I remember that because it was awkward to hop on my left foot. For a bet we raced, and I slid over a patch of ice. Kids had poured water over the packed snow on the pavement and smoothed it with shoes, for skating. All the streets were iced and the old people didn't dare walk outside.

"In the workshop, he stuffed the stove with wood. Your sister brought us tea with honey. A drop of honey stuck to his mustache, glittering. I remember that because when he rubbed his mustache with the back of his hand, he said he wanted to give me a raise. I protested, but he put wads of cotton in his ears and pressed blocks of wood against the saw to make soles. I sat on my chair, a log of beech, and nailed the leather into wood. Four strokes a nail—the fourth always made the deepest sound. The whole workshop shivered with the proud music of work.

"That's what I've been having nightmares about all week. When I saw you—you have the same eyebrows, same stubble as your father—I said to myself, 'Here's one of his sons. I'll dream about *Meister* again.' He walks into the shop, rubs his hand above the stove, and I am scared he'll see the shoe burning."

He lowered his brow, took off his sawdusty cap and slapped it against his knee.

His wife, passing by our bench in front of his workshop, said, "That's true, he dreams. And then he talks about it for hours."

The chains of his well crunched again. A woman in a red-and-white handwoven scarf drew the bucket.

"You don't know my Aunt Julia, do you?"

"He's ranting about the war again," she said. "And what does he know about it? He was just a kid." The ruddy woman poured the water into her bucket. "It was no worse then than it is nowadays. I was young and so pretty that the German officers invited me and only three other girls from the village to a ball. The officers danced with us and they didn't make passes or use dirty language. And while we lived for that evening like high society, I didn't know that the common soldiers outdoors had slaughtered three dozen of our people. My good looks saved me—and now they're gone."

"Not your looks, the Good Lord saved you, and I wish he'd save your soul too!" Nenad's mother squeaked like a stork as she walked by. She was in her eighties and still wore black for her dead husband. Many people, when faced with the atrocities of men, lose faith in God, but she strengthened hers. Her prayers in the church were the lengthiest, and her face bore more creases than any other, yet her eyes were calm and mild, and now they were caressing her son.

"Yeah," Nenad said. "There were seven or eight raids in our village during the war, and it's a miracle so many of us survived. One night *ustashas* went through the village, knifing young men and throwing them into a pit of wet mortar to make sure none of them would live to join the partisans. But two *ustashas* had gone stealthily ahead of the company and told the people to run for the woods. The two *ustashas* saved quite a few people—I don't know how they got into that vicious army, but there they were able to do more good than if they'd worked for the Red Cross."

"I marvel that you don't have war nightmares every night." I thought, He is an unstoppable storyteller. Instead of a writing program, I need a war. If I survived, I'd have enough stories to last a lifetime.

"I have more nightmares about your father. . . . No, I'm not complaining. It doesn't take much to see that since my father was killed, *Meister* became like a father to me. Almost all I know, I learned from him."

"Storytelling too?" I tried to interrupt him, but he followed his own train of thought.

"We were always together, day in and day out for twenty

years, working, laughing, swearing, hating each other's guts—we became a part of each other, we loved each other! That's it, we loved each other. I wasn't happy when Mother took me to him to learn a trade. She had first taken me to a restaurant to become a waiter, and on my first day I dropped a tray with drinks when a lady customer winked at me. At night I sleepwalked with a tray, balancing plates and glasses one atop another, and walked like that on a log fence. In the morning I juggled glasses until I shattered them all. I balanced pots, eggs, and pebbles so well that a circus would have employed me.

"At work I delivered cognacs like a magician pulling a pigeon from his sleeve. Dressed sharp, I felt like an actor—when serving people, a good actor is their king. But when Mother saw me practice winking in the mirror at home, she fasted and prayed for me in the plum orchard, loudly during the day and in whispers in her bedroom at night. When she lost her voice, she prayed in the corn fields, wheezing with asthma. I couldn't sleep. I clogged my ears with clay, but her whispers grew louder and more painful in my head.

"So I obeyed her to go to your father to learn an honest trade," Nenad went on. "I enjoyed work. *Meister* was quite a talker—never a dull moment—but never a word about the war."

"He used to tell us stories from *Don Quixote,* and . . ."

"Once he had just come back into town from a large fair on a muddy day. His clothes were all muddy, but he was happy, playing his tambourine and singing, because when the soil is muddy, the clogs sell like aspirin when there's toothache. His pockets bulging, he walked into a restaurant, but the waiters wouldn't serve him. He went home, changed into his Sunday best, and returned. The waiters now danced around him, bringing him all he wanted, and addressing him as *Sir* and *Monsieur.* When the table was loaded down with lamb, trout, caviar, cognac, and chocolate cakes—without tasting any of it—he stood up and walked out. A couple of waiters ran after him demanding he pay.

He ignored them, but they insisted, and he said, 'Who are you talking to? Me?'

" 'Yes, you.'

" 'No, it cannot be. You are talking to my jacket. You didn't serve me, just my jacket. But the jacket happens to have no money, so I doubt very much that it will pay you.'

"I don't remember how the story ended. Maybe he'd made it up. Anyway, twenty years later I set up my shop right across the street from *Meister*'s. He left the hospital where he'd been laid up with kidney stones, and he walked into my shop and said, 'Will you leave me now, now that I desperately need you? And if you leave, why don't you get out of my sight? Let us not compete. I don't want you to starve and me to go to the grave.' He did much better than I because he got a contract from the glass factory in Belgrade."

"I remember that," I said. "Before shipping the clogs in big Brazilian coffee sacks to the factory, he, Mother, my brother Ivo, and I stayed up several nights in a row. I hammered thousands of nails into the shoes though I was only nine. My thumbs were all blue from my missing the nails whenever I started to doze off."

"A couple of years later *Meister* said to me, 'You know, whenever I was mad at my family or business, I took it all out on you— you were my lightning rod. Can you forgive me?' I said I could, but I resented his asking, thinking, Here, he wants to make a clean breast of it in a minute, for hundreds of abuses—too easy.

"But it's never easy to ask for forgiveness.

"He was born-again then—he preached, prayed, and talked Bible. He gave money to the people he thought he had outwitted in business. To me he gave new rasps and saws. And then he died. . . . "

"I remember everything—he wrote his will with a steady hand, he said, 'I am going,' he looked up with so much longing that his eyes seemed to scratch the ceiling, and a trickle of blood dripped from the hairs of his nose onto his mustache, air creaked out of him, and he was dead." I cringed from the mucus-laden sound of my voice.

Nenad went on. "The night after he died, I thought I was dying. An invisible knife pierced my heart. I fell on my back in the middle of the room, I couldn't draw a breath, and my body tingled as if my fingers were stuck in an electrical socket. 'Don't be scared,' my wife said, 'I'm going to get the preacher.' The preacher! I must be dying. Otherwise she'd get a doctor.

"The doctor came with the preacher and gave me tranquilizers. The preacher sent me to Baptist brethren in the Slovenian Alps to breathe fir-smelling air. My attacks grew worse. I thought hell gaped, about to swallow me into its stomach of flame. I begged God to heal me, promising to become His slave. As I uttered the prayer, the knife was drawn out of my heart. I haven't had an attack since then, in twenty-one years, three months, and eleven days!"

I recalled the horrors of my dreams of Father dying again— slowly, putridly, falling apart under my touch, as if made without connective tissue.

"I remembered the promise I'd made," Nenad said, "although I had made it for the wrong reason—fear."

"But the fear of the Lord is the beginning of wisdom, isn't it?" I said.

"The fear of hell isn't. So, I tried to pay back everybody I had got the better of. But I couldn't do it—many had got the better of me. I had to feed my three kids and wife.

"From the town we moved to the village so our children wouldn't keep bad company. It didn't work. Two of my sons began to go to bars at fifteen. They picked up fights and girls. Zarko took up weight lifting and was the champion arm wrestler, and still one night in a brawl two guys painted him blue.

"Because I wanted my family to read books, I didn't want a TV set, but my wife, who hated the village, did. She smashed all the windows and doors and tables in the house with an ax. I begged her on my knees—before my conversion I wouldn't have been so meek—to stop. She screamed she would stop if I drove into town right away and bought her a TV set. I did. Mother was mortified that we'd have 'the blue eye of the Devil' in our household. She always turned her head away from the set. But once, as she walked through the room, there was a moment of quiet before a character shouted 'Stephanie!'—Mother's name. She faced the screen, and gasped, 'When did the Devil tell them my name?' It still pains her that she faced the screen.

"I spent more time talking Bible than selling wooden shoes. But in one village at a fair, three large Eastern Orthodox guys ganged up on me. One said, 'I have my God from the great-grand-folks of my great-grandparents, and where do you get your new god to sell to us like shoes?'

" 'It's one and the same God,' I say.

" 'No, it isn't. Don't insult mine,' he says.

"And the other two swore and cussed in such ugly words that the heavens were burning and smoking. They dragged me out of the village, tossed me in a ditch, and told me that if I showed up again, they would peel off my skin and rub salt in my wounds. The Bible says you should feel blessed when persecuted, but I didn't. There are three villages in the area I can't set my foot in."

I yawned, anticipating that he would start preaching to me in the good Baptist tradition.

"I know the war interests you more, but . . . " He spread his arms apologetically, and gracefully continued to stretch his right arm, to grip the fridge handle. He offered me beer in an iced mug. "I saw that in an American movie," he said, "you freeze your mugs."

"True." Finally I said a word. In his talking, Nenad had gained so much momentum that all I could do was nod my head, yeaing and naying, huhing and humming, like a young donkey learning to bray.

Nenad's tabby jumped, grabbed the rim of his cap, and tried to pull it out of his hands. Nenad scratched the cat on the head and said, "My dear kitty."

He patted her more tenderly than I had ever seen a man his age do, and he talked. "One night the Germans entered the village and were about to round up thirty or forty people to kill because the partisans had killed three or four German soldiers in the woods nearby. But the soldiers first axed some chickens to cook quietly at a house secluded in an apple orchard where nobody from the rest of the village could see them. There were some black cats there, and no black cats ever came to our end of the village. So, when I saw a black cat running down the road with a bloody rooster's head in its mouth, I screamed, 'The Germans are coming!' We ran into the woods and listened to the echoing of shotguns. The Germans killed ten, but most of the people in the village were saved—by the black cat!" He picked up his tabby, who looked like a camouflaged paratrooper.

Blue sheets of lightning shivered in the east, revealing the dark horizon; a steady roar shook the ground.

"But it's getting late and we'd better call it a night," Nenad said.

As I walked to the train station, the leaves in the woods—the tongues of the wind—murmured. The stones on the shoulder of the road crunched beneath my feet and told me how Jesus was tempted to make bread out of stones and instead how he later made wine out of water. The stones told me again how the vicious armies and the good people had passed. And I thought, If the stones can tell the stories, I can too.

Yahbo the Hawk

Instead of to the church, I walked to the nearby park one Sunday morning. Just as I was about to climb an oak, I saw my friend Peter walking down the path beside a grim partisan monument.

Peter used to lead Catholic funeral processions, holding a varnished cross, dressed in white vestments, his cheeks pink in the wind or the heat, while a priest sang in monotonous Latin. I respected Peter for his knowledge of Latin, which still did not prevent me from cornering him in our classroom and punching him like a boxing sack. I rented him for that purpose, a dinar for ten minutes of practice. Peter now carried a covered pleated basket.

"What have you got there?" I asked him.

"If you want to find out, give me five dinars."

I gave him a bronze dinar coin and peeped in.

"Don't open much; they might fly away!"

"Wow! What are they? Little ravens?"

"No. Can't you see? Hawks."

"Hum, and what will you do with them?"

"I don't know. Feed my dog."

"Look, why don't you give them to me?"

"Give. Are you crazy? They're not easy to come by!"

"Well, what do you want for a hawk?"

"It's a precious bird. You could train it to catch chickens, one a day, which would make three hundred and sixty-five chickens a year, and with that you could buy all kinds of things. . . . "

"I'll give you my sword."

"Come on! We outgrew that."

"My sweater and my jeans?"

"They would be too tight on me."

"You could stretch them."

"No, forget it!"

And he pretended he would walk on.

"How about a strawberry ice cream?"

Now I had him. His mouth began to water, he swallowed saliva, his eyelids drooped. "Three!"

We walked to the sweets shop. I bought him three ice creams and he lapped them like a cat drinking milk. Then he took out one hawk. I gripped it to make sure its talons, small Turkish sabers turned upside down, could not reach me. I was uneasy about the beak.

"I'd like the other hawk too!"

"That would be ten almond ice creams."

"How about three egg-cream cakes?"

"Four!" he said.

I searched through my pockets, and in the mess of nails, wires, cigarette butts, and several round pebbles for throwing at traffic signs and teacher's windows, I found one torn red piece of paper with a picture of a muscular factory worker on it.

"Let that be a deposit!"

I rushed home with the hawk in my hands, far in front of me. The hot bird pulsated with fast heartbeats; its whole body was one big heart with sharp edges and eyes atop its valves. As soon as I got home, I put it into a cupboard, stole some money that was kept in a prayer book to ensure divine protection, and ran back to the sweets shop.

Peter was not there. I learned later that he sold the bird to a cop's son, Nik. Next time I ran into Peter, I said, "Look, I paid for the hawk, and you gave it to Nik. Get the hawk back from Nik!"

"No, I want to be on good terms with him and his father because I still need to steal some things. . . . "

"All right, this is for the deposit!" I gave him a black eye, to which he responded by giving me a wonderful show of the firmament, with more stars than there are sons of Abraham, Isaac, and Jacob, flickering—giving me a black eye. In all fairness to the art of painting, which takes time, I must say that his eye was not yet black but red and purple, the following day it was green and yellow, and on the third day it was blue. Now I knew that you could get green out of blue and yellow, but that you could get blue out of green and yellow was a novelty, and it was not an exception proving the rule, because the area surrounding my eyes followed the same revolutions of color as his. In the end our colors were dark blue, like the most common sort of plums. Ashamed of my plum-eye, for four days I joined the pirates, wearing a greasy strap of leather across my head and over my colorful eye.

At home in the attic, my hawk's new home, I waited till my eyes would get used to the darkness. I made out the bird's silhouette on a cross beam; it was emerging from the dark, like a picture developed in a lab, sharper and sharper. It turned sideways toward me. When I began to approach the silhouette, it jumped and flapped its wings unsteadily to another beam. It nearly fell from the beam onto the bales of cowhide that my father had used for making clogs before his death. Along the walls of the attic, there were piles of wooden soles; newspapers and magazines, some with pictures of Russian spaceships and dogs, and one with Marilyn Monroe with her lips parted; jigsaw puzzles with missing pieces; and a flat soccer ball of leather.

I christened the hawk Yahbo, a man's name, feeling like Adam in paradise naming the animals. I was not sure what Yahbo's gender was, though I wanted to think of him as male. Still, I didn't ruffle through its feathers to find out, fearing that afterwards I'd have to rely only on my sense of touch, the beak and talons making my eyes flutter at the thought of coming close to them.

In the back of the attic sunshine streaked in, stronger and stronger, and particles of dust were brilliant, burning like stars in a downward Milky Way. Through the window, facing east, you could see the mountains and forests from which Yahbo must have come, from a no doubt very noble lineage stretching down all the way from the Garden of Eden and God's breath. If He made Adam of soil, He made hawks of leaves, detached leaves that winds carried aloft; with God's breath reaching them, the leaves ceased to be the helpless toys of the winds, and instead the stems evolved into seeing heads, and the outer parts of leaves into wings. And so came into being the great surveyor of forests, from the leaves' soft riblets.

I brought him water to drink. But he would not drink. I fed him liver meat, a quarter of a pound. I paid attention that it be bathed in blood because otherwise he would not get enough liquids. It was hot in the attic.

Several days later, Yahbo sat on a cross beam and stared. White film was covering his eyes, slowly, and withdrawing back somewhere beneath the hairs around his eyes. His beak was half open. He is dying of thirst and grief, I thought. I went to the library to find out whether young hawks drank water, or blood only, and I wasn't able to find anything on the topic. Since he would not drink water from a pot, I went to the junkyard behind the local hospital, where there were all kinds of syringes. I filled one with water and aimed a squirt into Yahbo's beak. Water would not pass down his throat. Drops trickled from his beak onto the dusty floor and coated themselves in dust, squirming and curling on the ground, like miniature hedgehogs. I dropped all shyness with Yahbo, grabbed his neck and squirted into his beak, again and again, until his Adam's apple went up and down without water spilling out of his beak. Afterward, he learned to drink from a pot of water. On hot days he soaked his legs and dipped his wings in the water. He shook all his feathers, water flying around the attic. He dipped his head in the pot too.

Yahbo was growing rapidly. I wanted to teach him to sit on my shoulder and to love me so he would not fly away into his forests never to return. I wanted to walk with him on my forearm wrapped in ox-hide. He would attack those who displeased him and pluck out their eyes with his talons, tear their ears off or at least pierce through them, making holes for earrings.

Then it was already summer, and, since there was no school, it was the busiest time of the year for soccer, biking, and reading. I often forgot to feed Yahbo for days. Suddenly remembering my neglect, I would run to the butcher's.

Even the hours I did have to train Yahbo I did not know how to put to use. I made a leather strap for my forearm. But Yahbo would not sit on it, growing irritated with my trying to place him there. A couple of times his beak started toward my eyes so I had to cast him aside. I am sure he had no sentimental impulses to kiss my ears or play with my hair locks—it was my eye he wanted to drink.

I imagined I should take him out when he was starved and tease him with some meat on a whirling rope, and he would fly after it, in circles, and learn to stay around me. But the taste of freedom, I thought, would be sweeter to him than blood.

To Yahbo I was a jailer more than a friend. I could not talk to him. He would not look at me. His head was always tilted sideways so I didn't know where he was looking. Perhaps he was looking at me, but I couldn't tell, and that did not do much for communication between us. Nor did he trust me. When I walked into the attic, he would often fly from the front beam far back into the darkest recesses under the roof. But sometimes he flew from the recesses toward me and let me approach him if I moved slowly. I caressed him down his feathers, with a quickening sensation in my whole body. Petting Yahbo was like petting a sword with sharp double edges, a perfect smooth cold surface of the sword on the sides, over which you glide your palms carefully. But he was not cold, he was very warm and soft. He seemed quite pleased then, his eyes growing shiny, teary, radiant hazel. His head moved a bit to the left and a bit to the right; he probably did not know what to think; was I being affectionate toward him? As if to ask me what it all meant, he opened his beak, but no sounds came out. In the beak I saw his thin red and pointed tongue, almost a snake's tongue. Overcome with sadness that he could not speak the language of humans, he stayed that way, his beak open, and the white film slid over his eyes like venetian blinds.

I often stayed in the attic for hours, just staring at the majestic bird. He was growing so large that I thought he might be an eagle. I doubted whether I could train him. It did not seem that he would want to be a servant. He was born to be a master, a count of the heavens, and who was I? Son of a clog-maker. How should I subdue this nobility? If he were a son of a banal human nobleman, I would gladly lynch him and humiliate him daily, make his nose bleed and tie him to a tree, a post of shame, the way I did with the mayor's son. After I'd been there for a long while, Yahbo would fly the whole length of the attic, swing around and smash straight into the glass window. Five laths of wood made twelve square glass surfaces too small to be shattered like that. Yahbo would fall to the floor, stand up, fly back to the opposite end of the attic and in a couple of minutes he'd be flying again, pointing his body straight to pass through the space between the laths. And he would crash down again.

In the morning he perched on the narrow ledge against the windowpanes, his beak open and uttering no sound, bewildered, perhaps not understanding what kind of air it was that would show you the wonders of your homeland and wouldn't let you pass through, homeward. He faced east like a Muslim toward Mecca or a Jew facing Jerusalem; for him the glass was the Wailing Wall, an invisible wall of wailing.

Time and again he flew against the window so mercilessly I was scared he would break his neck. His eyes glowed with wrath. I was tempted to open the window for him, but did not.

He needed fresh, winged food. When my cat caught a sparrow, I stole it from her. I threw the croaking, shivering bird toward Yahbo, and Yahbo missed it, unprepared for hunting out of the blue. Then he swooped down at the quarry, picked it up and wildly flew with it around the attic several times, whereupon he landed on his favorite cross beam, nailing the sparrow with his talons to the wood. He stood, dignified, with his head in profile, as if ready to be minted into a silver dollar, or a German mark, or some other aggressive country's currency. Blood dripped from the beam onto the floor and coated itself in dust, writhing. Then Yahbo tore the bird, his smaller nephew with the same color and same stripes as his own, and devoured it all, feathers, bones, eyes, everything, gulping hastily, his throat and eyes bulging out, and when his Adam's apple leaped over the last swallow, he seemed to regret that the pleasure was so short-lived.

Yahbo spread his wings like big arms of welcome. He opened his beak; his eyes increased in size and shot a beam of light; his snake tongue popped out. Then his body shook as if he were an alcoholic in delirium tremens. He opened his beak and vomited a chunk of feathers and blood. He cast another pallet. I ran downstairs to mother in the kitchen. "I have an upset stomach. Could you make me some garlic soup?"

"Of course you do. You take all the good food to that ugly bird."

She chopped cloves of garlic and tossed it into the boiling water with egg whites and charcoal bread. I put the soup in a syringe and spurted it into Yahbo's beak. He suffered it, now and then closing his beak to swallow, and opening it again, apparently asking for more.

Knowing that Yahbo needed fresh kill, I borrowed a rifle from a Hungarian boy, Janosh, with whom I fought nearly every day. I would hit him on the mouth, so his lips would be cut against his rabbit teeth; he'd fling chunks of coal, crushing my toes; I'd chase him through half the town, and, catching him by his long hair, choke him while he plunged his nails into my back until his hands grew weak and he seemed to swoon. Fearing for his safety, I'd release him, and he'd spring up and run away shrieking unprintable text. We were actually very good friends, and he lent me his rifle gladly. I tiptoed into the beech forest where I saw a weasel not far from me. I held my breath, slowly leaning the rifle barrel against the cold, peeled bark of a birch. The weasel did not seem to notice me. I aimed for the neck. Thup! The weasel jumped several times like a wild horse being tamed. I thought it would fall to the ground. It jumped onto another tree, almost missing a branch. I reloaded the rifle and followed. I tripped over a stump. I never lost sight of the weasel—its redness struggling to get onto another tree—I shot, missed, reloaded, shot, missed, reloaded. The weasel seemed to be picking up strength. I leaned against a tree, and pulled the trigger. The weasel shook. It stood in one place trembling but would not fall. I must have put five more bullets into it, and it continued trembling. Then a spasm passed through its body, and it shook no more. But it would not fall. Unsteadily I climbed up to the weasel. Its yellow fur was covered with blood, its neck torn, its eyes almost outside the sockets. I grabbed its bloody body and tore it off the branch and threw it to the ground. I slid down the beech bark and vomited. The green darkness grew darker and more radiant, and all I could see in the radiance was the red blood, screaming, like the blood of Abel, straight to God. I threw myself on the ground. I prayed to God, saying that I would never again kill any animals, except for mosquitoes, and ants that I was bound to step on—that I would never intentionally step on an ant, nor place, the way a friend of mine did, one ant's head against the neck of another to see an ant in panic biting through a sister's neck. I would beat a boy in my street for his having bathed a cat in gasoline and set it on fire; I would beat a boy who lived two streets away from me, who had killed the black cat of a ninety-nine-year-old widow by putting it into the washing machine.

I promised to God I would do all that on the condition that He restore life to the weasel. I waited, opened my eyes, and there was the weasel, as dead as before. I prayed more. I hit the ground with my fists, many times, until I hit something cool and slimy and when I opened my eyes, I saw I had squashed a snail. The weasel was as dead as before. I stood up, rubbed my slimy and bloody palm against the bark of the tree and against my jeans, and realized I had not completed my prayer, I said, "Amen!" The wind rustled around, invisible and ubiquitous, and the leaves trembled as it passed. With my bare hands I dug into the soft black soil; the soil stuck beneath my nails. I buried the weasel. So I returned home empty-handed. Yahbo opened his beak, turned his head in many directions quickly, in expectation.

I saw that if I was going to let Yahbo go, I should not hesitate. It was already mid-August, and the more time that passed the more difficult it would be for him to learn how to hunt.

The following morning with my bow and arrows I pierced the carton of an empty box that had held sunflower-oil bottles, and put Yahbo into it. I tied a narrow sheet of tin around Yahbo's right foot, having inscribed on it my name and address with a needle. We set out for the mountains, the way Abraham set out with Isaac, to slaughter him as a burnt offering to God. I did not have the donkeys, so I had to be the donkey myself. I hoped that Isaac would live, that an angel would stop my raised hand with a knife in it. We went through the park, past the vineyards in the hills, through a layer of beeches into an oak forest. On the way I saw no hawks and wondered how he would do, whether he would find any company.

In a windless meadow I opened the box. He jumped out awk-wardly, more like a chicken than a hawk. He flapped with his wings vigorously, making a wind like a helicopter during take-off. He flew in a semicircle and perched on a branch of a bumpy cedar.

Everything had changed now. He was free. I was merely a human with bare hands, and flap as much as I would, I could not fly. He hesitated, fearing perhaps that there was a glass barrier somewhere, against which he would hit and then fall, back onto the sandy floor of the stuffy attic. After several minutes of contemplating the forest and the sky, he sprang from the branch. He flapped up in circles, higher and higher, spiraling into the heavens. High above me he glided on a new wind, keeping his wings still for a long time. Then he made a circle out of which he darted straight for the mountain.

Every day I went to the attic and through the eastern window I stared toward the mountain, and wondered where he was in the emerald temple. During thunderstorms I feared a lightning bolt would strike him because of the metal I had put on his right leg. It is said that friends are one soul in two bodies. Well, that one soul was not in me; it was circling somewhere above the trees over the mountain.

Two weeks later a local forester came by and told me that his dog had found a most peculiar thing: a dead hawk with a dead weasel in its talons. The hawk's talons were sunk in the hips of the weasel; the hawk had missed the neck he must have aimed for. The weasel's teeth were still in the hawk's breast. The forester gave me the entwined bodies.

I made a hole beneath the cedar to which Yahbo had flown. The tree roots were wiry and tough to cut through with my stone-age tool, a sharp stone. Among the roots I placed the thin limp mess of fur and dark blood of the weasel, for there it belonged.

Then I collected dry branches of trees, made a bundle on the ground, and put the limp chunk of feathers, flesh, beak, talons, and dark blood over it. The white film covered his eyes. From my pocket I took out the Psalms on thin fine paper. I crumpled the pages, set them under the pyre and struck a match. The branches caught fire at once, crackling. The feathers smelled like a tire being burned. The flames fought through a thick layer of smoke and the smoke rose slowly. Some smoke touched my eyes, stung them; tears came out as if I had been gazing at a big naked onion. I took out a cigarette and lit it on the pyre. The circles of my smoke merged into Yahbo's smoke, and our smoke merged into the sky.

Yolk

Time: The first decade of the twentieth century
Place: Potgrad, a small town in Slavonia—the southern province
of the Austro-Hungarian Empire

Martha knelt to the forest ground and touched a soft moist round
mushroom resembling the bald head of a man. She scratched the
surface with her thumbnail to see whether it was an edible mushroom; if the color didn't change, it would be. The white matter
dimmed into purple. A serenity appeared on her face, and her
thin lips curved slightly into a Mona Lisa smile, if it could be
called a smile.

At home she cut a couple of logs with an ax in the cellar, and
put several splinters into her kitchen stove over the glowing embers. She sighed as she laid the mushrooms onto a knotty cutting
board of oak, and with her fingers broke the mushrooms into
small pieces the way a minister breaks bread in Holy Communion. Into each mushroom piece she tucked bits of garlic and
rose hips, and dipped the pieces in peppered olive oil. She cut
large onions in half and squeezed out one layer of onion after
another, making onion cups for mushrooms and chevre.

On barging into the room, Mr. Kovach, without greeting his wife, exclaimed, "Uh, what smells so delicious? Wait, don't tell me!" Sniffing like a bulldog, he said, "Hum, mutton, onions," and his voice lost its clarity, because saliva was getting in the way.

After Martha helped him out of his coat, Mr. Kovach sat on a chair, which looked woefully small for him. He rubbed his hands as if some agreement were about to be made, or at any rate something agreeable were to be done with his hands. He pursed his lips as if to spit into his palms as lumberjacks do, but he restrained himself. His hands were soft, without blisters: he was a clerk.

He put the stuffed onions into his mouth. You could hear his tongue parting from his palate, to which it had been momentarily glued by the melting food and saliva. He smacked his lips and grunted, while Martha shivered with disgust. Gulping another stuffed onion, he closed his eyes so that the sense of sight would not detract from the pleasure of smelling and tasting. When he opened his eyes, they were moist and hazy.

His wife stood at the table waiting to hear what palatial whim she must please next as his personal waitress and cook. As a matter of fact, they had met when, at the delicate age of forty and incapable of cooking for himself, Mr. Kovach ate at the restaurant where Martha was a cook. Her family had been poor and she had been destined to remain poor herself. She had had nothing to recommend her: she was not good looking, and though she was extremely bright, she could not count on a bright future because intelligence in a woman was considered perilous for domestic comfort. So she had been apprenticed at the Suckling Pig, where she had progressed so quickly that within a couple of years she had become a chef. Undone by her cooking, Mr. Kovach had sent her a letter.

Dear Miss Martha Berich:

My name is Peter Kovach. You don't know me but I know you. From the way you cook, I can tell you are a sensitive person

*with a fabulous imagination. Judging by how you use spices, you
are romantic. In that way we are similar—in being romantic—
except my imagination is not as good as yours, which is a guarantee that I am not making all this up; knowing that my
imagination is limited, I trust my judgment. I am an accountant
at the Central Bank and my income is good enough to keep a
family, yet I am a bachelor. I would like to ask you herewith to
become my wife. You need not make up your mind at once. If
you need to be acquainted with me beforehand, you could meet
me in the Flower Circle at three in the afternoon next Sunday.*

Yours with all his heart,

Peter Kovach

Martha hadn't been unhappy without marriage, yet she had accepted the offer as an opportunity for a change. The wedding
feast, at Martha's old home, left a humiliating pain in Martha's
chest for years. Mr. Kovach's relatives had, between moments of
drunken abandon, gathered enough sobriety to cast down super-
cilious glances at Martha's relatives, at their simple clothing, unre-
fined manners, and dirt floors. Although Martha's relatives held
good manners to be a device contrived to confuse and embarrass
simple folk, they had blushed.

Now, when he opened his eyes, Mr. Kovach looked vaguely
away from Martha toward a garish painting of a huge green wave
through which the sun shone. He pushed his wine glass forward
and said, "Some more wine!" Martha poured him some pale
green wine. He gulped it while staring at the wave, as if drinking
directly from the painting.

After dinner his face was as red as a sea crab. He lay on the
sofa with his boots on. He rustled the pages of the local news-
paper, and finding nothing of interest, grunted, "Could you take
off my boots?" Martha did as he wished. Both his big toes stuck
out through his woolen socks. Martha took off the sticky socks
and cut his nails. He was so rotund that he rolled from a lying

position to a sitting one, and demanded that his feet be washed in lukewarm water. She soaped his feet in a maple tub with a large bar of yellow soap and scrubbed his soles with a tough brush, while he laughed because it tickled him.

He lay back to continue reading the paper, which, several minutes later, fell out of his hands. His arms dropped and he began snoring. The expression on his face was one of utter satisfaction—of a baby who has had plenty of warm milk and was dreaming of more.

Martha washed the dishes, scrubbing the plates. She darned his socks. She washed the laundry by hand. The dirtiest laundry she put on the stove and cooked so that the whole kitchen was enshrouded in a cloud of steam, which precipitated against the window; drops of water swerved down the glass in jerks. Then she hung the laundry with wooden clips on ropes across the backyard—huge underwear, shirts, and trousers—which gave the impression of several broad, two-dimensional, invisible men hanging in visible clothing. She did all that to music—the symphonic result of the most sonorous snoring coming out of the windows, the grunting of pigs from the pigsty, the shrieking of proud egg-laying hens in the hay on the pigsty attic, and the screaming of a child on the next block who was most likely undergoing some essential lesson in acquiring good manners at the hands of his loving parents.

When she had some time to herself, she alternately gazed at the distant blue mountains and read from the Bible, including a passage about her namesake: . . . *a woman named Martha received him into her house. And she had a sister called Mary, who sat at the Lord's feet and listened to his teaching. But Martha was distracted with much serving; and she went to him and said, "Lord, do you not care that my sister has left me to serve alone? Tell her then to help me." But the Lord answered her, "Martha, Martha, you are anxious and troubled about many things; one thing is needful. Mary has chosen the good portion, which shall not be taken away from her."*

Martha exclaimed, "What a thankless guest! It was she who

invited him, not Mary, it was her house, not Mary's, and it was she who served him, not Mary!"

Then she flipped many pages back and read a shalt-not passage about cooking the meat of a calf in its mother's milk. Why should it be specifically forbidden to cook like that if it weren't very tasty and tempting?

Her thoughts were interrupted, because Mr. Kovach woke up and grunted that he wanted coffee. So while he stretched, yawned, and rubbed his thick eyelids and drooping eyesacks, she stood near the stove, crushing beads of coffee in a brass pot with a piece of iron shaped like a bone of the forearm. Afterwards, flames licked the pot directly through a small opening in the iron stove-plate. She laced the coffee with brandy because she knew that her husband did not want to run the risk of becoming alert. He merely wanted to be awake.

Since their sow had only one piglet now from the original sixteen—one for each of her teats—Martha easily milked enough out of the sow to cook the only remaining piglet in its mother's milk, without spice, plain as it was. The piglet made Mr. Kovach's blood boil with desire, grease making his cheeks and lips shine. Martha couldn't eat the same meal because she felt sorry for the piglet. She cooked cabbage, celery, hot peppers, parsley, carrots, and put piglet feet and ears in the same milk, and Mr. Kovach found that a delicate stew.

The good cooking was reflected in Mr. Kovach's body. First, after marriage, he had grown gracefully plump and his skin had been smooth—the general signs of well-being. His plumpness evolved until he became larger in circumference than his station in life called for. That kind of build would suit the county judge, the chief of police, and the main banker. With so much circumference—which is to say, with such a symbol of authority over a great domain—he looked misplaced in his office. He would have progressed in it, for by no means was he a dull fellow, yet because of his great and constantly gratified appetite he was too sleepy to work with concentration, and he occupied his lowly station with difficulty, hardly fitting behind his desk. Since in those days people did not have cars, prestige had to be gained by investing in something else that was visible. The most assuredly conspicuous place for investment was the belly. Wherever you went, you could make a statement of being prosperous enough to eat well and to relax well.

The reputation of his kitchen spread around the town. Wherever he passed in the streets people turned round, conversations hushed, and instead of admiring his status by his bulk, they whispered about Martha's craft. He became ancillary to his wife, a walking proof of her great ability precisely because he could hardly walk.

He began inviting distinguished members of Potgrad to have dinner at his home, and no one declined. So the best physician, lawyer, banker, and even the count came to pay the pleasant tribute to this phenomenon of culinary art.

One such evening he ate and drank with his guests, a physician, a banker, and the Orthodox priest. They joked, embraced, and sang, and then ate again. Martha was so busy cooking and serving the party that she had no time to eat, and it simply wasn't conceivable that she could sit at the same table with the elevated gentry. She had to serve them in style, with platefuls lowered onto the table always from the left of their shoulders, empty plates lifted from the right; with wine poured with a quick twist of the wrist so that no wine would trickle down the bottle like dark red tears and leave purple stains on the labels. Martha hurried. Now and then her large brown eyes flared, and she whispered "What simple creatures these people are. All they want is to eat and laugh." And that is what she offered, both hearty and tickling meals.

She learned how to combine subtlety with substance from her talent for timing, molding, and combining, and from the Hungarian cuisine that, unlike the subtle French cuisine, offered enough substance to hide the spice for the hide-and-seek game of testing. She created a smoke screen of glaring spice so that the most intriguing spices passed unnoticed beyond the throat where they spread their intoxicating influence. In grilled mutton she smuggled shredded and raw nettles into the stomach (relying partly on hasty chewing by the debilitated teeth of the gluttons), where they would creep out and begin their commando action, tickling ever so lightly. The tickle in the stomach needed to get scratched—which is to say, more food was needed—and the more scratched it was, the more it tickled and the more scratched it wanted to be, and Mr. Kovach, who had demanded that his servings be particularly spicy, rose from one pitch of laughter to another, until he suddenly lost his sense of humor and keeled over.

The crimson color of merriment drained from his face, and only purple remained.

His funeral procession was very long. Martha shed some tears at his grave pit as the recipe for sending a husband into an uncertain eternity required. Mr. Kovach's relatives looked at her from time to time in silence, examining her carefully. Many people wept around the grave pit; it was hard to tell whether they wept for sorrow or for joy. The death of a banker, even of a lowly bank clerk, is always a complex matter.

People observed everything that was going on at the verge of the grave pit. In the small town there were many seasoned funeral goers—old people and housewives—for in funerals they could have previews of their own deaths, they could daydream about their beloved spouses put in coffins, and enjoy the highest achievements of art. If catharsis is the essence of art, then there is more art in a graveyard than in hundreds of museums and concert halls; perhaps it is with that guiding knowledge that museums are arranged like catacombs and concerts like funerals, with pianists like morticians and pianos like caskets. While thrilled by the sight of a casket being lowered into the ground, many old inhabitants of Potgrad were alerted to their keenest awareness and perceptiveness. They studied the family structures knit and torn around the deceased. One could see how much each mourner wept, and one could not immediately decide whether the tears were faked.

One had to study the tear-shedders: if their grief passed quickly, one couldn't believe its authenticity. After many careful studies, one developed intuition so that one could judge at the grave without a follow-up study. According to many such astute psychologists, the tears of Mrs. Kovach showed a real bereavement, but since she was a masterful cook, they supposed she could produce, without being bereft, tears of real bereavement, if called for by the occasion. The occasion certainly did call for them.

Mrs. Kovach inherited Mr. Kovach's house. She wore black for 366 even days and after the length of the odd year expired, she opened several letters, one from the physician and another from the Count of Potgrad, and while walking through her living room, she read that the count asked for the honor of her hand. When she reached that point in the letter, she was near the fireplace. She let the letter glide into the fire and admired how the flames turned from red to blue, and from blue back to red. A slight smile appeared on her lips, warmed by the flame.

Everybody in the county was invited to the wedding feast that followed, even the peasants. The feast raved for three nights and two days; the third day was a stillness after the storm, a trembling and shivering in hangovers. Amidst the valley of Potgrad there was a navel-like hill, and atop the hill the castle, surrounded by a park richly endowed with bushes from which, for three nights, came calls and shrieks of birds from all sorts of zones: tropical and subtropical, moderate and immoderate, Arctic and Antarctic. Ever since then, the biological genealogy of the town-dwellers has been a speculative science.

The count had the largest barrel, eight yards long, brought out from his cellars and cut in half; the halves were joined to form a figure-eight-shaped wine pool in which he and Martha took their conjugal dive. After they had climbed out of the pool, the townspeople were free to jump in the pool, and when they got out, the peasants could swim there too.

The town dogs devoured everything that fell from the feast tables. They interrupted their gustatory pleasures now and then to chase cats, who appreciated the wisdom of the Creator for creating trees and at the same time doubted the very same wisdom, for the existence of dogs was definitely at odds with a good design of the universe. And the squirrels, mistrusting the invaders of the kingdom of leaves, rushed toward the periphery of the park, flying from one tree to another. The trees around the castle became fruit trees on which cats' eyes grew. Thousands of eyes glowed with fire. On the highest tree there were no glowing eyes until near the top, where a pair of Owl's eyes flamed. The eyes gave rise to the legend:

> that Owl was one millennium old, and that the wild feasting
> brought Owl so much remembrance of early birdhood and
> of the days when the unchristianized Slavic nomads arrived in
> the valley and feasted, that Owl's tears began to fall as fire
> drops onto the ground, where they sank, bringing terror among
> the worms of the soil. One tear went as deep as the place that
> the oldest snake of the hill lived. The tear touched the snake's
> eye, and the snake went blind in the one eye, the only one that
> it had; the other one it had lost when it had crawled too deep
> in the ground and seen a glimpse of the fire in the center of the
> earth. Those Owl's tears could never die: there was too much
> grief in them. Even now the tears warm up the soil beneath
> Potgrad—and if you doubt it, go to Potgrad, and you'll see the
> vapors that arise out of the ground. That is how the town became
> a hot springs spa whose waters cure sclerosis and insincerity.
> There are very few who dare bathe in the spring waters.

Even today people retell the legend in Potgrad.

Late at night the overfed dogs fell asleep, and the cats fled down from the trees and had their fill. For years later the towns-people claimed that the cats organized themselves into an army and concertedly attacked the inert dogs. That was the explanation for why, for more than a decade after the feast, most dogs in Potgrad were ugly—crippled, blind, and without ears.

Martha's bony face, crooked nose, and deeply set eyes looked noble against her elegant clothing and the splendor of her new surroundings. She had no duties—she had several servants—except that the count often begged her to cook for him. He ate, drank, hunted, and wanted to be entertained by funny stories. But it seemed to him that no one in the region except himself had any sense of humor, and so for entertainment he resorted to retelling stories. No one laughed at them, but he didn't know that. He roared so much with laughter at the end of each story and his eyes were so filled with tears that he could neither see nor hear anything except himself.

What a waste, thought Martha, as she looked at the count and the large room; this huge building to serve only one man, and not much of one at that!

Several times a week Martha cooked hearty and tickling meals—venison, pheasants, wild ducks, rabbits, and whole nations of ants, snails, and other sylvan inhabitants, as well as crabs, caviar, eels, frogs—all boiled in butter and lard. The food, while being served at the table, was placed above a flame so that it still hissed, twisting in its oil as the count landed his fork in it, and continued to twist even in his mouth. The count became more and more buoyant with food; his body leapt to all sides, as if wishing to claim more space.

Martha guided him in his expansionistic tendencies like a martial arts master, using his own momentum, helping him along his chosen path. She mixed foods and spices so that gas would expand his belly. While dropping juicy wild blackberries coated in Belgian chocolate into his mouth, he laughed so loudly that he drowned out the popping of champagne corks.

His expanded belly pressed against his heart, but his heart wouldn't yield its rightful territory, and it accepted the race of expansionism. His heart stretched itself out in all directions and exploded. The explosion was so powerful that it tore the count's rib cage. Pieces of his heart muscle flew; a couple of them stuck to the wall. One piece of his heart shattered a windowpane and when it fell on the ground outside, a kitten caught it and tossed it around, and then ate it.

Apple

One snowless winter morning before going to school, I collected sawdust in baskets in Father's clog shop and dumped it out in the yard next to a walnut tree. The circular saw was running in his shop, yet I saw no father behind it. I found him in a corner, behind a pile of wooden soles, prostrate, praying. I was terrified of his praying.

Late that evening as Father drank warm milk and chewed dark bread, he told our grandmother how he'd heard someone calling him—the way Samuel was called—and yet he could see nobody. It was an angel of God calling him to prayer. That afternoon he had also felt someone touch him on the shoulder, and when he had turned around there was nobody. An angel of God had been there to strengthen him.

Grandmother said that she was glad to hear it, and then she coughed. When she didn't cough, her bronchial wheezing had a soothing rhythm to it, and I listened to it more than to my father's stories, which went on all evening.

The next morning, Father walked around the town and begged everybody for forgiveness "in the name of Christ" for all the wrongs that he had wittingly and unwittingly committed. He gave his former assistant, who now had his own shop, two bales of ox-hide. Earlier my father had sold him a rotten bale, creating a bad reputation for the assistant's new business.

Father brought home an astonished old peasant, forcing him to take a large sum of money because, several years before, Father had forced the peasant to sell him wood too cheaply—the peasant had wept, to no avail, that he and his children could not make it through the winter on so little money.

The following Sunday, even though it was my father preaching in our Baptist church, I was bored, and made deep creases between the grains of the soft bench wood with my thumbnails, each crease representing one year—that's how long it seemed that the sermon lasted. Stealthily, I read a chapter from *A Journey to the Center of the Earth,* which I had stored in the Bible. A retired electrician and distant relative, who sat behind me, tapped me on my shoulder to make me stop. My father preached Christ's giving up His ghost on the cross, and in the middle of the sermon he wept.

Father had played the bass in the church orchestra and sang with the deepest voice in the choir. When he shouted at home, the whole household, including the cat, ran out into the yard. When he missed shaving for just one day, his chin was black; he often rubbed his raspy cheeks against mine, laughing—if he had pressed harder, he would have swept off my skin. The same man now cried in front of more than a hundred people. I blushed.

But at home, as if aware that I was ashamed of him, he said to me, "If you understood God's grace, you would have to weep." He took me out into the moonless night, and from the apple-scented garden he pointed to the stars swimming in moist, dizzying blackness. "See, God created the stars. It takes millions of years for the light to reach our eyes, and God's thought is everywhere in no time at all. God's thoughts are right here with us."

"I can't feel it," I said.

"You are lucky you can't. Moses could see God's radiance only from behind as It passed. We would die if we saw nearly as much. You cannot be close to God and live!"

It was January 6th, and snow stormed outdoors, slantedly. When I looked through the window, I had the feeling that the household floated into heaven sideways. The big patches of snow resembled the down of a huge, slain celestial bird, whose one wing covered our whole valley, and the spasmodic wing must have been flapping, because it was windy. As soon as the snow touched the ground, it melted.

After a day in the clog-making shop, Father stepped into the living room, solemn and luminous. Ivo read comic books. Father said to him, "Don't blaspheme against God by reading trash. Why don't you read the Bible, or study math?"

"I don't feel like it," said Ivo.

The cat, who was sleeping on the roof of a large clay stove, stretched herself and blinked, her pupils contracting in vertical slits, coiled her tail as if scared Father would deliver her a blow, and jumped off the stove. Usually she rushed to sit in his lap. Now she sat on the Bible on the chair next to my bed and licked her paws, now and then looking at him mistrustfully.

"And you," he addressed me, "how can you allow this dirty animal to sit on the Bible?" As if to punctuate his question, the cat twisted her body and licked the root of her tail. I chased her off the somber book. Mother's slow, heavy steps resounded in the corridor, against the cement, louder and louder. She walked in with a basketful of wood and, breathing heavily, knelt in front of the stove and stirred the thin ashen embers with her bare fingers in such a quick way that she did not burn herself. Her method of doing it always disturbed me.

"Sons, why do you let Mother carry the wood? Why don't you help her?"

We made no reply.

He addressed me, "Yozzo, bring me an apple from the attic."

I went to the attic over the creaky wooden steps, and the

flashlight didn't work. I was scared of the dark. I knew the attic very well, so I found the apples and pressed them with my thumb to find a large one, neither hard nor soft, but crunchy. Taking the red apple with his large hand from mine, he said, "I didn't know we had such beautiful apples—you surely can choose! I hope you choose your wife so well, so you won't look at other women and sin in your heart. Hum, there's nothing more joyous in this life than the beauty of a woman."

My mother said, "That's no way to talk to a child!" He replied, "It is."

"Will I ever be able to speak in tongues?" I asked him. "He can do it"—I pointed at Ivo—"though he reads garbage!"

"Though I speak with the tongues of men and of angels, and have not charity, I am become as sounding brass, or a tinkling cymbal. And though I have the gifts of prophecy, and understand all mysteries . . . and though I have all faith, so that I could remove mountains, and I have not charity, I am nothing. Don't worry about the tongues, son."

"But if I spoke in tongues, then I'd be sure to go to heaven."

"He who wants to save his life, will lose it, and he who loses it for my sake, will gain it. Don't worry about salvation."

He looked at me for a long time. Then he dug his teeth, some of them made of gold, into the apple, his gray mustache spreading like a brush on the red skin of the fruit while he was biting. Saliva collected in my mouth as if he had chewed a lemon. He ate one half slowly and left the rest on the plate. A haze of brown soon covered the white crystal apple meat. His face suddenly lost color, turning ashen gray, and he said, "I don't feel well."

"Let's go to the doctor's, then!" said my mother.

"No, I don't want to go there."

"Let me go fetch him."

"No. Maybe I'll go there tomorrow, if God wills."

"You speak strangely, let me go."

"No, it's no big deal—everything will happen the way God wills it."

My mother didn't look pleased at his conversation and she left for the bedroom. In the doorway as he was leaving the living room, he looked long, sadly, at Ivo, who continued reading the comic books, and at me, as I patted the purring heathen goddess. He closed the door quietly.

In *The Secrets of Paris* I read about drunks and wondered what it was like to be so drunk in a cellar that you sing without noticing that you are doing it. I fell asleep, the book sliding out of my hands.

Late at night I heard a scream. Ivo was shaking me violently. "Father's dying!" he shrieked.

It was pitch black in the room. I sprang out of bed, and both of us ran to the bedroom of our parents. "Where's Mother?"

"Gone to get the doctor."

There was a feeble light from the night table casting an orange hue over our father; the corners of the room stayed dark. In the double marital bed, two beds put together, he lay in his striped blue and gray pajamas. His gray chest hair stuck out through the unbuttoned top of his pajama shirt. He was propped up on a pillow. His eyes were closed and he breathed slowly, inarticulate sounds coming from his throat. Above the bed was a photograph, framed in wood: he—in military uniform—and my mother at their wedding, cheek against cheek, both of them handsome and unsmiling.

His breath was partly a snore, partly a sort of choking. His face was pale, and as he hadn't shaved that day, his chin was blue and gray. Ivo and I were so terrified that we couldn't go to his side of the bed; we went to our mother's side. We started screaming prayers, whatever came to our minds, to the Heavenly Father, to let our earthly father live. We had been taught to keep our eyes closed when praying. So I was closing my eyes to pray, and opening them to see how our father was. His gurgling noises came from his throat, as if he were using a mouthwash. White foam appeared on his lips, and began to trickle down his chin from one corner of his mouth. We shrieked.

"God, don't kill him!" I yelled.

"God, let it be your will to let him live! We cannot change your will, but make it your will, if . . . " Ivo shouted.

A drop of blood trickled from our father's nose, onto his mustache, and from it onto his chin, and it dropped onto the hair of his chest. A loud breath came out of him, and it lasted long, without him drawing in another, and when the body was silent, again, some more air wheezed out of his throat and red foam appeared in the corners of his lips. His head dropped forward. Ivo and I grabbed his left hand. He had taught us where to find the pulse, hoping we would wish to become doctors in order to find all about the ways of the heart. I pushed Ivo's fingers away, so I could feel, he pushed mine, so he could feel. No pulse. His hand was cool and swollen. Ivo, green in face, pressed his palm against Father's chest, kneeling on the empty side of the bed.

"Nothing! His heart's stopped!" he shouted. "It's finished."

I looked at the clock next to the preserved cherries and blackberries on the dark brown cupboard—grains slanting into trapezoid forms. The large hand of the clock covered the small hand.

"Midnight!" I shouted. "And it's the midnight between the sixth and the seventh days of the month! Isn't six the number of man, and seven the number of God?"

"Yes! Yes! That means he went to God!" Ivo said. "That's a sign!" We stared at his face. It bore no expression, neither joy nor sadness, neither peace nor war; he looked as if he were listening to something attentively with his eyes closed, like an icon in which ears and not eyes see you.

Ivo said, "Look!" and pointed at a piece of paper—Father's handwriting was on it, in blue ink. "In his last hour, when Mother had gone to the doctor's, he called me and asked for a piece of paper. He wrote down his will calmly. See, his handwriting is no different from usual—just read, see how clear his mind was!

"Then he said, 'Look, I will die very soon. Don't forget to love God with all your heart, mind, and soul, don't ever forget that, and all else will come from it. Let us pray.' We began to pray, he prayed for all of us, except for himself. Then he grew quiet and closed his eyes and began to breathe heavily. I began to pray for him aloud. He opened his eyes, and said, 'Not for me, pray for yourself! You are remaining on earth, and now leave me in peace, I must breathe out my soul to God.' Then he lay back on the pillow, like now."

My body trembled and my teeth chattered. I looked around as if to find a getaway, but the windows and the door could not do. There was no way out.

"So I prayed again to God to spare him," said Ivo. "He opened his eyes once more, and said, 'I am going!' He meant he was going to heaven. He said it with certainty." Ivo's face was yellow green and his eyes slanted, as if he had changed his race to Mongolian. "What will become of us?" he asked me. Our father lay no longer a man but a corpse on the bed; blackness of the night was seeping in through the windows. The clock ticked like a time bomb.

We went into the living room, turned on the lights, and didn't dare to leave the room. I prayed to God to revive my father as He did Lazarus—I would serve Him all my life then. Yet I was scared that Father would indeed be brought back to life, but not be the same as he used to be; instead, he might have something heavenly in him, something that would kill me on the spot as soon as I beheld it, turning me into ashes.

The doors opened. Mother, wet from snow, came in with the doctor. Ivo and I stood in the middle of the room in our long spacious flannel pajamas, with broad blue vertical stripes, in the fashion of Turkish soldiers from an old picture book. With the doctor came in the stink of tobacco and booze. "Where is he?" he asked without breaking his stride.

"He's dead," I said.

"But where is he?"

"He is in heaven!" said Ivo. "You won't find him anymore."

"Oh, my God," cried our mother in an unearthly chilling way. And she ran with the doctor following her into the bed-room. We watched from the door. The doctor listened with his stethoscope, searching for sounds on the chest of our father. "It's too late!" he said.

Our pale mother said, "My God, what will I do with these ones?" and looked at us. Besides being terrified, I was scared, if that makes sense, that aside from a big fear of death, I had a smaller fear, of the future. How would we live? The doctor walked out, his chin on his chest, and several men walked in.

The man who used to help my father make clogs, Nenad, opened his mouth as if he would say something, but he said nothing. The uncle, a hefty man, breathed heavily, went to see the corpse and stayed there for a long time. He came back and grunted, as though he were asleep and snoring. He lifted me onto his knee and rocked me up and down thoughtfully. His whole chest rising and falling, he said, "One thing is the other life, and another this life, and we don't have him anymore."

When Ivo and I went to our bedroom, Ivo switched off the lights, and I switched them back on. "Why do you want the lights on? You can't sleep with the lights on."

"I'd be scared in the dark," I said.

"What more is there to be scared of ?" he snarled.

"I want the lights on," I said, and he let me have my way. Soon he was wheezing, asleep. I couldn't sleep. What if I die too? I couldn't breathe well. Maybe I am dying? No, children don't die just like that, unless they have a high fever. I touched my forehead, and it felt cool, but feelings could lie. But why should fever be dangerous? Fever should be healthy, the farthest away from death—death is cold. I shivered under my covers. I looked at the window—a big blue-black square in the wall. I propped myself up in bed, realizing I wouldn't be able to sleep, realizing my father had died in this position. I lay on my side, but the black windows behind my back disturbed me; when I faced them, they disturbed me even more.

What if God doesn't exist, and here we are almost envying our father for having died a holy death? I looked at Ivo with envy. See, he's a good Christian, he has peace. He has seen the whole death, and I missed it. When I came in, Father was no longer conscious; maybe he was already dead, or in the last stretch of dying; perhaps he would have told me something, the way Jacob told his son Joseph.

Still, the way it was it seemed it had to be. I felt ill in my stomach, and didn't dare to move out of my bed, lest I should injure the holy balance of reality, its finality.

I heard firm boot steps on the staircase, and then in the corridor. My older brother Vlado, who had been serving as a physician in the army in Novi Sad, stepped into the room, and said: "I heard it. Don't be afraid, everything will be all right. Why don't you switch off the lights, it's daybreak?"

"Look how dark it is." I pointed at the black square in the wall.

"No, it isn't, look!" He switched off the lights, and the square changed into light gray-blue. "And if I turn the lights back on, it'll look dark outside, but it isn't." He was in a green uniform, a cap with a red star on his head. He had a benevolent, encouraging expression on his face. Then our mother came in and said, "You know, that lout of a doctor, Slivich, was not at the hospital when he was supposed to be. He had left a message that he was at the Happy Cellar but went instead to the Last Paradise on Earth. By the time I found him, drinking and gambling, Father was already dead." She pointed in the direction of the bedroom with the corpse, tears in her nose. "Cerebral hemorrhage, he said."

Vlado went to see the corpse. He came back and said that it was a heart attack, and that Father could have been saved with a timely injection of adrenaline.

"But he didn't want me to get the doctor," she said. "Everything that happens is His will, he said, and not a single hair falls out without His will. Maybe it's better this way. He had ruined his health—two years in the army before the war, five in the war in the rain, sleet, snow, and sun ruined his kidneys. He had taken so many medications for kidneys, high blood pressure—his heart loomed so large on X rays that it always astonished doctors. And then the religious seizure—he did not even sleep, he prayed and prayed for the last two months!"

"He could have lived on—a large heart is not necessarily a terrible thing," said Vlado.

Now it was bright outdoors and we switched off the lights. The sun began to shine.

I walked out of the house and sat on a felled tree trunk—and with my thumbnails I peeled the rugged bark. The windows on the house loomed black. My mother called me in for breakfast. Nauseated, I put my finger on my tongue.

A friend of Ivo's, Zoran, walked into the yard and sat next to me on the bark and peeled the bark. "Now we are the same!" He seemed to be glad—now we could be real friends. His father had been killed while defending a woman from a rapist, who had shoved a bayonet through his chest. Zoran had grown up without a father, without any recollection of him whatsoever. Often in the middle of shooting arrows at trees, playing Robin Hood—he was Will Scarlet; I, Little John; Ivo, Robin Hood—he'd asked me, "How is it to have a father?"

"I don't know how to tell you—I don't know how it is not to have a father."

Now I said, "Yes, now we are the same."

"You'll find out how it is to live without a father," he said.

"Yes."

"But I still won't be able to find out how it is to have a father, and you know that," he said.

"Yes, now I'll know nearly everything I wanted to know," I said.

"So we are not exactly the same." He tore a thorn from a roseless rosebush, and cleaned his teeth, pushing the thorn between them, and he did it so violently that he spat blood.

"So we are not exactly the same," I said.

Several hours later more than a dozen relatives in the living room discussed the dead man. My sister-in-law said, "When we saw him last at the train station, he waved to us for a long time, as if he knew he wouldn't see us again. He had joked wittily, played with his granddaughter"—a blond little brat who at that moment dug her fingers into the soil of a flowerpot, and began to knead it into a cake—"and lifted her onto his shoulders. I thought, What a healthy man!" Everybody evoked their last images of him aloud and it was all said in a tone of regret, amazement, and, at the same time, admiration for the integrity of his death. I thought I could contribute. "Ivo shook me out of sleep in the back room, he screamed, 'Father's dying!' I leaped out of bed, and there he was, purple foam trickling down his chin, gurgling noises coming through his throat, and then he choked, and the blood trickled from his nose. . . . "

Everyone in the room frowned. I became quiet. There was silence. I thought I had said something wrong; I put my right shoulder over my chin, to hide my mouth. Yes, they didn't like hearing anything from me; I wanted to impress them with how much I'd suffered and with how much my father had! I should have told them something uplifting, like Ivo when he tells them the religious stuff, like "I am going," and that stuff about the midnight between the sixth and the seventh days.

During the day, my mother washed the corpse and changed it from pajamas into a suit, his Sunday best, which he had worn on the way to the church to preach about the death of Christ. Now, however, he had no hat on his head. His swollen chubby hands with two purple nails (from hammer misses in work) were intertwined as if in prayer, though when he was dying they had lain at his sides. Maybe the hat should be put over the hands, I thought. He lay in a casket on the dining table where he used to sing, joke, and play the guitar as well as tell us Biblical stories, adding to them things that I couldn't find in the Bible, like more and more adventures of Jonah. The undertaker, who had brought the casket with Father's name and age in golden letters, put some disinfecting white dust into Father's ears and nose, and then plugged the ears and nostrils with cotton—to keep the death inside.

The curtains were rolled down. Mother went to the neighbors across the road, to an old woman whose husband, also a clog-maker, had died three years before, and returned with the black flag. I went into the street to see how the house would look with the flag. Above the swallows' nests that Mother had shattered with the flagpole in the fall to prevent the swallows' return in the spring, the black flag came out between the red tiles where Father used to stick out the flag of our Socialist Federal Republic of Yugoslavia. The house looked like the tower of a missing castle, with a very simple and ominous emblem.

I recalled a dream from five years before. In the dream, Father and I sit in the living room next to Mother's casket. He says, We'll have to live without her. Can we live without her? I ask. I think so, he says. At that, I had screamed in my dream, and when I opened my eyes I was relieved that it was dawn. My mother had asked me what was wrong, and I couldn't tell her that I had dreamed she was dead, so I said that a pack of wolves was tearing me to pieces.

Hearing from my father about the prophetic powers of dreams, for years I had feared that my mother would die. And now Mother and I were sitting with Father's corpse, wondering how life without him would be.

Many people came to pay homage. Mother led them into the living room without turning on the lights. There were no candles at the side of his head. Some light came through the half-opened door and through the curtains. A strong disinfecting smell stung my eyes and nose. And what was the smell there for? To disinfect the dead one from death or from the last traces of life?

I wanted to touch my father again, but I couldn't, as if death in him would devour me too if I touched it. His cheeks were growing purple; the capillaries around his eyes were breaking open. His chin was covered with white and black stubble. Yet he still looked somehow good-natured and attentive, with his arched eyebrows and the clean parallel lines on his large forehead. His relatives and friends gathered around the casket. Some crossed themselves. Some wept. It made me glad to think that others were sad too, but I wished they wouldn't stare like that—it was obscene, they looked at my father as if he were a new species. Ivo and I stood in the corridors all day long and asked each other, "Do you want to see him one more time?"

"I think I couldn't anymore," we would say and go back in.

The day of the burial arrived, cold and windy. "This is your last chance to see him," our mother said to us. She walked to the casket and kissed Father's purple corpse, her tears dropping onto his ear. The mortician, a dry bony man whose mustache was white on the sides and yellow beneath his nose from smoking, said, "Time to go!" He seized the casket cover, which had been leaned against the wall like some great gilt shield, and laid it atop the casket. He took a hammer and nails in his hands. Vlado snatched those away from him. As a child Vlado had worked with hammer and nails, helping with the work of nailing leather onto the wooden soles. Even Ivo and I had had to do it, and several times we had stayed up all night to meet the glass-factory deadline; we all took pride in being the best hands with hammers and nails.

Vlado hammered the nails through the yellow metal holes on the side of the cover. He hit with measure. Both the living man who was hammering and the dead man who was being hammered in must have hammered millions of nails each, the dead one more than the living one. The sound of the hammering was dull; there was no echo from the box because the box was full. Our mother wanted to take Ivo and me out of the room so we wouldn't witness this, but we wouldn't let her. I wondered why I wasn't crying. I could barely breathe, there was pressure on my chest, and my body was cold and electrified.

Four people carried the casket through the doors, down the steps of white, black-spotted stone. Masons from the Dalmatian Coast had made the steps, smoothing them out for days, and they had shown me pictures of women's pubic hair, and I hadn't believed them. I had thought women had pearls in shells there, not hair. The crowds parted before the casket like the waters of the Red Sea before Moses. The casket was carried through the varnished oak door of the house entrance into the yard, with the carriers maneuvering and panting as if with a heavy piece of furniture. There was a crowd waiting next to the thorn bushes, next to the cherry trees—no leaves—and next to the flat wall of our neighbor's house.

That wall carried no windows except a small one of the larder, with iron grates over it. People used to point their fingers at our neighbor—he had been in the wrong army during the war. Now he stood against the wall, gray, ghastly, as if waiting to be shot by a firing squad. In the midst of the yard stood a black hearse with a silvery cover. Two black horses with blinders stood in front of it, and steam rose from their backs, from the areas not covered by black satin. They did not move their tails—probably the function of tails is mostly to chase away flies, and in January there were none. They bowed their heads, as if there were grass among the wet gravel, or as if they reacted to the human emotion and gave it even better expression than the people could. The casket screeched onto the hearse. The horses moved their ears as if the noise had tickled them. The screeching brought a chalk whiteness to my sister, Nella, who had just arrived from West Germany, where she was studying to become a nurse. I used to irritate her by driving big pots over cement, because I knew that she hated the screeching of dry chalk on blackboards, and pots on the cement. Men in black, a variety of relatives, hooked green wreaths with purple tapes onto the feeble top frame of the hearse.

A procession formed. Mother, two brothers, I, and two sisters stepped behind the hearse, and behind us, three uncles and five aunts. One uncle was missing because he had loved cars so much that, as the first mechanic in town, in the middle of the winter he had lain on the ground beneath the cars and had caught pneumonia and died. I chose to walk next to Nella rather than Ivo. The procession was very slow. Now and then I turned around to see how my uncles were. They all looked thoughtful. The steadfastness of the pace held a lesson for us, some lesson anyway, as we shifted from one leg to another. Howsoever slowly we went, by howsoever many places, we could not deviate from the crooked path that led into the graveyard. We went across the railroad tracks, the casket bumping up and down. Then over a hill, past the shabby house where Father and his nine siblings had grown up. As the oldest son, he had helped his father in clog making and had attended only four grades of elementary education, though he'd been declared the best pupil of his class two years in a row, and though the school principal himself besought my grandfather to give his son a chance. "I'd be delighted to," replied my grandfather, "If you, Mr. Principal, replaced my son in the shop to feed all these children." The grandfather had died of cancer—because of his strong faith in God he had refused to go to the hospital to have a growth removed. The house had been sold a long time ago. Now in the backyard many white geese greeted the funeral with hissing. We walked around the cemetery onto a hill with three crosses in imitation of Golgotha: Jesus crucified between two robbers. Jesus was missing, somebody must have stolen him. But the robbers were on the crosses, white pigeon paint making stripes down their cheeks, as if they were weeping.

The Baptist cemetery was fenced off from the Catholic and Communist cemeteries—the Eastern Orthodox cemetery was on another hill—corresponding to our isolation in the community. Wherever we went, fingers pointed at us and hushed whispers followed us; we were called the "new-believers" in derogatory tones of voice—meaning the "wrong-believers."

The hearse got stuck in the muddy ditch between the road and the Baptist cemetery. The coachman whipped the horses with a thin leather whip to inspire them to pull the hearse, and the hearse nearly toppled over. My three uncles and a grave digger carried the casket off the hearse. The horses pulled the hearse out of the ditch.

They bowed, staring at the ground, but now and then they lifted their heads and watched the burial with their large moist eyes, their foreheads contorting into sad, thoughtful expressions.

In the Baptist cemetery wooden crosses, cracked from heat, rain, and cold, tilted in the soft soil, the names erased. Others, made of old thin stone, collected moss on their northern sides, as though to protect them from the winter winds. Ivy climbed them snakily, making them resemble the emblem of medicine. Some graves did bear tombstones, but most of these had sunk half their height into the soft earth and dry weeds grew around them. Over the edge of the hill on the western slope, facing the "Whore of Babylon" (as the minister called it), Rome, the Catholic cemetery sprawled, filled with large stones, marbles, and fat little angels like Cupids—all they needed were bows and arrows. Between the graveyards from several cedar trees pigeons descended onto the ground, probably in the hope of getting crumbs of bread. I took the pigeons to be doves, and their descent a sign from God.

Beneath one cedar two fresh heaps of yellow and green soil arose like wings, and between the wings blinked no bird, but a rectangular hole, the grave. I was glad my father would be buried under an evergreen tree on the highest point of the cemetery— even better than Robin Hood beneath an oak. People gathered all over the soft cemetery, trampling old graves, sinking into them in their best shoes, totally disregarding the ones who had been dead, and paying attention only to the newcomer, or, rather, the new-leaver.

The minister stood right next to the tree, turning his back to the Catholic slope. On his left were about ten members of the church choir. They sang about death, heaven, faith, grace, and all the rest, addressing my father in his coffin. After the singing, the minister shouted a sermon, and some foam appeared over his lips, and trickled down his closely shaven round cheek, which was pink in the wind. The parallel lines of his shiny hair showed the distance between the picks of his comb. "We cannot even sing about how we miss him, because without him we don't have a good bass! We all miss him, but dear honorable citizens and comrades, brothers and sisters, I tell you, there is no point in our being sad, for this man is alive!" Saliva sprinkled out of his mouth like sparks of fire. He paused for effect. His thunderous voice echoed behind our backs from a steep hill, covered with apple orchards, beyond the cemetery.

I looked at the coffin, expecting the lid to break open.

After a hush, there was a commotion and murmur in the crowd, especially at the edges of the crowd, where the non-members of the church, including the Communists, stood.

My toes freezing, I wished the minister would stop his speech—he said we hadn't had such a good death in years, and went into the details of my father's death, nearly verbatim from Ivo's account—there was no way of stopping him. From the corners of my eyes I observed the crowd. My school classmates with our main teacher were there. A couple of girls wept, some boys looked gleeful, others nudged each other with their elbows. They were scrutinizing me and taking bets—whether I would cry or not. I learned that later from a friend. I wished I could throw stones at them. I turned round and stared at the crowds of familiar faces with animosity.

Two grave diggers, who had been waiting impatiently for the speech to be over, shifting their weight from one foot to another in soiled rubber boots, leaning their hands on the shovels, dropped the shovels, and with the help of two uncles of mine, withdrew the planks of wood from beneath the casket and began to lower the casket on ropes into the soil. The casket dropped out of my sight, and I had a sinking sensation, as if my heart had sunk into my intestines. The ropes grated against the casket, sounding like dull saws cutting into wood.

Mother and Grandmother, arm in arm, walked to the grave, and Mother leaned to the ground, picked up a chunk of soil, and handed it to the mother of my father. The old woman tossed it into the grave. A loud thump on the wood. Then Mother tossed some of the soil into the grave too. A loud thump. Great pressure in my chest. Behind my nostrils, below my eyes, it burned—it felt similar to the anesthesia for my tonsillectomy several years before. Having seen the red mesmerizing light and felt the scorching sensation on awakening I had screamed, "Am I in hell?" A doctor had had to intervene because my scream had made my throat bleed.

Vlado and Ivo threw pieces of soil, and so did my older sister Nada, tears flowing down her cheeks. Nella and I refused to throw. I walked to the grave, and Ivo wanted to stop me, pulling at my coat, so that I slid, on the edge, fighting for my balance and staring into the muddy water: atop the casket sat a bloated green frog, a beating heart.

Grave diggers avalanched soil over the casket. The thumps grew less and less loud, and more and more dull. The grave diggers sped up their work, and one of them spat into his fists—as though sealing some good agreement—to avoid getting any blisters.

From the hill you could see how the people dispersed, church-bound, or pub-bound, or home-bound. We too walked away from the grave, even though the grave had not yet been filled with soil to the top.

A warm wind lifted Nella's hair from her eyes. When I didn't watch myself, I began to skip my steps, hop. I wondered at the inappropriateness of my cheer. Nella sang "Silent Night" in German.

"Did they pray for you so you could speak in German tongues?"

"No, I learned it from tapes in a classroom."

"That's too bad. Did you see any murders in Stuttgart?"

"What a strange question!"

"I heard Germans were murderers, so I was afraid you'd never come back."

"No, they're nice."

"Impossible. Have you seen our history book? Our people hanging from the trees, houses burned, children shot to death?"

"Those were the Nazis. Modern Germans are very cultured."

"But they kill the soul in Germany and America, my teacher says. They don't believe in God, do they?"

"Most of them do, more than here."

"Uncle Pero says their bread is made of plastic foam."

She continued to sing.

In the church the minister told the congregation they should all hope to die like my father. "Who among us has prayed as much as this man had? I had a quiet minute at his side, and as I prayed for him, a voice whispered to me to stop praying and to look at his knees. I rolled up his pajamas above his knees—they were coated with a thick layer of blood crusts. So let us give praise to God for such a wonderful death. Our man is now in New Jerusalem."

As soon as the sermon turned to more general terms about the glories of heaven, I began to stick my thumbnails into the bench along the grains. The minister broke the bread, and the electrician passed it around in a small basket; wine followed in a silvery bowl resembling the Cup of Marshall Tito trophy that my favorite soccer club had won. I was glad that I couldn't participate in the ceremony—I hadn't been baptized—because I couldn't imagine salivating on the rim of the cup with a hundred old men and women. I liked the smell of wine, though.

On their way out of the church, a variety of old people stroked my hair with their dry hands—as if dipping their fingers into the sacristy, reverting to their Catholic habits—and the sacristy was my hair.

At home dozens of relatives ate the chicken paprikash and cakes Mother had somehow managed to prepare amidst all the confusion. I knew it was she who did it, because nobody else made such poppy seed cakes, cheese pies, and apple strudels. I laughed though there was no joke being told, my sister told me to stop it, and she pulled out a smooth yellow German toothbrush, and brushed the poppy seeds from between my teeth. That tickled me and made me laugh even more.

The cat, who had been outdoors for three days, scratched her back against my shin, blinked flirtingly, and purred as if everything were in the best possible order and none of us were missing. She could not count; if she had four kittens and two were taken away to be drowned, she continued purring, apparently not noticing that some of her children were missing. But if you took all of them away, for days she would moan so sorrowfully and dreadfully that you had to shudder. There were enough of us left for her. Perhaps soon I too would be used to there being one less among us, to having no father. I slipped her some white meat beneath the table when nobody was watching, and she devoured it without chewing, momentarily interrupting her purring, and continued to blink for more.

Even though Vlado, Nada, and Nella were there, Mother kept repeating that the house was empty, and I agreed—there was more echo on the staircase. "Wherever I open the door, I see him there, sitting and reading the Bible, or kneeling, or pacing around the room," she said.

Mother raised the tombstone to my father. She inscribed my father's name on it—the same as mine, to my displeasure. And to my horror, she engraved her name with the date of her birth, leaving the date of her death empty, so when she died, only one date would have to be cut in the stone. After erecting the tombstone, she walked to his grave almost every other day.

I avoided the cemetery. But willy-nilly I came to the grave a year later after drunk Uncle Pero had fallen off a barn, breaking his neck. The smooth stone, black and spotted with gray, reflected my shadow. And, as became a beekeeper, his tombstone bore a honey-colored inscription; *Death, where is thy sting?*

I feared the room where Father had died. My brother Ivo didn't. The unsmiling brown wedding picture of my parents stayed above the bed, both of them looking alert.

For years I couldn't eat apples, my father's last supper. When I did try to eat them, I choked. Every 6th of January for several years I remembered what had happened. I kept the lights on then, fearing that I myself would die.

On the first anniversary I was certain that I would die at midnight, though I knew that my belief was irrational. I put Father's Zenith watch next to my bed. I prayed, opening and closing my eyes. Thirty seconds left, ten seconds left. My heart skipped beats and pounded against my chest like a hawk in a glass cage. I was sure the glass would burst in a couple of seconds. When it was a second past midnight, jubilant, I thanked God. And so every year until my reason began to prevail.

I couldn't control dreams. Father would still be in the workshop, made of Styrofoam, lying between two chairs like a magician, without his body bending.

In one dream he appeared in his room and called me to his side. Come, Yozzo, I'll tell you something.

What will you tell me?

You are the only one who knows that I am alive.

But we buried you, you are dead.

Yes, you buried me, but I am not dead. I am about to die now.

For the second time?

For the second time. But first bring me an apple, and choose a beautiful one.

I brought him one that looked like a heart, and pressed my thumbnail into it—it was crunchy.

I walked out and wondered how we could bury him for the second time. What would the police say when we took out his second corpse? How could we hide him? Could we bury him in the garden? When I came back he was propped up on his pillow, the room stank of dead fish, and he, barely lifting his eyelids, said,

Son, no rush, I'll be here for months. I am not going to die quickly like the first time.

Nobody knew that he was alive except me, and I kept him in the back room like some monster. One day I wanted to take him out for a walk, but when I touched him, his flesh fell to pieces, scattered on the white sheets, without any blood.

Wool

In Vinograd Village one morning a girl named Anna rushed out of her backyard when she heard a high-pitched murmur, her hazel eyes turning green as she looked through the slanting rays of the sun. A lake of sheep was flowing down the hill toward her in waves, each wave with many voices, all voices together becoming a huge sorrow. (After spending the winter in the Pannonian plains near the Hungarian border, the flocks were returning to the Bosnian mountains—this was in 1969, a long time before bridges over the River Sava between Croatia and Bosnia would sink.) Shepherds with long sticks, dressed in rags, walked along their flocks. Black dogs bullied the sheep. Rams with mud in their hair often bucked thick back-twisted horns into empty space before them. Ears hung on the sides of mothers' faces as if the mothers had grown tired of listening to bleating, though it was they who bleated the most. Little lambs struggled to keep up with them, bleating several octaves higher. Anna's neighbors stood on the roadside, at the edge of grassy ditches, and chewed pipes with their yellow dentures. Her father, Noah, stood behind her, leaning on a hunting rifle, his small blue eyes vanishing into the redness of his chubby face. "If any of these damned sheep run off the road into my vineyard, I'll blast the hell out of them." He probably forgot that the rifle did not work—it was rusty and jammed with mud. His free hand lifted a bottle of crimson wine to his wet lips.

Anna asked a shepherd if she could hold a little lamb, as small as a cat—its legs were long so that it looked like a cat on stilts. It had black nostrils and black circles around its eyes among white wool. "Could I have it?"

"Give me three hundred dinars, and it's yours," the shepherd said.

"Dad, could you . . . ?"

"Hungry monster, aren't you?" Noah said.

"I'd like to have a pet."

"What good can a pet do? You should . . . "

"The flock's not gonna wait," the shepherd cut in. "Take it or leave it!"

"Three bottles of wine?" Noah said.

"Four."

Anna ran into the house, brought five bottles from the moldy cellar, and was about to hand them all to the shepherd, but Noah snatched two and said to her, "Can't you count, ass?" and to the shepherd, "Take it or leave it."

The shepherd looked down the road at the flock, which had passed, brown dust rising above it, and said "Blood is worth less to you than wine?"

"What can you do with blood?"

The shepherd wiped his dusty lip, and his Adam's apple rose and fell with a click. "Fuck your planets, my friend. You got me!" He snatched the three bottles, and Anna took the lamb from his forearm, where it had perched chewing imaginary future grass. He walked in quick strides after the bleating brown cloud.

"Kid, we got us a steal. Have a sip!" Noah offered wine to his child. Anna rushed inside the house to play with her little lamb.

For days Anna groomed the lamb, gave it milk, walked it in the vineyard down to the creek, and rolled with it in the cricketing grass. She buried her thin aquiline nose in the wool. Surrounding the lamb with her long coppery hair, she created the illusion that her face and the lamb were in a luminous tent.

The lamb was clean and averse to mud and could have slept with Anna if it had not rolled little steamy bronze-black droppings all around the living room. Her mother, Estera, wanted the lamb to sleep outdoors, on a chain, like a dog.

Anna set up the lamb in the empty pigsty, in a nest of hay and old sweaters. The lamb often broke into the garden and ate lettuce, cabbage, tulips, and white roses. Estera was dismayed at the damage. Anna dragged green branches of various trees to the lamb; cherry leaves were the lamb's favorite, so Anna climbed two large cherry trees in the garden, and sawed off branches and tossed them to the lamb, who wagged its tail and hopped like an antelope.

Anna often crawled around the animal on all fours, as if she were a lamb too. She scratched her head against the lamb's, pushing a little. At first the lamb dodged her head and ran away into a bush of budding flowers, but soon it began to press its head against Anna's. For weeks they gently pushed each other around the yard, but the lamb was growing stronger and stronger, and for all Anna knew it could have been a ram. She decided, however, that it was a female, and named it Tanya. As soon as Anna came back from school, Tanya would lower her head, dig her hind hooves in the sandy soil, and grind her teeth, as if she'd chew Anna. Anna laughed at the challenge and went down on all fours, imitating her teacher, who catapulted and flew to collide with Anna's forehead. The impact of the collision threw Anna off balance, so that she rolled on the ground. Anna had a splitting headache, and tears went down her cheeks.

Anna invited neighborhood children to play the same game with Tanya. They were astounded at the violence of the sheep, and none of them wanted to have their head butted more than once.

Soon it was summer, and Anna thought the best part of her life was over. For Anna unfortunately much more than the friendship with Tanya was going on that summer. Every Saturday night, her father got drunk. The first Saturday night in June, he came home at midnight. He shouted at Estera, accusing her of sleeping with the chimney sweep, and hit her with his fist over her mouth so that she bled.

Anna's younger brother Mato—he was eight, she was almost eleven—and Anna stood in the corner of the room, their teeth chattering, while their father smashed a chair over an old cradle, where instead of a new child Estera kept jars of plum jam. The cradle cracked, the jars burst, and the dark sugary tissue of plums oozed onto the splintery floor. "Coward!" Estera said. Noah charged after her and slipped on the jam, while Estera jumped out the window. He ran after her down the gravel road into the woods. In nightgowns Mato and Anna ran after them, screaming to their father, "Don't, don't!" They caught up with him. His tobacco breath rasped, wheezed, and he doubled over, and panted, "My liver, my liver!" Mato and Anna did not respond.

"Don't you worry about your Dad?" he said.

"You bet!" Anna said.

"How dare you worry about me? I don't need your sympathy! Chimney-sweep bastards!"

He grabbed Mato and Anna by their hair and knocked their heads together and kicked them, and his knuckles struck Anna on the cheek so that her face blazed with heat. Anna ran to the pigsty and moaned, while her knocked-out salty molar swam in blood around her tongue. She cuddled up with Tanya and fell asleep.

The next morning when Anna woke up, Tanya was sniffing her hair and wetting her eyebrows and eyelashes with her cool nostrils. That refreshed Anna. When she walked out, she saw her mother sweeping the entrance to their red brick house; the polished stone steps glistened. No evidence of the previous night remained, and Anna thought that perhaps she was crazy to think that all that helter-skelter had gone on. But it was odd that her mother wore cherry lipstick; though her lips were full, her lower one looked too full now, so she must have hidden the bruise.

Noah was repairing old wine barrels, taking off rusty rings and putting on new ones, then hammering them. His hands were unsteady, and the short nails kept falling from between his fingers into dust, where he could not find them. In his hangover imprecision he missed most of those that didn't fall and he hit his thumb; he groaned and jumped around the yard as though he'd hit his toe. He stood at the side of the spindle-well, sticking his hand into a pail of cool water.

Anna helped her father mix chemicals, for spraying the vineyard, in a cemented hole in the ground with walls as high as her waist. The chemicals turned pale green. Noah saddled the copper carry-on pump on her back. In wooden shoes she walked down the slope between the rows of vines, sliding here and there over snails. She kept pushing a handle with one hand and with another waved a metal-capped hose with small holes, smaller than needle eyes, so that the spray came out as a haze that bit her eyes. This went on for two days. Sunday Anna hated it, but Monday she did not mind because she could skip school, and her father would write a note saying that she was sick, which, as it turned out, she was, with a cold—headaches and a nose-drip—so she skipped Tuesday too, free to play with her friend the sheep.

When her father did not watch, Anna took Tanya to the vineyard, and spread the leaves of the vines so she could chew young bundles of green grapes, which, out of their sheaths, looked like homeless peas. Tanya loved the baby grapes, chewing quickly, rubbing her ears against Anna's knee, looking at her sideways, flirtatiously, with big moist eyes. Anna petted her, and each swallow the sheep made was to Anna as though she herself had swallowed ripe apricots. Who knows how long their idyll would have gone on if Noah hadn't sneaked up on them, grabbed Anna by the hair, and dragged her into the yard. Tanya fled into the pigsty, but Anna couldn't, though she kicked her father in his hairless white shin. He pulled his belt off his pants, tied her to the youngest cherry tree with a rope, and whipped her, mostly over the back, with the metal part on the belt cutting through her cotton shirt. It was as though fire licked her. For a while he did not seem to know how to stop, though he took several momentary breaks to pull up his unfastened pants.

So Anna became feverish and her sores became infected. She lay on her stomach and her mother rubbed plum brandy into her skin to disinfect her. Anna gasped with the pain, and then fell asleep, brandy sinking into her blood from everywhere, so that she woke up drunk. Anna missed a whole week of school, and then got an F in math upon returning—she had forgotten the multiplication tables. While Estera cooked a vegetable stew, Anna now had to sit at the bread cabinet and recite the multiplication tables not only up to ten, but to twelve. While Anna hesitated at eight times nine, Mato, who'd been cutting his initials in the table leg with a Swiss knife, shouted "seventy-two." Anna could not think what eleven times eleven made, and while she was coming up with the answer with help from pencil and paper, Mato shouted "one hundred and twenty-one," and added that thirteen times thirteen made a hundred and sixty-nine. The whole day afterward he put on airs of being the smart one, and Anna the dumb one, until Anna trapped him below the lowest wire of a row of vines. Sitting on top of him, she opened his mouth with her hands, put a stone between his upper and lower molars so his mouth would stay open, and spat into his mouth until her throat went dry, and then she held his white tongue down with a stick and lowered a brown spider on its silky string onto his swollen tonsils. That would teach him to shout his tables!

Noah stayed on the wagon for the whole summer. He and Anna often sang folk songs from Zagorye, to his tambourine accompaniment. Every day he and Anna went into the vineyard, pulled out old rotten posts, put in new ones, and nailed the wires to them. If a wire broke, they mended it, using a long eight-wire twist to connect it. Her father ordered Anna to tighten the fence between the garden and the vineyard so that the sheep wouldn't eat the grapes. But for that, Tanya attacked the garden all the more zealously.

The whole side of the garden of flowers was eaten. Tanya had laid the backyard and garden to waste. Big and beautiful, she pranced around the yard like a race horse, challengingly looking at the stray cats and dogs, who kept out of her way.

In the beginning of the fall, the grape harvest took place. For a week Anna missed school and tore grape bundles off bumpy vines, tossed them in a bucket, and carried them to the barrel at the top of the hill. Afterwards, she, Mato, Noah, and Estera danced barefoot in the barrels, sinking through the grapes, while the grape juice flowed through holes into smaller barrels, where it would mature—or degenerate—into wine. Their feet stayed purple for days.

They boiled grape skins and distilled the steam into a pale brandy, almost as strong as pharmacy alcohol, certainly as poisonous.

After the harvest, Noah went into a tavern down the hill, and when it closed down, he brought home a dozen drunks, including the bartender. They slammed the doors and hollered and swore, so that they woke up the family. Through a slightly opened door, Estera and her children lined up their heads, one above another, and stared at the red-faced men. Several of them arm wrestled; others sang into each other's ears with spent voices.

The morning afterward Estera and Anna went to pray in the Catholic church in the next village—the peculiarity of Vinograd Village was that it had no church of its own. As if to compensate, the villagers had scattered a bunch of porcelain blue-and-maroon Mothers of God and thorny bloodied Jesuses, sometimes amidst a vineyard, so that the incomplete Holy Family looked like scarecrows, but far more durable than the raggedy ones in rotten colorless dark hats with Stalinesque mustaches made of horsehair. During the sermon Anna detested the smell of ordinary, non–vine-growing peasants: a mixture of garlic, hay, sweat, and manure. She stared around at their venous swollen blistery hands, which, as if ashamed of themselves, often clasped each other. The thumbs with the blue nails of a peasant across the row from her kept circling around each other. She could not follow the priest's slow reading, though now and then she grew excited when the words *sheep* and *lamb* floated and echoed in the dank space above twisted candles.

My sheep wandered through all the mountains, and upon every high hill. . . . my flock became a prey, and my flock became meat to every beast of the field, because there was no shepherd, neither did my shepherd search my flock but the shepherds fed themselves, and fed not my flock. . . . I will require my flock at their hand, and cause them to cease from feeding the flock; neither shall the shepherds feed themselves any more; for I will deliver my flock from their mouths, that they may not be meat for them.

Anna was disappointed since the words did not honestly mean what they said directly, but something beyond the sheep, about Israelites and Christians. She thought this was abusive to sheep, to use them as pictures for people's own purposes. But she liked the verses that the priest read afterward. *The Lord is my shepherd; I shall not want. He maketh me to lie down in green pastures: he leadeth me beside the still waters. . . . Yea, though I walk through the valley of the shadow of death, I will fear no evil: for thou art with me; thy rod and thy staff they comfort me.*

Anna sneaked out of the church. She climbed the large un-steady stones of a ruined Turkish fort, stared at glowing amber forests, and listened to the shushing and murmuring of falling beech leaves, each leaf floating like a bloodshot eye without a head to illumine. The fleeting shadows of the falling eyes gave Anna shivers because she had the impression that flocks of mice were running at her and up her legs. The flat eyes drifted into a swerving green river, and the river turned red.

On the way home she passed her father's favorite tavern, with the cries of drinkers rising above the clanking of silver and china. She smelled grilled meat, and inhaled deeply because the smell was pleasant. She read the sign: "Today's Special: Lamb."

At home she called Tanya out. No answer. She looked for Tanya everywhere. She walked back to the tavern, and peeped in. The red-faced bartender, with his greasy brown beard, laughed.

"What do you want, girl? Would you like some diced lamb?"

"Where did you get it," Anna asked, her throat parched.

"Where? Your dad sold it to me; I gave him a good price, a very good price! We neighbors have to support each other. . . . "

"You are a shitty pig!" she shouted, and the tavern owner ran after her. She grabbed a sharp stone from a heap of gravel on the side of the dirt road, and aimed at the bartender's forehead. The blue stone hit its target. His face was bathed in blood, and like the blinded Cyclops after Odysseus, the bartender bellowed threats.

At home, Anna called her Father names that he clearly could not believe she knew, though she had learned them from him. He grabbed her and knocked her head against the blue-washed wall. Anna kicked him in the stomach. He tied her to the chair, and talked:

"How do you think I feed you, brat? That sheep costs me a barrel of wine, with all the grapes you ripped off for her. And how do you think we're gonna feed ourselves? Don't you know that our grape harvest was lousy? I won't be able to pay taxes, and the government will steal our vineyard, and we'll starve."

"You're a murderer! A beast, pig . . . "

Father poured himself wine into an aluminum cup, and drank it, tears in his eyes. He got up and pulled out a sheep's leg from the bucket, still bloody, and said, "Dear daughter, I'm gonna cook it. This is a delicacy, grape-fed lamb!"

Anna tried to spit in his direction, but her burning mouth could produce no saliva, and when he offered her a slice of lamb, she closed her eyes and screamed.

Noah sat with her a whole day. He chewed lamb stew with onions, smacked his lips, drank wine. And he talked. "During the war I had to boil my leather shoes and eat them. I chopped them up in a thousand pieces. In the famine after the war, we got only Red Cross rice, so I became as thin as a rake and got TB. And look at you, how lucky and thankless you are, brat!" He sighed and then sobbed. "So eat, my daughter, eat, while you can."

Anna listened but still would not eat the lamb, not even on the second day. Her father slept by her side, and prevented her mother and Mato from bringing her plums and walnuts. He let Anna drink, but only wine. On the third day when Noah fell asleep and snored in deep unrhythmic bursts, Mato fed her bread and milk, but Anna was so dizzy she could not keep her head up. In the evening her father woke up and tickled her nose with salt-ed slices of grilled lamb. "Don't you want it real bad? I bet you do. Have a bite!" And with his thick fingers he pried her mouth open and pushed in a slice of lamb. She slammed her jaw shut as hard as she could, biting his thumb and forefinger. She spat out the flesh and blood—more blood had come from her gums than from her father's fingers.

Noah was so taken by surprise that he did not react. Estera came in and shouted. "Enough is enough! Sure, we could not have let her carry on with her sheep anymore, but you better stop!"

"She bit my finger to the bone!" Noah howled. "Quick, alco-hol!" He dipped his fingers in a cup of brandy, and Estera ban-daged them.

"I'll teach you a lesson yet, crap shooter!" he said to Anna.

"If you haven't yet, I don't think you ever will," her mother said. "You've taught her nothing but to hate." Her mother walked out, turning her rosary beads, and muttering.

That evening Anna grew so weak and drunk that she could not resist her father pushing lamb into her mouth. Almost asleep, she chewed the meat and gulped it with wine, and it felt amaz-ingly tasty; the amazement alerted her senses, and when she real-ized what was going on, she spat and vomited. She wept in misery, for she had eaten of her friend.

It was nighttime, and as usual in the fall, a power shortage resulted in a blackout. A lantern on a chair cast a light, so that Anna saw a light from below pass through her father's upper lip and nostrils, both made orange by the light that stayed in them. The shadow of his nose cast a pointed triangle across his bare forehead. He said nothing. He stood up, untied her, and marched out of the room.

Anna did not go to bed because she was afraid that when he got back he would beat her. She trembled for three hours, and as the church rang a brassy midnight, she grew calm. She could hear her father singing on his way, hoarsely, lyrics of some forbidden regional folk song. Anna grabbed the old rusty rifle from behind the pigsty, and when he opened the yard gate, she struck him on the back of his head with the heavy handle. He fell on the brick-laid path. Anna feared what he might do if he got up, so she hit him again, as hard as she could. Anna kept hitting and hearing crackling of bones, but she did not dare to stop.

Rust

I walked through the chirpy green tranquility of the park toward the baroque castle—my school—past a partisan monument. The partisans' noses were sharp, lips thin, cheekbones high, hands large and knotty; everything about them was angular—a combination of social realism and folk art. This type of sculpture was common in most Eastern European towns; the larger the town, the larger the proportions of the custom-made sculptures. But there was something unusually fierce about this monument.

The monument was made by Marko Kovachevich, a sculptor educated at the Moscow Art Academy, who had been a Communist before the war when it was dangerous to be one. During the war he fought against the Germans, and was awarded several medals. After the war, the Party commissioned him to erect the monument to those who had fallen. He received so little money for it that his expenses for the materials were barely covered. Marko excommunicated himself from the Party, flinging the red book of membership into the garbage in the town hall.

Since in a poor socialist society nobody could afford sculptures, except for the Communist government, and he no longer wished to work for them, Marko Kovachevich could not make a living as a sculptor. He became a tombstone-maker, specializing in the tombstones of deceased Party members.

Kovachevich moonlighted as an art teacher and, as such, was loved and feared by us children. His presence was imposing: tall and heavy-boned with a massive hooked nose like Rodin's and with rising eyebrows like Brezhnev's. His hair, the color of steel, was cut several times a year to a centimeter's length so that it looked like hedgehog bristles. His hair grew quickly, leaping into several shocks and cowlicks. Even when it was long, his donkey ears stuck out with some hair of their own atop each lobe.

Whenever he entered the classroom—a room with greasy maple floors, high ceilings, and chandeliers—he shouted our assignment—to draw a tree whose branches in the wind scratched the windowpane, or something out of our imagination, something we had never seen. He often assigned us to print inscriptions, HEREIN LIES IN PEACE . . . The ones he liked best he used on tombstones.

After giving us our assignments, he would pull four chairs together, take off his boots, put one beneath his head the way Jacob had put a stone beneath his, and soon the room resounded with sound snoring, as if a tank were tearing up the road, whereupon we would sneak out of the classroom into the park to climb trees and dig with branches into the soil for small Roman, Byzantine, Turkish, Hapsburg, and Croatian coins. Waking up half an hour later, he would shout out the tall windows for us to come back.

Before the end of the two-hour lesson, he'd stroll down the aisle, looking at our drawings.

"What's that?" he asked me.

"A tree," I answered proudly. I had paid painstaking attention to details.

"I don't see it. A tree lives, has a soul. Yours is a bunch of doodles."

He took a pencil and drew a line down the tree. The graphite pencil tip broke and flew off, hitting the windowpane. Marko continued to draw the line, unperturbed, through the core of what the tree should have been, and sure enough, it now looked like a firm tree, irrepressible, ready to resist tempests, challenging them to howl.

"See, you give it marrow. This is no beauty salon. First you make a tree, and what you do with it later—whether you put lipstick on it, eyelashes—that's incidental. But let it stand, for heaven's sake!"

He gave the tree a character distinctly his: uncollapsible grand simplicity. How, I wondered, does one learn to impart character with one stroke?

Marko Kovachevich took advantage of his job as a teacher to rest, and he let the children raise hell, wrestle, and jump through the windows. But now and then, quite unpredictably, he shouted, "Back to work!" Once, when a boy shattered a lamp on a post outside the window with a slingshot, Marko shouted, "Come here, beast!"

"No, Comrade, it wasn't me."

"Come here, you animal, I'll show you your God!"

The boy leaped to run away, knocking over several benches. Marko grabbed a coal shovel and hurled it. The weapon struck the wall half a foot above the boy's head, digging a hole in the loose mortar, while the boy rushed out of the door. The mortar sand hissed as it trickled to the floor. Marko's gray eyes glared fierce and savage and he ground his teeth as if the boy's bones were there to be chewed—Poseidon chewing a member of Odysseus's crew fallen overboard. Had the weapon struck several inches lower, it would have cracked the boy's skull. But, so far as I know, he killed no pupils. He was mostly pacific and ignored us the way a bull ignores flies. Of course a bull's tail now and then whips horseflies away.

Kovachevich the tombstone-maker chewed gingerly, like an old wounded lion, telling us that our region was poor in fluoride. I used to bring him apples from our garden just to see what trouble eating them gave him. One day as soon as he entered the classroom, he shouted for silence and stood on the table. In the posture of the partisan on the pedestal who was doomed to shove his rifle into the air as long as the bronze lasted, Marko pulled out his front teeth and shoved them toward the gasping children. "Comrades, asses! I'm a new man. I have new teeth. They will not give me pain. If I get tired of them, I put them in a glass of water. When I need to chew or give a speech, I put them back in. Progress! Do you hear, that's called progress!" Then he fitted the upper teeth back into his mouth and grinned the pink and white at us, closed his mouth, and masticated so that the muscles on his jaws kept popping, making a seesaw pattern, his jaw clanking. We watched silently, our eyes popping. He called my name. "Bring me one of those damned apples!"

I leaped to the window and lowered myself into the park, and was soon back with a crunchy apple. Marko slowly chewed it in front of us, grinding the teeth sideways, the way a bull ruminates, turning his head a little to the left, a little to the right, so we could all see how it worked. "That's art, my children. It makes life good, that's what art should do. Now you can go home. You've learned enough for today."

One spring day, he stood on a chair and shouted, "Comrades, you need some real life, some hardship." He pointed at two boys and me because we were the largest in the class. "You go to the junkyard, and ask for Marko's cart."

As we pulled the laden cart, the junkyard keepers laughed at us, calling us donkeys. We heard the chilling screams of pigs being slaughtered at a nearby slaughterhouse. The cart squeaked under the weight of chains, parts of engines, crowbars, and the bones of old school buses, whose blue and rusty bodies lay outside the yard like tired elephants. Panting, we hauled the metal uphill, through and beyond the town, where the park turned into forest, to Marko's home.

The redness of his house's bricks cried against the green forest. Its massiveness cast a long shadow over the backyard, prostrate and vanishing in the darkness of the underbrush. What was in the shadow attracted even more attention, so much so that the bright house sank into a shadow in your mind, while the darkened objects in the backyard began to glow—planks of wood with bent nails sticking out, rusty train wheels, cats, tin cans, empty cement sacks, tires, winding telephones—and formed a buffer zone in greater disarray than Berlin had been on May 2, 1945. The backyard too seemed to witness the collapse of an empire. Marko seemed to be entrenched in a war of sorts, with chaos gaining the upper hand.

One half of the house was finished, the bunkerlike downstairs with rusty rods sticking out as if a cage had been cut through. As I approached the house, tripping over empty cans of paint, the door silently opened a little. A woman of worn-out countenance peeped out the door, clearly expecting nothing but evil from the outside. She wore black as if her husband, Marko, was dead.

I used to wonder what the point of hoarding rust was, but I found out what some of the metal would do: Marko had erected two pillars carrying a steel beam and a pendulum, which was connected by chains and a whole series of cogs to a large smoke-emitting motor. I thought he was building some kind of modern sculpture, something he had learned in Russia. It looked like an updated guillotine.

He placed a large whitish stone beneath the steel base of the pendulum. With a chisel he cut grooves into the stone to fit the blade, switched the motor on, and the blade rasped over the stone loudly, while he stood on the side, masticating contemplatively, constantly adjusting his teeth. Now and then he poured water over the stone, as if baptizing it, though of course it was too late for baptism: it was a tombstone. His cats ran into the woods, but returned, and, transfigured into hedgehogs, stared at the monster who consumed stones.

I stood there for half an hour without saying a word. I thought he didn't see me, but he turned to me, and said, "Could you pour water over the stone every third minute?" He gave me the aluminum cup and the aluminum bucket of water.

I mentioned Plato to him because I wanted to appear smart; I had heard Plato knew the truth better than anybody else. Marko flung his hammer and chisel on the ground, and motioned for me to sit on a pile of logs. He sat down too, and said: "But you know why his Socrates died? He raised his voice against tyranny. That's how it was then, that's how it is now. Nothing's changed. Our government is a bunch of tyrannical crooks."

"But there is more to Plato . . . "

"Yes, there's less to Plato. He wrote with tyrants around him. You must learn how to read it. There's crooked politics wherever you turn. Do you think I like making tombstones? I used to hold a high post in the Party. I was about to be elected the Minister of Culture of Croatia, but I spoke freely against their Mercedes limos and champagne. Since I had contacts in the Soviet Union, they discredited me as an informer. They sent me here, behind God's back. This is my Siberia. But enough of this, there's a living to be made, I must support the old hag and the young hag. See, my daughter is pregnant, the fucker has left her. I need to make her a room upstairs. She'll need the space for her bastard." He spoke with acerbic, Serbian bitterness.

He walked back to his stone. He hit the broadened head of the chisel with his heavy hammer. Bluish steel cut into bluish gray stone, stone dust flying, clouding up the image. With his gray hair, bluish stubbly cheeks, he blended into the grain of the stone, and all I saw after a while was a stone with a pair of upwardly curved eyebrows. The metal rang dull in a mesmerizing rhythm, my ears felt pressure and pain as if we were landing in a plane, and I stared at the tombstone of a yet-unnamed dead man, with a face of eyebrows and stone—no nose, no eyes, no ears.

"Is there eternal life?" I shouted. Marko didn't reply, I repeated my shout, and he turned round and looked at me as if I had seriously misunderstood something.

"Why do you always work?" I asked him as if he had misunderstood. How could it be that the man I admired most for his freedom was a slave to work, more than any other?

"God works six days a week, and who am I to work less? The whole creation travails, works—and so must I."

"But if work is punishment, can't you avoid it, rise above it?"

"Nobody can rise so high as to oppose God Almighty. In the sweat of your brow . . . that's how you have to live. If you fail to accept your punishment, God will *destroy* you." He looked like a bleak judge pronouncing a sentence of life imprisonment in the Siberian labor camps.

He grabbed the hammer aggressively as if he would smash my skull. I was more dejected than the rich young man who asked Jesus what more he should do to be saved and was told to give up all his riches to the poor. The work I did—homework, hauling wood, and nailing leather over clogs—tormented my body and mind, and interfered with my daydreams.

He chiseled away rough edges from the stone. I felt self-indulgent in front of his hard labor, his hard features, and his past hardships. Blue and purple nails stuck out from his knotty fingers—perhaps he had hit them with the hammer. His tendons went prominently into his fingers; blue snakes of his veins twisted around each tendon into semblances of the symbol of medicine. Chiseling into the stone, he wrestled with time, wishing to mark it and catch it. But time evaded him with martial arts methods. Luring him to cut into the bones of the earth, into rocks, time would let him exhaust himself and run out of time and out of himself. He was being spent in epitaphs. Gray widows would stare at the outlines of the epitaphs to find the ghosts of their beloveds in the bleakness of the stones under faint moonlight and above candlelight, expecting that something in the stone would begin to flicker into life. Marko, and all of us, would be no more than the whistle of the wind in the pines, an octave higher than a screech owl's.

Later, in 1971, on the Day of the Republic, when there were nationalist tensions between Croats and Serbs, he interrupted a vague pompous speech by the Mayor, and shouted: "Comrades and Comradesses, enough bullshit. God created us equal. In front

of Him we are all blades of grass and ashes. So why all this nonsense, why do some of you shout, I am a Croat, and others, I am
a Serb, what the hell's the difference? Who cares? Let me tell you,
God doesn't." And he proceeded to preach in the middle of the
atheist, Communist assembly and nobody could stop him. Religion and proselytizing were strictly confined by law to the
churches. Religion was considered a disease, a crutch for those
who had no courage to face the finality of life.

When he sat down, there was silence, marred by throats clearing phlegm. Thick blue smoke hovered like a large wreath above
the assembly. As a Baptist I had seen many religious people of
considerable courage remain silent in public gatherings. And here
a Communist whom I thought was a nonbeliever had spoken
out. I felt proud of our shared faith in God. Shivers ran down my
body into my shoes.

Because I went away to study I did not see Marko the
tombstone-maker for years, but once when I visited my hometown I did see him amidst fireworks and crowds of people, in the
shade of a kiosk, for the Fourth of July, the Yugoslav Day of Inde-
pendence. He crossed his arms, stood up straight, and in his gray-
ness struck me as Jonah awaiting the destruction of Ninevah.

I greeted him, *"Zdravo."*

In lieu of greeting me back, he exclaimed, "Sodom and
Gomorrah! Just look at it. All these girls running around naked,
and the guys don't even look at them. What immorality, godless-
ness!" His comments surprised me.

His daughter claimed that he was strict and puritanical.
Throughout her childhood he'd kept an eye on her. In her teens
he had often locked her up to keep her away from the town
"dogs." She eloped, and her fiancé left her pregnant after half a
year of free love. Marko, who had anticipated it, became extra
moralizing, which made it no easier on his daughter, despite his
helping her materially. His influence, however, was so powerful
that she herself became an art teacher, a painter, and a sculptor.

Rumor had it that if you were a virgin, all you needed to do was visit her and she would initiate you in ten minutes.

His daughter's promiscuity hurt Marko's pride. I guess he was a bitter old man. But in his bitterness there was intrepid grandeur. He never laughed; like a medieval portrait he displayed sorrow, grieving for what came of it all—the country and the family.

Now, when the fireworks crackled and shed light in many colors, I saw the lines on his face, just like the lines he had drawn on my trees to make them trees.

His sunken face startled me. Although his new, slightly changed appearance was powerful and immediate, the old Marko who was vividly present in my mind seemed stronger. By what force did the weaker Marko suppress the stronger one? Time had been chiseled into his face so steadily that I think I should have been able to tell how many years had passed just by looking into his face, had I been woken up from a years-long comatose sleep. In the whole impression of his face there was a little less, a little less of what? A little less flesh, but not exactly; even if he had gained weight, there would have still been a little less something, a little less Marko. His flesh had lost vigor, the vigor had moved into his eyes. But even his eyes seemed to have shrunk; they were a little grayer, as if with cataracts, as though he had begun to turn into a pillar of salt like Lot's wife.

The work of time is black magic. Time drains the tissue from under the skin, drains it down the lymphoid channels out of the body until only the skin and the bones remain. But time does not stop, it thins the skin, empties the bones of their marrow. Only the broken skeleton remains under the tombstone. Seeing the shrunken Marko, who had struck me as permanent as the tombstones he was making, I was afraid to look into his face.

We shook hands. He masticated as he used to, his jaw muscles popping up, and said, "For God's sake, where have you vanished to?"

"I live in the United States; I'm studying philosophy for a Ph.D."

"Philosophy in the West? They cannot teach you nothing. Come on, visit me in my workshop, and I'll show you what philosophy is!" He spoke in his sharp take-the-whole-world-by-the-throat voice. "I'll tell you some things that I have understood, something no one here or there understands. If you listen to what I say, you'll be able to demolish all the philosophers over there by the force of your arguments. You'll sink them!" He spoke calmly, spreading his right arm forward and moving it level with the horizon, with a distant look in his eyes, as if he were leveling the American cities to the ground. I chuckled; he had become even more bellicose and preposterous than before, despite his shrunken appearance.

A year later, my wife and I walked through the park to the periphery of the town, toward Kovachevich's house. Where there had been piles of rust, there was now a garden, and in the garden sat his daughter, reading a book; a child was swinging on a swing, hung on a branch of a large oak.

We walked into the garden and asked about her father. The swing stopped, the child ran into the house, and bumblebees buzzed, bending stalks of flowers. She closed her book and told me he had died several months before.

He had been ill for months, skin and bones, and he had sunk, as unbelievable as it sounded, into the ground on his sixtieth birthday. In the war, in the mountain forests, sleeping in torn tents in snow, sleet, rain, and mud, his kidneys had rotted. Appearing to be a man of steel, he was a man of iron, rusted inside, though standing embattled and firm as if the war had not ended.

The Jehovah's Witnesses wanted to bury Marko Kovachevich in their way, the Serbian Orthodox priests in theirs, and the Communists in theirs. Kovachevich had left a spoken will with his wife. Mrs. Kovachevich warded off all the groups that fought for the right to bury Marko Kovachevich—no easy task since there was no written will that dictated how he should be buried. Now that Marko was dead, it was easy for the townspeople to claim he'd been one of them and to be proud of him. Kovachevich was buried according to his spoken will, without a star, without a cross, without angels, and without food—as is the Serbian custom—on his tomb.

Atop his grave was placed one of his own products, a cubic tombstone from his own machine, formed by his own chisel, with the inscription cut by his own hand. His stone arose among many stones, sticking out of the ground like a tooth among many sparse teeth on the lower jaw of Mother Earth—a molar crown among canines.

Petrol and Chocolate

Milan was the despot at home. If he wanted to nurse, he merely raised his voice in an inarticulate cry. He didn't have to strain to express his desires; it was up to his parents to figure out what he wanted. Milan began to speak very late. His parents, who considered him retarded, showered him with noise-making toys of all sorts that they bought in the town miles away. Milan climbed tables and clanked pots against each other, and threw plates on the floor to hear them burst, and his parents admired his liveliness.

After his mother's absence of several days, a rosy stranger appeared, swathed in white—a doll with a very loud screaming tape in it. The parents and visitors surrounded the cradle and admired the baby's widow's peak, little nose and little mouth, and family likenesses. Nobody noticed Milan, and Milan understood that drumming on the pots with a ladle would not help.

Milan was only six when his family loaded up most of their belongings on a cart pulled by two snorting crimson horses. A long ride followed: a lot of whip-swishing and screeching of screwed wooden brakes. Suddenly around a curve overgrown with rose hips appeared a horseless buzzing iron cart, hooting and going uphill all by itself. In terror, Milan jumped off the cart into the rosebushes. His pants and skin were torn as if a dozen cats had climbed him in a rush, but, still, he fell in love with the self-moving cart at first sight. It took his parents two hours to find him and drag him back on their horse-drawn carriage. The steel-ringed wheels crunched limestone and gravel, until the road became smooth. For the first time in his life, Milan saw asphalt. His mother told him the asphalt was there not for the people and horses but for the self-moving carts.

With the loss of familiar sounds and smells, Milan definitely lost his primacy. His brother was now the despot. It was enough that the baby should sigh at night, and their mother would rush to its side; Milan's screams won no attention. What infuriated him was that his baby brother Nenad *was* a loveable child. Milan often leaned over the cradle, pulling the baby's little pink fingers gently so that he laughed happily. And then in a moment of jealousy, he'd pinch his ear so that he would cry. Their mother rushed into the dark bedroom to change the diapers, and finding them dry, she gave Milan a stern and suspecting look. But that happened rarely. It looked as though Milan was devoted to his little brother, and in a way he was. When the parents went to Mass, they left him to baby-sit. Milan gave the baby a suck from the bottle— chamomile tea laced with plum brandy. His father, Jakov, kept a bottle of brandy behind his bed so he could take a swig first thing in the morning, saying that nothing wakes you up better than happiness. After tea, Milan gave milk to the baby, so that the plum brandy couldn't be smelled. He had a sip of the tea too. When the parents came back from church and found their six-year-old and one-year-old laughing, they rushed to Nenad, to pet his soft brushy scalp.

Several years later Nenad confiscated all Milan's childhood toys—that is, the ones that Milan hadn't taken apart to see what made them tick and those that he hadn't decapitated or mutilated in one way or another. In addition to that, Nenad received electric trains and flying helicopters, the sort of toys that had not been available before the electronic revolution when Milan had been a toddler.

Having lost ground at home, Milan sneaked out into the streets though they menaced him. A few self-moving carts rolled along in all sorts of colors, sounds, shakes, and smoking habits. Milan hid in a ditch among neighboring homeless dogs and waited for cars to pass by. Whenever one did, he ran in the pack after it and barked. The car raised a dust screen (the street in front of his home was still a dirt road). It wasn't clear whether the persecutors barked or coughed, but the car certainly roared with laughter.

Milan noticed that cars had a tendency to herd in the center of the town. He did not dare touch them. He could not even peep into them because his eyes, when he stood on tiptoe, reached only to the keyhole, through which he could not see anything. He repaired the shortcoming by piling up several bricks from the building site of the cinema; he stood on the precarious elevation, staring into the cabin, marveling at the variety of clocks in it. He could not see how clocks would move the car, but he could not grasp how clocks could move their own hands either. Maybe many clocks put together could move the car? His forming a more elaborate theory on the relation of time-making machines and motion-making machines was roughly thwarted: the owner of the coveted object slapped him over his soft pink cheeks so hard that big fingerprints stayed on them for several days, clear enough to demonstrate to the police whose they were. Although Milan had heard that adults could be punished for beating children, he did not believe it.

Ashamed of the palm prints, Milan hid in the woods near the town in a cavelike partisan bunker, despite his fear of the dark. He stayed there for two nights and ate wild cherries. Meanwhile his parents put Milan's photo in the major papers all over the Socialist Republic of Croatia, offering a reward to anyone who found the sweet missing child. When Milan, starved, returned home, he got a new set of fingerprints, this time from his father. But his

love of cars did not diminish. On the contrary, the idea of mobil-
ity gained an additional attraction, and he often knelt behind
idling cars at the gas station, burying his head in the blue smoke.
The sharp smell in his nostrils tasted to him of big roads, leading
to big cities and big countries.

But Milan was not often left alone to roam wherever he liked.
His father locked the yard gate and expected him to study math.
As a factory worker, Jakov wanted his son to become an engineer.
"The whole world will be your toy," he said.

But Milan did find toys: frogs in a large pond at the end of the
garden. Frogs relaxed on the edge of the brown-green water, visu-
ally merging with the soil, grass, and water, and you wouldn't
notice them if their bodies didn't pulsate like hearts. Their cosmic
eyes—beady periscopes—protruded, registering the landings of
bees onto floating hay as well as the jerky zigzagging of dragon-
flies, which walked better than Saint Peter on the Sea of Galilee.
Milan spent afternoons catching frogs with his bare hands.
Though their cool slippery bodies repulsed him, he liked catching them and tossing them back in the water, to see their joy at
escaping back into freedom, deep into the water till he could no
longer follow their swimming.

Milan heard that Italians ate frogs, so in an attempt to feel like
an Italian, he put two frogs in the stove together with wood that
was supposed to cook the meat. Only ashes remained and those
did not taste good. For May Day, Milan's mother grilled several
rabbits, and, watching her, Milan learned how he could grill frogs.
Ordinarily they ate very little meat because meat was expensive,
so Milan was always hungry for its taste. Nobody in the house
knew that he ate frogs. He felt sorry for the frogs but they grew
like mushrooms. There were so many of them that sometimes
they climbed on top of each other. The whole bank of the pond
was covered with two floors of frogs. Cats hid among lettuce
leaves several yards away from the pond and stared at the frogs
with pale green eyes, wide open, with vertical slits for pupils, like
rifle-aims. Suddenly a cat would dart. In their greed, cats would

often lose their balance and fall in the pond. They would then swim out and lick their fur methodically to clean the green film of the pond away. Milan chased the cats away and so, in a way, he saved more frogs than he killed.

Of course, Milan went to school. On the way he passed by a junkyard, where he picked up a car tire. He got the tire for the capital investment of five kilos of rusted metal he had stolen piecemeal in many forms from the junkyard through the fence. Now, every day—six days a week—Milan ran to the school with a tire ahead of him, slapping it with his palm and skimming it forward. He parked his vehicle in a narrow passageway at school between wooden barrels. One summer day he smelled the smoke of burning rubber, and ran out of the classroom like a mother on hearing the screams of her drowning son. Some classmates had set the tire on fire. It took him a week of stealing iron from the junkyard to buy another tire from the junkyard keeper.

Milan often skipped classes to go near a car-repair shop, where he lustfully gazed at the dismembered cars, their very bones, and his eyes shone in the wonderful smell of gasoline and oil. How great it must be to see it all, where the wires go, and to touch it all! Every day he summoned more courage to come closer until oily apprentices drove him away, casting screws at him.

So, for a while, Milan went back to the frogs. Nenad, now about five, began to hang around the pond to watch Milan catching frogs, which made him laugh. But he was scared of the pond and stayed away from its edge. Milan lured him onto the bridge that made a crossing over the long and narrow pond. "Come, come here, Nenny, you'll see how they swim, like women." Nenad wouldn't come.

But when Milan took out a chocolate that he had gotten for his birthday and unwrapped the silvery foil, Nenad's lips shook the way cats' cheeks quiver when they see a bird out of their reach. "If you step on the bridge, you'll get a bar," Milan said, kneeling above the water. Nenad crawled gingerly onto the bridge. He cried from fear, but he couldn't resist the chocolate. He got one square of the chocolate when he reached the first quarter of the bridge; two, when he reached the middle; and none, when he came to the end, because after all, then he no longer had any choice. He cried at the end of the crossing because he thought he deserved more chocolate, but Milan thought he was spoiled. Whenever Milan got a chocolate, he didn't eat it. Once a day Nenad made crossings for his three chocolate bars. On one occasion, a splinter entered his knee and he cried and cried, so Milan gave him a whole new chocolate and pulled out the splinter and made him promise he wouldn't tell on him. But Milan couldn't afford the game, until he began to steal chocolate from a supermarket just several days after it opened with all the pomp in their town: the town's first supermarket, just like in the West.

Milan once got caught and pulled by the ears in the storage room, among sacks of sugar and salt, and cartons of sunflower-seed oil. The next time he stole, his hands trembled, and he blushed, but he went ahead anyway, expecting to be caught. The cashier looked at his blushing face. He couldn't look her in the eye, so he looked lower at her knee so that she would catch him doing it, which would explain his blushing and protect him from the suspicion. She asked, "Is that all?" when Milan asked for a hard roll, the cheapest item in the store he could buy to legitimize his being there. As she moved to get the change, her skirt slipped up, and her flesh fascinated Milan more than he had expected. In reply to her question, as he stole glances at her body, Milan gasped and hissed like a threatened goose. She laughed, stroked his cowlicks, and Milan felt that she knew everything, that she knew that he stole but let him get away with it.

At home, Milan climbed the large walnut tree and stood in a fork of branches, swinging with the wind, so that some nuts in their green coats fell on the ground with dull thumps. Milan cracked open the shells, whose green tart juice stained his fingers like a chain-smoker's. Nenad came out.

Milan lured Nenad onto the tree, with a chocolate on a

thread. Nenad cried because he was scared of heights, but he wanted his chocolate. And when he was high in the tree, Milan left him there among quivering leaves. The child clung to the tree like a little bear and moaned. Then along came their mother and threw stones at Milan on his thick branch. She climbed to get Nenad; snot hanging from his nose stuck to the cool, smooth gray bark like a slug trail.

Mother whipped Milan with a thin weeping-willow branch, and his father with a thick leather belt. Now every afternoon, instead of playing with Nenad, Milan was locked in his room with nothing but math books. Meanwhile Nenad ran all around the yard, kicking his new leather soccer ball. Milan made a rope out of his bed sheets, tied it onto the window frame, and went slowly down, his feet rappelling against the wall. He found Nenad in the garden, eating strawberries with soil on them. Milan wanted to be good to him, so he told him the stories from the Bible, the few he remembered—the Great Flood, Israelites crossing the Red Sea, Jonah living in a whale, and Jesus driving a herd of pigs into the lake.

They played the Great Flood, using an old wine barrel as Noah's ark. They filled the barrel with a chicken and a rooster, two cats, two frogs, two snails, a turtle (turtles live long enough; besides, they could find only one), a crippled dog, two bricks, and two rabbits. The creatures shrieked, fur and feathers flew up, and after them the animal kingdom, splashing into the pond. Only the turtle, the snails, the bricks, and the dog stayed in the boat; the snails hid in their twisted houses, the turtle under its shield, and the dog was shaking, as if with the vibrations of a large ship engine.

Milan and Nenad went back to the game of chocolate. Milan promised Nenad a Swiss chocolate if he would walk over the bridge. Nenad used to crawl over the bridge, and now, though weeping from fear, he walked. Milan saw that Nenad could easily make it. Just to make the passage a little more challenging, Milan slightly shook the bridge. The edge of the pond was muddy from recent rains, and the bridge slid a foot or two. Nenad lost his balance and fell into the water. The water swallowed him with a splash; waves spread around in a circle as if a stone had fallen, and Milan stood there, mesmerized with horror. Milan couldn't swim. He pulled out a string-bean pole from the soil, and pushed it into the water, hoping Nenad would catch it. But he didn't. Milan shrieked for help. Nobody came. His mother was shopping, his father working. Milan climbed back into his room, untied the sheets and ironed them. He trembled with fear, yet he worked on his homework, so he wouldn't be caught. For months his parents looked for Nenad. No one but Milan knew that Nenad had drowned. Nenny stayed in Milan's mind, swimming and leaping in his brain folds like a hybrid of a baby and a frog.

The parents again showered Milan with toys and love, but Milan forgot how to play and how to be loved. He sulked and tried to do math day and night. Jakov said, "Oh, my son will be an engineer if not a nuclear physicist!"

Whenever he could, Milan ran out into the streets. Seated on a bench between the Catholic and the Orthodox churches, beneath a linden that smelled like expanding tea and buzzed with bees like an idling and extremely precise engine, Milan observed cars cutting the curve on the cobbled hill. He loved their ways: the slanting, downshifting, screeching. In the town there were about a thousand cars, and he knew them all. One could tie a shirt over his head and eyes and ask him to identify an approaching car. His nostrils opened wide, his large ears moved back and forth like the wings of a buzzard about to land on a rock, and he could report the make of the car, its owner's name, its license-plate number, acceleration, deceleration, gas mileage, and maximum speed, as well as ills the car suffered. If an accident occurred within his earshot, he could tell who the protagonists were. Naturally, he was a favorite of the police, and though the butt of many practical jokes, he was free to stroll almost wherever he pleased—no oily apprentices dared throw screws at him anymore.

Ten years later, Milan's free palm stroked the empty seat on his right and he exclaimed, "How good it is to have a car!" Of course, it was not a surprising discovery; he had yearned to have a car ever since seeing his first one.

He chuckled smugly in his Ford Mustang. Trees passed by him, and his thoughts spun from the past to the future and back, and the fields of green grazing grass with black-and-white cows, who all faced the missing sun, turned also. He had failed to qualify for apprenticeship because it was an inherited power position in the dynasties of car mechanics. The only way to become a car mechanic was to make your own shop on hard currency from West Germany as a *Gastarbeiter*. After serving in the army, Milan went to Germany, hoping to work for Mercedes, and instead became a railway worker. None of it seemed bad now as he stroked the leather. He liked his future even more, rushing into it faster than anybody around him. He watched the way the road seemed to be devoured, disappearing into the mouth of his car beneath him. What a pleasure it was to press the pedal, and what a thrill to feel you would fly off the curve like a stone from the sling of David if the Pirelli radials hadn't clung to the asphalt, squealing like a lonely elephant!

When he crossed into Austria, the blue sky turned gray; dense white patches like bursting cotton sank to the earth, silencing the road. The sky and the earth were so gray and dim from the snow that he could hardly see ahead.

Since people pulled their cars off the road, Milan drove safely alone with the snow falling; it seemed to him he was being dizzily lifted straight into the gray heaven. In the Austrian Alps, the tires often turned without pulling him up, but he went on. Where it no longer snowed, it was icy. He drove like a skier, changing his direction gradually; he never braked but often downshifted. The third gear opening resisted his push at one point, and the car growled like a lynx whose prey a wolf wants to steal. Well, so what? Isn't third the least important one? With great acceleration like this, I can shift from second into fourth, as easy as butter, so what's the need for third anyway?

But after he lost—before the border of Yugoslavia—the first, second, and fourth gears, he despaired until he realized that he could still drive in reverse. He maneuvered the car back onto the road and delighted in the properties of reverse: as much power as first and as much speed as third!

At the border crossing, a policeman with a red star on his cap asked him, "Comrade, what's wrong with you that you drive backwards?"

"New Year's joke. If I go backwards in time, I'll grow younger."

"A joke? You mean something political?"

"No, no, just a joke. Everything is the reverse of what it should be—so, driving backwards straightens it out."

"What do you mean?" The cop ordered him out of the car, and inspected it for smuggled coffee and pornography.

In Slovenia Milan varied his methods of driving. He turned his head left and right, and so looking backwards sideways, he went forwards, back to his home. His hands steered the car behind his back; when that grew tiresome, he scratched his back against the wheel, and steered like that. He drove safely if not thanks to his skill, then to other people moving aside. Children hollered from the sides of the road.

The reverse did not fail him. He backed into the center of his hometown and parked the car. Many people gathered and admired the car so much that they did not even notice him. "What a model! How fast can it drive? Two hundred? This is an American car, these are miles! That means three hundred kilometers. No, four hundred. No, you are thinking of nautical miles. And what's the acceleration?" And their faces puffed vapors in the cold, as if their heads were exhaust pipes. Milan watched, proud, the way a father listens to the praises lavished upon his son, or, better, the way a son listens to the praises lavished upon his father's strength.

Around that time, the house where Milan used to live was torn down to make space for a new post office. The pond was

emptied and dried. Green bones of a young boy lay among cracking soil.

Milan wanted to leave the town. The car, however, wouldn't
leave; it stalled as stubborn as a donkey with very thick skin
whom no rod can prod. Milan sold the Mustang to the junkyard.
The old junkyard keeper remembered him, laughed at the collapse of his transmission, slapped him on the shoulder, led him
into the tilting aluminum office, seated him for slivovitz, and
explained to him that he was without an heir. Amidst a lot of
coughing, wheezing, and phlegm spitting, he asked Milan to suc-
ceed him in the junkyard dynasty, and Milan did.

After people laughed at Milan's new position—once you
worked in Germany for a while, you were expected at the very
least to open a glossy tavern—they got used to him. Milan collected parts and assembled them. Several years later he established
a thriving business, converting rust into gleam. It still thrives.
The story must end here because we have come to the present
tense, and as for the future, who can smell it? Who among us can
prophesy?

The Eye of God

"We decided you are not sincere," the minister said in an earnest voice. Breathless, I was seated in front of the Baptist congregation in Nizograd, Croatia, about eighty of them, trying to avoid their eyes, yet meeting them all.

"So, we'll wait for a couple of years until . . . "

Great, I thought. They aren't going to baptize me. I can still break into the cinema, skip classes, write fake notes, and steal combs and mirrors at the town fair.

A slap on my shoulder nearly blew me off the chair.

"I was only kidding." The minister gave me a more powerful slap on the shoulder in his clubby friendliness. His teeth shone at me, especially a gold molar. "Everybody is touched by your decision." He sprinkled particles of saliva. I wiped my face with a sleeve and stared at the congregation, where I noticed some handkerchiefs wiping cheeks sympathetically. I wanted to tell them I wasn't crying but just wiping off the minister's spittle.

I was scared of the people I was facing, scared of their strict goodness.

Some people coughed, my grandmother gasped asthmatically, my oldest brother scratched his high forehead, and my uncle arched his eyebrows almost to his hairline, crumpling his forehead.

The minister improvised a lengthy prayer on the spot, as did several other members—we were supposed to pray as the spirit moved us, not as the memory blessed us.

I wondered what had made them accept me. They knew I was bad. I wished to be worse, but didn't have enough courage to steal motorcycles—I didn't even have enough courage to ride them, let alone steal them. But still, I shattered school windows with stones. I had waged war against old women several years before. From behind the gate of my home I had struck a woman in black on her back with a bean pole from our garden. She chased me into the yard, and, unable to catch me, she wanted to complain to my father, but his assistant Nenad begged her not to, saying I would be flogged. She listened to him. I obviously needed more distance from the enemy, another old woman, so I improved my technology, making a spear no larger than an arrow from a bike spoke sharpened at the tip, a thin bamboo stick from the marshes, and turkey feathers. The spear struck into the buttocks of my target, who ran with great agility after me. Probably she wasn't that old despite wearing widow's black. I ran into the park and climbed a well-trusted oak. She spent the afternoon aiming at me with stones. I couldn't call it exactly a victory and I was ashamed of myself—I really was rotten and knew it. Though it had happened four years before, I still blushed at the thought of it. And that the elders of the church would accept me now as good—well, but that's the point. The conversion: the worse you are, the more believable it is. How could you be converted if you had nothing to be converted from?

After the prayers, the lights were switched back on, and as I squinted and rubbed my eyes, I believed I could become a new person. I would study hard. I would not quarrel with my mother. I would try to love everybody, even my biology teacher.

A week later on the day of Baptism I walked to the church in my uncomfortable new clothes. Sunshine soaked my cheeks, goodness in the form of heat reaching me deeper and deeper. A German shepherd with a torn ear came along and sniffed me, and somehow I couldn't trick him; he smelled the old wolf in sheep's clothing, and growled through his throat, to convey to me that he would like to tear mine. Two winters before, I had struck him on the muzzle with an icy snowball. Since then he would pass by me at a respectful distance, but now he was at a foot's length, his, not mine, showing me his impressive incisors. I walked past him, but he followed me, growling, and when I turned round he leaped and tore through the front pocket of my pants into my skin. I jumped away on a heap of gravel, and grabbed a sharp-edged stone. The German shepherd squealed and ran away, and I ran after him throwing stones and swearing obscenities.

A silver-haired deacon honked from his VW Bug, nodded his head sideways, and raised his index finger toward heaven, a sign to mind things heavenly rather than earthly. Only then did I notice there were quite a few church-goers on the other side of the street, mostly widows in black.

I wondered whether to give up the whole business of salvation, since it was so hard. But, according to the minister, I would never again have a chance to be saved if I didn't take it now. So, I walked to the church, my right hand in the torn pocket, trying to hide the hole.

It was very hot in the church. Many sermons were delivered and many songs sung before I was ordered to walk into the back room and change into a white gown. I walked with my hand in my pocket, and could see the stern look of my mother.

Several people sat in the back room, in robes, waiting their turns to be baptized. Behind a partition in the room a naked peasant boy about my age looked toward my penis analytically.

"A dog bit me," I said, explaining the deep scratch.

"How long is it supposed to be?"

"I don't know, almost a meter . . . "

"That long? Gee, we'll never make it."

I realized that I was speaking about the dog, and he about the normal penis size. I laughed while he looked more and more worried, until he yawned in resignation. He had probably decided that since his penis wouldn't be long enough, he might just as well become a Baptist. I didn't try to explain the misunderstanding to him; somebody was saying, "Shush!"

I waited in the steamy room for an hour while people walked, one by one, through the pool that stretched into the main church room beneath a curtain—mostly peasants from the hills, who wanted the prestige of America if not heaven. Rumors had it that rich Texans financed our church and gave each Baptist a bag of oranges in the middle of winter, and a washing machine for a wedding present; another rumor was that the church was a nest of CIA agents. Many other attractive rumors circulated around the town about our congregation.

Waiting, I was tempted to pray like Christ in Gethsemane for the cup to pass me by, unless it was unavoidable. Unlike Samuel who heard his name called out even when it very likely wasn't, I didn't hear mine when it was, so the silver-haired deacon's heavy hand grabbed my arm and dragged me down the steps into the lukewarm water. The curtain opened. The flashes of cameras blinded me. The lightning was upon us, blinding me like Saint Paul. Dark chambers of East German cameras would immortalize the moment of Baptism in film silver. The minister, standing on my side, pronounced a blessing, "In the name of Jesus Christ." I expected a long prayer, so I breathed at my leisure. The minister put his hand on my forehead and suddenly tripped me over his leg backward into the water, which entered my nose and mouth and sinuses. I tried to come up, but he pushed me down as if the old man literally needed to die not only in soul but in body. I tried again. He pushed me back. I kicked, trying to strike the minister so he would let go, because the issue of salvation, from the fantastic, had reached very concrete proportions. I missed, and my legs made noise as if I were swimming. I forgot where I was— I was drowning again in the sea, sinking through time, with starfish below and a brilliant haze above. When I got out of the

water, I gasped, coughed, sneezed, and the water leaked out of
me, from wherever it could, like it did out of the whale who
threw up Jonah onto the shore.

"Like a newborn baby," commented the minister, and the
congregation laughed in unison benevolently.

So, I'm saved. At what moment exactly did it happen? It
couldn't have been when I tried to kick him. It couldn't have
been before, since kicking was still my old reaction. So, then, as
I was getting out. But I wasn't thinking of Christ. Maybe that
doesn't matter. As I walked out, water still flowed out of my ears
and nose. Organ music played, and the congregation broke out
into loud singing, dominated by Marinka's voice—Marinka was
an enormously fat woman who sang powerfully and enthusiasti-
cally, and was excommunicated each spring for carnal sins, and
received back each winter. Though it was springtime, she was still
with us.

I rubbed my back with a wet towel. I had barely managed to
get dressed when deacons escorted me into the second pew with
the other novices. I hid the hole in my pocket, and the dog bite
burned. The sun's rays bounced around the church, lifting the
gathering above the clouds.

The minister read from the Bible, "And this you shall do in my
remembrance," and broke thin slices of bread into small cubes in
the aluminum plate emblazoned by the rays leaping back and
forth between it and the sun faster than the speed of light—at the
speed of God's thought. It disturbed me a little that I knew who
the baker was: Machek, a large Czech, puffed up as if with yeast,
and pale, as if made of dough. White powder usually covered his
beret and his blond eyebrows. I shook off the banal association so
that the white, unwhole-wheat bread—the de-blooded body of
Christ—would work to bring my spirit to life. I chose the largest
cube in the basket, because I was starving. It turned out to be two
cubes thinly connected.

I closed my eyes, and my thoughts about salvation now focused on my mouth—saliva soaking the bread and my decaying teeth. I am supposed to think of Christ now, I am thinking—am I thinking? He's not in the bread, of course, not physically. The main thing is to feel *something*.

Then the blood of Christ came. It was before the grape-juice years in our church, when wine was wine, and Holy Communion intoxicating. The blood came in the trophy cup.

The first in the pew was a newcomer from the hills. This would be her first Holy Communion. She lifted the cup like a tournament winner. Flushed in cheeks, she turned to the congregation and shouted, "*Na zdravlye! Zhivilli!*" To your health, cheers, live it up! Before the deacons, like security guards during an assassination, could intervene, the woman lowered the cup to her lips and gulped while some wine flowed down her chin into her bosom. The deacons snatched the cup away from her, and took her aside, whispering to her. The children from the back rows giggled and laughed, while their angry parents turned round aggressively, the bench wood squeaking.

I overheard the silver-haired deacon whisper to the minister that there was no more wine left. The minister announced that before we continued with the Communion, we would sing a song of joy and thanksgiving. I bit my lips not to chuckle, and lowered my head, praying so God would save me from laughing. But Marinka sang even more loudly than usual; no laughter and giggling could be heard. The minister put his forefinger on his forehead and after much thought, his face lit up. He whispered to the deacon, who walked into the back pews to my red-faced uncle Pavle, the woodcutter, to talk into his ear. The minister talked into his other ear.

Half an hour later Christ's blood was back. By now I had almost swooned from exhaustion because I hadn't had breakfast, I was thirsty, it was hot in the church, and the service had already lasted more than four hours. The cup passed from one member to another, after each had a sip. I was squeamish about putting my lips onto the thin metal edge, thinking of the saliva of so many people. But wouldn't God protect us? So with much faith I drank a large gulp of the sweet wine, and as it went down my throat, despite my knowing its banal origins from my uncle's vineyard, I concentrated on the divine. The warmth of the wine shot straight into my eyes and cheeks.

On the way home I breathed deep. The broken-eared German shepherd wasn't around. I felt saved, but I didn't know from what.

At home my cat ran away from me and hid beneath the sofa the way she used to at night when Mother wound the alarm clock before throwing her out into the yard. I caught the cat, lifting her by the tail, just to tease her, after which I gave her a cup of fresh milk and thought, yes, I will be good, you will see.

I spent several days in elation.

In the church one song often shamed me: "Leaves, I bring only dry leaves to Thy Altar." The leaves were souls. Dry leaves were dead souls, or rather, no souls. To bring green leaves meant to save souls.

In the park, one hot afternoon, so hot that the tongues of dogs hung to the ground, I saw an old man with white stubble coming out of his chin, like the remains of wheat stalks in the soil after harvest. His hair was white, his face soulfully creased, and his eyes amazingly small, as if he were turning into a bird, ready to take off in a migratory flight to the cold lands. But it was summer—perhaps he had missed the migration and was now alone. He breathed heavily.

"Good afternoon, Mister. How are you?" I asked him.

He looked up, and though startled enough that his body shrank back, he couldn't lift his eyelids much. "Not that good, young Sir. I just came out of the hospital with no good news."

"Well, I have the good news. Do you believe in God?"

"Ah, I used to, but in the war I forgot about Him."

I talked to him about God and heaven, and the old man breathed easier, light was in his eyes. It was as if he were a child and I his grandfather telling him tales. He said he was glad to find that there was kindness in the town. He had thought that no one cared to talk to anybody, and was glad to see it wasn't so.

"Yes, thanks to Christ," I said to him.

He looked at me almost disappointed. Nevertheless, he heartily clasped my hand in his rakish bluish hands with torn nails—he looked as though he had been tortured by medieval means, which after all, I guess, peasantry as well as Christianity, and alas our medicine, were.

A day later, because the old man came from a Serbian village where everybody used to be Eastern Orthodox, I bought a Cyrillic Bible. I packed it in white paper from the butcher's, tied it with a raw rope in a knot, addressed it to him in printed letters, and gave it over to a sneezing clerk in the post office.

A year later I saw the old man's obituary on a lamppost. I was happy to see a cross presiding over the obituary; I thought the cross was there because of my sending him the Bible (Communists adorned their obituaries with red stars.) Perhaps he died with faith in God. I was glad that I had bragged to nobody; it was a secret between God and me.

So, when I was about to be excommunicated from the church on several accounts, in my mind I clutched at the conversation with the old man as proof that I was not all bad. Let them excommunicate me. God knows I have served Him, at least that once. But I was not excommunicated. The explanation was that, since my father had died when I was eleven, it was natural that I should be a little disturbed and unruly.

I talked about God (whom in my mind I chose to distinguish from Christ and prefer) to many people. When the minister asked me what I wanted to be, I replied, "An evangelist like Billy Graham. A Billy Grahamovich."

We read books by Billy Graham, and one day Billy Graham himself, in all his glory, was to appear from a black limo in the Square of St. Mark in Zagreb, the same place where four centuries before the leader of the Peasant Revolt in Zagorye, Matija Gubec, now our national hero, had been beheaded by foreign (Hapsburg) executioners in front of several thousand spectators. Now people would be seated in stands, and, in the middle of our anti-religious country, they would listen to the word of God in American English. All my relatives and nearly all the members of the church traveled a hundred miles to listen to what they believed over loudspeakers in a foreign language. On the same day my favorite soccer team, Hajduk of Split, played the most crucial match of the year against the Red Star of Belgrade. The match was televised, and I could see it in the pensioner's club. I spent the afternoon in a smoky room with the rattle of walking sticks falling to the floor. The roaring TV trembled and slid sideways on the table (it was so loud that the deaf too would be able to hear).

The minister often asked me whether I had any new sins to confess. "It's very likely, you are at that age, how old are you, twelve?"

"Thirteen."

"Aha! Well, so?"

"Hum. Yes, I have sins to confess."

He led me into his study and waited.

I said, "I skipped classes two days last week."

"I know that."

I was startled, wondering how he knew that, but went on, "I cheated on an exam. I read all the answers from my shoe—a friend passed them to me."

"We'll pray for that. What else?"

I kept silent.

"Nothing more?" The minister insisted.

"I don't think so."

"Don't kid me. You don't, you don't . . . ? Here, read this." He handed me a pamphlet about masturbation—if you do habitual self-abuse, your spine will dry up, your eyes will sink and lose their glow, you will stammer from brain damage, and won't be able to walk upright but will stoop like a monkey. I got frightened, my breath quickened, and the minister, who scrutinized me, lit up. "So?"

"I . . . I . . . don't know what they are talking about."

"Come on! So, why are you turning so pale?"

"I really don't."

"You probably do it, but just don't know the name—masturbation, self-abuse." The minister opened his palm, put onto his palm a yellow American pencil with a rubber eraser atop it—a great luxury item—closed his fist, and slid it up and down the pencil. "See, if the pencil is your thing down there, and you squeeze it, and pull at it, then you are doing it. So?" His cold gray eyes opened wide, fixed on mine, as though to see into the back of my mind.

"Why would anybody want to do it?"

"The devil makes it feel sweet. So, you say you don't do it? Anyway, don't let anybody teach you how to do it—sooner or later someone will try," he spoke in a prophetic manner, and his eyes beamed with the power of an X-ray machine.

I blushed at that much scrutiny.

He smiled, his eyes wandering over my red face. "All right," he said gently, "all right. Don't lie again. Any other sins?"

"Not that I can think of." He prayed for me on his knees loudly so that he didn't notice when I opened the door and left— I had to go to school in the afternoon.

During the tedious English class—This is Mary. Is this Mary? Yes, this is Mary. And that is a tree—I kept wondering what self-abuse felt like. As I tilted backwards, to appear all the more negligent in the English style, I put my hands in my pockets. The material parted noisily. I scratched my balls while the voluptuous teacher tilted her neck, smoothing her hair over her ear, a fleshly whirlpool of sound. She crossed her legs, and the darkness beneath the thighs beyond the vanishing line lured me. The more unkindly I pulled, the more kindly my penis responded. It stretched out, straining to see through its Cyclopic, vertical eye. He asked me what I saw, I asked him what he saw.

A couple of weeks later, the minister wanted me to confess again. I went through the usual list of stealing, lying, spitting, swearing. But he kept insisting.

I knew full well that he wanted me to confess that I jerked off. He knew that I knew. After all, he had taught me! That I blushed more than before encouraged him. "So?"

"I shouted at my mother"—I didn't need to lie, it was true— "I know I should respect my parents lest my days on earth should be shortened, but I . . . I just cannot control it, when she tells me I should shine my shoes . . . "

Now, the sin of disrespecting your parents, mothers particularly, always worked with the minister. He asked for no more. At once he fell on his knees and prayed for me with enormous exertion. Half of his sermons were about motherly love, about sons who failed to acknowledge their love to mothers, coming to their graves from faraway lands, now that it's too late, and tearing their hair and beards in grief, lamenting over the soil. But too late. No more. He often recited "Mother" by Yesenin. He composed and recorded songs about motherly love and sold them in many churches of all sorts. In Catholic village households I often saw the well-fed face of our minister on record covers beneath the words "Love Thy Mother."

He was praying and sobbing for such a long time that I began to daydream about caressing my English teacher's breasts. I raised my voice to confess my sinful daydreams. At least the sin committed during the confession I could confess, in the true Protestant tradition; after confessing for six hours, Luther begged his confessor to let him confess all the sins he had committed during the confession, but the confessor besought him to spare him. The minister now hushed me and showed me the door. He stayed at his worktable, with tears flowing down his cheeks, devastated at the thought that his mother would die. The fact that, when he had been a little boy, the Nazis murdered his father carried no weight in comparison.

But the corpulent minister was not always so easy to deal with. Late one evening, with all the street lamps turned off because the country suffered a shortage of electricity, I was walking homeward, listening to the echoing of my steps from the other side of the street. Not a soul besides me was in the street. Suddenly, from behind a corner a big man leaped at me, grabbed the collar of my jacket, and lifted me off the ground.

"Gotcha!" I had no time to respond, but fought to inhale air, which now smelled strongly of cologne.

"I know where you've been. Tell me?"

"I played chess with a friend of mine."

"Yeah? That was yesterday. You've been to the cinema, in the congregation of the nonbelievers and blasphemers."

My, how does he know that? I stammered: "Yes, I was at a . . . a teacher mentioned it . . . it was historical . . . yes, a movie."

"The Devils of Louden." He emphasized each consonant.

"It's a famous movie."

"The Devil is famous. Watch out where you step. You think you can hide in the dark? God's eye sees in the dark better than the eyes of Owl—it sees through your flesh better than X rays, it sees through your soul."

He suddenly dropped me from his grip so that the back of my head hit the wall behind me, and I saw stars. Wiping his forehead from sweat, he said, "Amen!" and his ghastly purplish face turned away and his silhouette walked off. When I recovered my senses he was already gone. You could hear only his militaristic footsteps on the cobbles; his leather soles were fortified with iron crescent moons.

One May Day Bruno, a member of our church band, ran in, looking for my brother Ivo. He grew pale when Mother told him she didn't know where Ivo was. His blood returned to his face when I told him Ivo was in the toilet.

Bruno knocked on the toilet door. "Ivo, I have something private to ask you. Can I come in?"

Bruno asked Ivo to pray in tongues—if Ivo could do that, it would be a clear sign that God's grace was still upon earth.

Ivo came out, fuming. "No, impossible, impossible, it would be a sacrilege to pray in the toilet!"

"But can you still pray in tongues?"

They walked into the garden, where a swarm of buzzing bees had formed a congress in a grapelike bunch around their queen bee, on a rough-barked pear tree. Ivo closed his eyes and strange consonanted throaty sounds came out in an electrifying torrent. Bruno fell on his knees, kissed Ivo's hands, and shouted. "Great, Christ hasn't come yet! I couldn't find the preacher, couldn't find the deacons, couldn't find anybody born-again. So I thought they were all gone to heaven, and I was left here to suffer the seals of God's anger!"

That I had been there could not have served as proof that the saved had not ascended.

Several months later, without much announcement except the noise he made climbing the tree, Bruno jumped through my window, breathless, the whites of his eyes leaping out at me. It was déjà vu; he had jumped through my window like that a couple of years before, after his release from the military service. His chronic sinus headaches in the middle of the winter hadn't been enough to obtain him freedom. Instead, he had simulated insanity, with more success than he had bargained for—now, classified as a "paranoid schizophrenic," he couldn't get a job.

"Is there a God? What do you think?" he asked.

"You need some spirits, not a discussion." I walked to the larder to fetch plum brandy. My older brother Vlado as a doctor got slivovitz from peasants, who believed the drink would make him work better. I chose a bottle smelling of fresh plums.

Bruno sniffed the drink, made an expression of true beatitude, into which his face, scarred as it was with acne, startled as it had been, relaxed. His skin shone. I felt privileged that he came to me—and not to Ivo—to ask questions.

After his third shot, he asked, "So, frankly, Yozzo, what do you think? Is there a God?" He grinned broadly.

I had had a moment of doubt on my own in the middle of a long prayer in the church. I had sacrilegiously dared to open my eyes. Tortured peasants and workers had piously bowed their heads, muttered, and the strain to believe had twisted their foreheads into a wedge, a sort of anchor perched above the nose with a net of creases over elusive, shelled sea creatures, sifting through the bottomless indigo ocean of Christianity with its multi-headed, multilimbed, and multitongued monsters. The thought had flared up in my mind, God probably doesn't exist!

"To what other 'peoples' did Cain go when his family was the first family on earth?" Bruno left his mouth wide open after the statement, as a rhetoric portrayal of stupidity.

"I know. And why is there a genealogy of Christ from David to Joseph, when we are told Joseph is not the father of Christ?" I contributed. "And how come we have night and day on the first day of creation when God creates the Sun and the stars on the fourth?"

"That's it!" Bruno shouted, and tapped me on the shoulders. "I knew it, you don't believe!"

I feared that he had taken me in, just to see what I really believed—he'd report me to the minister and I would be excommunicated.

My mother showed in the door, her small sunken eyes blinking, with gray, kinky hair in disarray around her head. Against the corridor darkness behind her, the bright gray hair made her look like a disturbed saint woken from dreams. "I knew it," she said. "It's you, Misfortune." The people she despised she didn't call by their names, but by the names of vices and states of corruption. "Can't you keep your disgusting voice lower?"

"All right, Sister, I'll try, I'll be good," Bruno grinned, emphasizing the word *Sister,* the church title.

"And you, Misery," she addressed me, "Why did you let this miscreant in?"

"Sister, that's no way to talk about your brother in Christ!" Bruno exclaimed in the spirit of devilry.

"It stinks of booze. Don't you know, Misery, you have an exam tomorrow? In the afternoon you should help me finish the clogs for the town fair. You should be fresh for that."

"Leave us alone! We are having an important discussion," I said.

"Out! Out, you ugly Misfortune!" Mother shouted at Bruno. He and I doubled over with laughter.

Mother left, muttering. We sat at a polished maple table, where my father used to teach me to believe, where he had told me the stories of Joseph in Egypt, and where he had lain seven years before in his coffin. I shuddered at the memory.

Then Bruno whispered to me a verse from the Gospel according to Saint Mark: "And he said unto them, Verily I say unto you, That there be some of them that stand here, which shall not taste of death, till they have seen the kingdom of God come with power.'

"So almost two thousand years ago Christ promised his followers that during their lifetimes the kingdom of God would come. But those guys who hung around Christ are obviously dead, and we are still waiting for the kingdom of God. There's no kingdom of God." He kept whispering, louder and louder—as loud as some people shout.

"Maybe the kingdom of God is a metaphor, and it did come."

"In that case the whole Christianity is a metaphor. Poetry doesn't interest me."

"Yes, yes, I know. It's all human invention."

Though short, Bruno joyously leaped and touched the ceiling with his fingers. "Hush!" I said and we walked out, with the bottle of brandy in the pockets of my sheepskin jacket, which I had put on because it was fall.

"We are free!" I shouted, smelling the aroma of evergreens blown from the hills.

"No heaven, no hell. Don't you feel light?" Misfortune asked.

"Yes, like feathers," answered Misery.

"Christ, I was so stupid, Oh, pardon me, no Christ . . . sweating at night with fright . . . "

What I had failed to feel in my Baptism—the vanishing of gravity, the pull heavenward, the uplifting power of spirit—I felt now. The brandy was excellent.

We ran through the town, bringing the good news to an uncaring audience. Most people professed, as Communists, or Communist-pleasers, that they did not believe in God. Just as we used to suspect the professed believers to really be atheists, now we suspected the professed atheists to be closet believers. We assailed whoever was around with arguments for the nonexistence of God. The reasoning was based on a fundamentalist sort of understanding of God: the Bible reveals God. God is truth. The Bible is all true. But look, it contains contradictions; therefore it is not true. So, God doesn't exist or doesn't reveal Himself through the Bible.

For hours I tried to deconvert a friend of mine, Mirko, the only soul I thought I had brought to Christ with proofs for the existence of God. The whites of Mirko's eyes popped up like Ping-Pong balls; he frowned and blinked. After the example of Kovachevich the tombstone-maker, Mirko and I had kneaded cool clay into noses, cheekbones, eye-arches, jaws, and Adam's apples, never really finishing a single bust—we just hadn't had God in us to blow spirit into clay, to make living sculptures. Mirko now ceased to go to church.

The church elders, who had been so quick to reprimand me on each of my little transgressions before, were strangely quiet. I thought I would volunteer to excommunicate myself, but I didn't. I thought I didn't want to offend my old mother, but the fact was that the edifice of faith, not comprised of rational arguments, could hardly be eradicated by counterarguments. In my mind, among the ruins at least three thousand years old, mausoleums with mummies of the ancestors of ancestors, a dreadfully grating sand blew but failed to cover the ruins.

Mausoleums don't have much power during the day. But at night the Mausoleum of the Father and the Son, though I suspected it to be robbed of the Corpses, hooted and echoed.

I listened to my dreams and considered myself a superficial atheist and essential theist. I needed to reconcile the two. So I resumed my faith in God in a way, but the pictorial faith of my childhood, with Peter walking on the water, was gone. Though my faith sprang from tradition, now I could rely on no tradition. Jacob's ladder with dancing angels, after being climbed up and down, had fallen out of my reach.

To Baptists I was now an atheist, to atheists, again a believer. To myself, I was a believer without a congregation, a mason without a wall.

A year after flattering myself that I had deconverted Mirko, I saw him walk into an Eastern Orthodox church, and, unobserved, I too walked in. He prayed next to the melting candles. Orange light spread around in a steamy, waxy heaviness; the light gently touched gilded eyes of icons, which stared at you from all sides. An Orthodox priest with yellow teeth said, "It doesn't matter that you see the icons: stand before those eyes so they can see you."

God watched through the icon eyes akin to two fishes swimming toward each other. The priest prayed in Church Slavonic, his back to the congregation. The tall candles, crooked from the heat, twisted around each other, bowing like contrite sinners and dropping their hot and clearly transparent tears. The tears, as they jerkily and indecisively slid downward, lost their clarity and gathered around the feet of candles like knee-deep snow, choking light and hiding the shoes. I walked out, stepping through dry snow, which moaned beneath my shoes.

The Address

Big cities make people miserable, and more so those who do not live in them than those who do. The same applies to big countries in relation to small ones. The fact that there were big cities and that I lived in a small town of a provincial country (Nizograd in Croatia, Yugoslavia) drove me up the wall, the way a trickle of honey from a wall cupboard drives a cockroach up a lengthy journey across the wall. The clamor of big cities worked like the smoke of dry mushrooms that grew on lindens. My father used to blow fungus smoke from an accordion-like mechanism made of wood and leather; the incense gushed into his beehives and the bees buzzed away, their paths crisscrossing like an illusory vibrating net while Father installed a new queen bee. The sound of big cities, blown over the rolling hills, deceptively smelled of incense, and drove me out with the suffocating strength of smoldering mushrooms.

Every night I listened to the *Voice of America* on the short waves. It slid away and I shifted the dial after it; often the *Voice of Albania* overshadowed it. I was reluctant to turn off the radio since I believed I could pick up English unconsciously. Late at night I woke up with cold sweats, to hear pulsating buzzing and hissing, as if creatures from outer space were trying to reach me.

As agitated as a smoked-out bee, one rosy dawn I climbed into a steam-engine train. The train crept through tunnels and glided over bridges. Deer fled from the steel dinosaur into the dank woods. Hawks supervised the slow progress of the train as though it were a meaty monster of charcoal flesh, breathing its last with terrible gusts of steam, about to collapse and be feasted upon. I pulled down the window and breathed in the smell of coal and felt the wind begin to freeze my lips. I looked toward the steam engine as it appeared and disappeared in curves. Particles of coal smarted my eyelids. A dry old man with sunken lips touched me with his crooked walking stick, and raspily begged me to spare his health and close the window.

In the warmth of the closed space I leaned against the window, separated from the woods by the transparent membrane of the mobile womb, the train, which offered me the chance of rebirth in a new place. Steamy smoke crept into heathers and disheveled grasses.

At the first station—one whitewashed house, not much larger than a chicken coop—many old people entered and sat on the wooden benches of the train, carrying brown eggs wrapped in newspapers, live black turkeys, red chickens, and butter in grape leaves.

Children spread their noses over windowpanes, rolling their skulls against the hard surface—they reminded me of dough that bakers roll over wooden boards. Pencils peeped through holes in their schoolbags, sliding and hanging lower and lower. Boys wrote love messages on papers, made airplanes, and threw them at girls, who did not deign to notice, and the planes boomeranged. The boys weren't yet good enough. The girls braided and unbraided each other's hair. Daydreaming, they knitted a surprise present for a prince, a mitten, wishing to envelop the prince's fingers in lamb's warmth. In several years after the princes would have failed to appear, the boys would become desirable.

My forehead against the cool windowpane, I breathed against the glass, making it hazy, as if I did not wish to see the familiar anymore, as if out of the vapors a new world would precipitate, not so peasanty and shabby. The glass dried and I stared into the woods and saw the reflection of my eyes gazing at me as if they were the eyes of the forest. What is behind the woods? That I knew. The mountains. And what is behind the mountains? That I did not know. Mountains hid mysterious worlds from me. If there were no mountains, there would be nothing to see but the plains. The name itself says plain, unintriguing. Why do mountains promise more on the other side? Is it because they separate peoples? To go from one valley to another, at least it used to be so, was to go from one language to another, one history to another, one religion to another, to a new hope from an old illusion. Religions came down to us from the mountains, from the clouds, when it grew cold and the vapors on the top condensed into stone tablets, promising another world beyond the mountaintops—promises in the form of thunder and terror. Only fright can thrill us to imagine a new world; only when your life is at stake do you sense that it could become something else, something unknown and greater than life—death, negatively described; and positively?

I became nervous on the approach to the border, my first border. The police looked for my name in a book, and then stamped my passport against the train wall, which shook. I smelled the wet ink on a new stamp, a trophy, as the train crossed the Italian border.

The train soon moved quickly and smoothly. The friction of the reality as I knew it was glossed away.

In the morning, I dreaded Rome, my first big city. As the train slid, clicking sparsely over the minimal rail gaps, I hoped it would never arrive at the station. The metal wheels squeaked piercingly and the train shook into a full stop.

I had ignored my brother Ivo, who traveled with me, but his insisting that we leave the train and find a music store brought me out of my daydreams. Ivo fingered varnished classical guitars—he wanted one to play church music (death-contemplating Bach). He listened to street musicians and exchanged tidbits of technical know-how with them, and I rushed to see Saint Peter's.

Rome looked dry. What Romans called a river was evidently a monument to what once upon a time had been a river—most things in Rome were reminders of what had been but was no more. In the celebrated River Tiber, or rather, in the river bed, sleeping stones and a bit of liquid garbage held some vague olfactory promise to lean cats, who languidly moved about, finically choosing their stepping stones.

I was so thirsty when I reached Saint Peter's that I did not bother to look around but searched instead for water fountains—and I found none.

Having returned to the train station on time—we were in a rush, in a month we wanted to cover as many miles on my Inter-Rail pass as possible—I found a place to sit and left my bag on it, and the earlike plastic handles of the bag shrank. Through the window, a sign on a building, BANCO DI SPIRITI SANCTI, scandalized me: mixing holy spirit and finances—it was blasphemy against the Holy Ghost!

On the platform people were seeing each other off. Women rested their cheeks on men's breasts as if from one second of such rest they would remain fresh for days. Some leaned their faces sideways as if to listen for the heartbeat, suspecting departing lovers to be heartless. Some probably feigned big loss, others disguised it.

Some wept, others laughed, many shouted, some were silent and somber. Almost everyone was leaving an embrace of parents, lovers, brothers, friends, grandparents, children, perhaps to land in another one, a secret one, at the destination.

It was time for the train to depart. I leaned through a window and watched the minute hand on a large clock settle with a jerk into the twelve to show it was two o'clock. I had expected the motion of the hand to convey itself to the train, with a jerk, and to knock people off balance in the corridors. The parting was at its climax: lovers were kissing each other last kisses, deep and dreamy. Now the insincere lovers were doing their utmost to display real passion and the sincere ones were on the verge of fainting.

A quarter of an hour later, the train still stood still.

"That's ridiculous!" shouted a blond passenger. I wondered what "ridiculous" meant, but by the motion of an impatient and angry face, with a blazing eye, I was beginning to guess. His staring toward the engine, as if the sparks from his eyes could ignite it, laid the foundation for my grasping the meaning of that monumental word. "That's ludicrous!" he shouted.

After an hour and a half the train was still motionless. The lovers who had feigned emotion had given up, going away and shrugging in resignation, as if saying, "It's not my fault, I kept it up as long as I could." The lovers who were too shy to show love, had now no need of hiding it anymore because none was left. Those who had been kissing in ecstasy chewed bubble gum. Some people still wept, but there was such a note of impatience in their weeping that they probably wept because the train had not brought an end to the togetherness. A young man—blond hair, black beard, golden glasses—his *Portable Lenin* sticking out of his quasi-military jacket, burned blankets in front of his first-class sleeping car. The girls who had taken catnaps on the firm chests of their heroes now cast charming sideways glances at other young men; and the heroes no longer controlled their necks but examined all the examples of womanhood within the radius of visibility. That resulted in name-calling, and I was privileged not to understand Italian.

The train was suddenly seized with violent paroxysms. Backpacks flew onto the heads of their masters as if to teach them some basic relation between geometry and statics via dynamics. Eggs flew out of overturned sacks, showing their true consistencies—some burst into yellow slime, others let their green yolks roll around the corridor.

The old emotions resurged instantly; parting loved ones cried and shouted. A cool breeze carried a sensation of triumph and relief.

Handkerchiefs waved. The train, still in jerks, moved from the scene. Whoever could, leaned through the windows and waved just in case their beloved ones were not nearsighted. Those who were parting from nobody in particular waved to Rome as if the city lounged in the Termini station.

The morphology of Rome is easy to describe. In the center: ruins. Then a circle of firm buildings. After this, again ruins or buildings about to become so: mortar falling off, roofs missing, shaggy trees growing out of walls, shooting their roots through cracks.

The ridiculous/ludicrous blond man talked to another American; I was certain they were American because they sounded like John Wayne and Jack Nicholson. The men's long vowels demonstrated that, self-confident, the men needed neither to flee nor rush—in contrast to half an hour before. Since it was impossible to stay shy and be on Italian soil, I addressed the blond man. I had otherwise feared to address anybody in the language of Rock, that powerful music that made your ribs resonate, each rib to a different high frequency, and your forearm and shins to different deep ones.

The American smiled benignly as if he could understand what I was saying. My numerous dependent clauses never got to the main clause on which they hinged—the way one, in a lawsuit, never arrives at the Supreme Court, but only to the dependent courts.

I thought the safest way to express a meaning would be to choose a long word and to stick to it a couple of prefixes and a couple of contradicting suffixes, producing all the nuances that my point needed and all the ones it might turn out to need. So to express the idea that there could be no noise, I would say, "Nonunnoisesomelessably," and bury the word in multiple layers of *if* and *nevertheless* clauses.

Having heard my nonirreproduciblesomelessive sentences, the American left the corridor and sat next to my brother Ivo, who slept—his mouth open, his eyes half open—and soon leaned his head on the American's shoulder. The American shrank back. I stared at the rocky fields, which seemed to rotate.

As I mused about the rocky wealth and vegetal poverty of the landscape, I heard a clear feminine voice speaking English—a young woman talked to a priest. She spoke so gently that my skin, if there had been more hair on it, would have resembled that of a cat facing a wolf with no trees in sight. My lips dried up, playing smart—they needed to be moistened. My blood cells heard her voice—they forgot to store oxygen in the furnaces of my body, a steam engine, where carbon, coal, should burn. My blood cells stood still at the edge of my heart and then leaped with suicidal excitement into it. In the chambers they found nothing but emptiness—and each other. My heart kicked against my chest as if saying, "Hey ass, what are you waiting for?"

I jumped over people's knees in the crowded corridor, barely managing to keep my physical balance and failing to keep my mental balance. I was approaching her like a feline beast, albeit not so gracefully—hiding as if attacked while attacking. Well, it was obvious where I was. Still I hid my focus on her by pretending to be looking through the window. The priest, whose collar must have been white several weeks before, used some Slavic words—the rest English, Latin, Esperanto. If Esperanto has anything to do with hope, he spoke Desperanto.

"You are from Poland, aren't you?" I exclaimed. "I am from Yugoslavia!" I paused, expecting a joyous impact, along pan-Slavic lines. After a silence, during which the coach wheels noisily skipped rail gaps, he said, "Aha, from Yugoslavia," and frowned.

She repeated, "Wow, from Yugoslavia!" My ears caressed her voice. The priest asked us, "How you amare moy Englisch? I never parlo esto before. Solo read."

"It's lovely," said the woman, and the broad creased forehead of the priest beamed a pink shade of pride. I did not speak but felt some complicity between me and her. The priest looked at us and smiled with an air of generous and inevitable renunciation, and I loved him immediately, the way Jesus loved the rich young man when He believed that he would give away all he had; He loved him at first sight. I loved the Polish priest at the third, seeing that he would retreat. He said to us, placing one hand on my shoulder, and another on hers, "Por que non amare one andere, eh?" She looked at me and said, "We do!" and touched my cheek lightly. I metamorphosed into another creature on the spot, an ass, most likely. As I looked at her wavy radiant crimson lips, peripherally seeing her breasts lifted upright by her dancer's posture, I stood in admiration—as did something else. She parted her full lips slightly, turning her green irises toward me, and the Cupid disguised as a priest grinned devilishly and slid into his compartment.

We were alone in the corridor. I shivered, it seemed so natural to embrace each other—the year was 1974, the Autumn of Love. Her voice, barely touching her vocal cords, came from within her chest, arising directly from her soul; a touch of her lips, a flutter, crowned her words. My cheeks brimmed.

"How did you get out of Yugoslavia?" she asked.

"It wasn't easy. I swam across the Drava to Austria with a brother of mine one stormy night, so the police dogs could not detect us. Yet we were espied, and the guards fired at us and killed my brother."

"Oh, how terrible," she exclaimed in alarm and sympathy, and held my elbow in her hands gingerly as if it were dislocated.

"I was only joking. Yugoslavia is a free country. You can leave it as you please."

"Don't they choose your occupation when you are five years old, and if you don't follow their plans, you go to Siberia?"

"No."

"But your government wants you all to have the same things and wear the same clothes."

"That's fine. Your work is what matters."

"Work? What if you don't like to work?"

"Then you are ill. Work is a beautiful phenomenon." Whenever I had argued about Communism in Yugoslavia, I was against it. Now that I was abroad, I surprised myself by praising Communist ideologies. "If you work on what you like, you enjoy it."

"I could see that if you are a musician, a painter, but what if you are a dentist?"

"Well, teeth are sculptures. Dentists can concentrate on making the best vegeto-carno-dynamic form, giving vent to ingenuity, which would give them a rewarding feeling. . . . "

"Provided you didn't bite into their fingers!"

"Yes, the creative process . . . " I was about to go on in praise of unalienated dental labor, when my tongue expressed its own opinion. It did not want to move into the twisted English vowels and consonants, from which my jaws ached (the origin of the language must be very gluttonous). Instead, the tip of my tongue got stuck, just as I was about to pronounce the famous English "the," in a sizable hole in an upper molar (if it could be called a molar; it was a ruin that testified to there once or twice having been a molar). My tongue rebounded and struck against the upper front teeth.

"That was good!" she exclaimed. "Your *the* sounded like an Englishman's."

My tongue squirmed and would not budge; I gurgled sounds. My lips tingled for hers. Of course, the American Dental Association had released her to kiss freely. But I wasn't sure that I could proudly display the secret ways of Communist dental work. So I withdrew into sadness—a carnal grief—and didn't look into her eyes but rather at the darkening skyline with vineyard sticks on hills, like needles over needle-pillows.

I suddenly began preaching—some kind of defense—about God. She stared at me in disbelief. I took her disbelief as doubt in His existence; in fact, she was not sure about mine.

"You know," I said, "the greatest ideal is Love your neighbor as yourself. In it all Christianity and Communism could be fulfilled."

"I agree."

"But," I said, "it's not a call for promiscuity. You cannot have sex with your neighbor because you cannot have sex with yourself."

"Can't you make love to yourself? Since you want to be so

literal—if you masturbate, you should jerk off your neighbor as yourself, right?" She laughed.

My interpretation of Love Thy Neighbor as Thyself was undergoing a crisis, and I realized that I was working against my desire. "The verse is not a call to promiscuity. You should have sex with only one person."

"But there are many neighbors, and you should love them all. I see nothing wrong with sleeping with several people," she said.

Wow, I thought, we could do it, where? I looked around to the ends of the corridor. The red bathroom light for "occupied" was on, on both ends. We could go to another coach? I was thrilled as if stealing, on the verge of being caught. But the lights on the bathrooms stayed mercilessly red. What a socialist country Italy is! I wished to see some green.

"What's wrong with sleeping with several people?" She asked, taking my looking around for a sign of embarrassment. "Don't you know that God is One"—I'd been so used to arguing that I went on against my wish—"and He wants our love to be one—for a man there should be only one woman and for a woman one man, one flesh. Fusion of two souls results in a new soul, a child. Only a perfect monogamous fusion can form a good soul, a healthy human being. . . . "

"How about twins?"

"Sleeping with many people is cynicism." I ignored her challenge to the oneness theory.

"It just occurred to me! We don't even know each other's name! Mine is Deborah."

I told her mine. She told me that she majored in music, wanted to become a psychotherapist—music therapy—and that I looked stunningly like her cousin that she admired.

I was intoxicated with English—the ethereal language I had for years longed to speak—and there it was, the language incarnated as a beautiful woman.

It was dawning. I had not conceived that our conversation could end. Out of a blue mist and green pastures rocks arose;

somber pines covered the mountain below bald blue rock, and there was snow atop it.

"It looks like New Jersey, where I come from, but our mountains are not so high." She leaned against the window, looking high up, her breasts spreading against the windowpane.

Suddenly she turned toward me, her face brightening. "If you come to the States, you could visit me!"

"Visit you? No, I couldn't."

"Why not? I am inviting you!"

"No, no. It costs too much to get there. I will never see America . . . and I will never see you again."

"No, we will see each other! I feel it. In America we say Everything is possible."

"Well, we too say Everything's possible, but we mean that in the catastrophic sense."

The blue morning spread through the mist directly from the sky over wooden shacks of bluish gray wood, straight into my soul, if I had one, and to me it seemed the greatest tragedy that I would not live to see the same scenery in New Jersey one day— I didn't know that nobody would.

"Look, it's dawn and we haven't had a wink of sleep!" She touched my left cheek with the dorsal side of her fingers, and she let her transparent nails slide down across my lips.

"Yes, but I am not tired."

She lingered a little in the door of her compartment.

After her, the corridor appeared desolate and chilly, Alpine chilly. Yet I was jumping up and down, and I walked on my arms for joy. From a compartment six Italian soldiers shouted, "Bravo!"

They tapped me on the shoulders, offered wine, happy for me, pointing toward Deborah's apartment and winking. Then they began to look serious and pushed me out of the apartment without comments. Deborah was back in the corridor.

"I couldn't sleep!" she said. "Where are you going to after Vienna?"

"To London. I want to see hippies. I've never seen one."

"I am going to Hungary. My roots are Hungarian."

"Really? What's your last name?"

"M———."

"That sounds Japanese. Could you write it down?"

She did, and I added, "And could you add your address to it? I'd write you almost every day."

"You are crazy!" she said merrily. "I'll write you too, but you write first. But look, why don't you come along to Hungary?"

"Hungary's not covered by Inter-Rail."

"Never mind. I'll lend you some money."

I nodded, sadly, in refusal, and thought how Ivo, who spoke no English, would react if I dumped him and rushed after a woman.

"You are afraid to miss out on hippies, ah?" she laughed. "There aren't any anymore. I used to be one, and hanging around me is as close as you'll get to one."

I still nodded side to side.

"What's your ethnic background?" she asked me, as if ethnicity should explain my pride.

We were in the outskirts of Vienna. People were getting their backpacks ready. When Deborah stretched to get hers from the rack, she looked tremendously lithe.

At the train station Deborah embraced me vigorously, and I embraced her. We looked into each other's eyes for a long time.

I was sorely aware of my brother standing on the side.

Her fingers slipped away from mine, and she was gone, rushing into a green train, to Budapest.

"Who was that?" Ivo asked.

"None of your business."

"Man, you should have gone with her!" Ivo nodded.

I had known my brother so little; I saw him as the keeper of my Baptist conscience.

Ivo insisted that I loan him some money. I did. Since Ivo wanted to buy a Yamaha guitar, and I seemed to be in a daze, he asked me for two hundred DMs, all I had, two hard blue papers, rustle-y and elastic, which I considered to be some kind of jewelry you kept forever rather than spent. I threw the money at him, and walked away. From a distance I could see that he picked up the money and started toward the bank; such is the power of music that it takes pride away.

I rushed now to the train to Budapest, but the train was pulling out. Why didn't I go with her? I felt guilty, stupid. I stared at her handwriting reverently without reading it, like an illiterate medieval Christian gazing at a copy of the Bible. I walked into the park and slept in the sun, and later, back at the train station, I saw a large olive-colored train arriving. The letters on the side of the train read in Cyrillic, MOSCOW–WARSAW–WIEN. A train from the Slavic East! I'd traveled in the West, learning the language of the West, longing for a Western woman, and I had neglected the lands of my forefathers and foremothers. I was put to shame. I wanted now to reverse my longings toward the East; the Cyrillic stirred me.

Near the train engine I noticed a pale woman of about fifty with a broad face, high cheekbones, small closely set eyes, and a creased flat forehead. Her face shone above a big bouquet of red and white flowers. I sat not far from her on a wooden postal cart. She did not notice me. She did not notice anybody near, but gazed only ahead, coaches and coaches ahead. How eagerly she awaits a beloved one, a brother, sister, son, husband, friend!

Suddenly she dashed forward shouting a name I didn't catch. Then she stopped, petrified, and the features of happiness contorted into pain. Slowly her happy expectation reappeared on her face. People passed by. There were fewer and fewer to come. Her face still smiled. There was now only a trickle of people to come. Her smile stayed as if she were afraid to change it. She grew pale and gray. Her smile still stayed on and then her face was rent with twists of pain, her eyebrows and eyes collecting in one dark blur, a silvery tooth glittering bluish hues out of her mouth.

A railway man in greasy blue, walking listlessly along the train, hit the wheels with a small hammer on a long handle, proofing for cracks in the iron. The striking was loud and cold, and each wheel left a dulled, high-pitched buzz, hurting my ears. Each new strike of the hammer jarred her, as if she were a nail, and the hammer was hitting her on the head, sinking her deeper and deeper into the wood. Now she looked at least sixty. The flowers in her hands drooped—no longer a bright bunch. I thought she would die of a heart attack then and there.

In the shade of a park's trees whose crowns were manicured into cubes, I checked my pockets to admire Deborah's address in her cardiogram-like handwriting—to memorize it by heart. It was not in my left pocket. I panicked. Never mind. I often panicked. It was not in my right pocket and not in any other one—I still had hope, but less and less. I checked my pockets systematically, and then hurriedly, unsystematically. I had lost it! Despair struck me.

I took a train toward Norway, no-way. I wanted to go as far as the railways went into the icy country. I wanted to leave reality. Going off the map (sort of)—where geographers can't keep the measures straight, where everything is broadened and distorted, beyond the Arctic Circle—would be the closest to leaving reality. I would pass through each place simply to say to it, I will not be here. Even before my existence could appear in a place, I would be gone away. Travel is a form of vanishing, of nonexistence. It is the best substitute for suicide.

I saw no fjords and no ice caps. I gazed at the countryside with my forehead against the windowpane; trees and grassy hills used my eyes to gaze back at me. I whispered "Deborah"—at the end, instead of an *h* there was a breath, a sound of the vanishing rainbow, aspirated expiration into infinity. I wrote a letter to her, in my head—it came from farther away than I could think and was going farther away than I could imagine. There could be no envelope for the imaginary letter, just as there could be no womb for seed spilled in dust. My eyes plucked the Norwegian landscape and put it together into her ghostlike image—emerald eyes with patches of night sky drowning in them. She became a natural deity, permeating all the environment—and I, a pantheist pagan. My letter was three thousand miles long, three thousand miles of smooth iron.

I tried to concentrate my thoughts so they would lead my mind toward her, by telepathy, to Hungary. If I had enough faith, I could move mountains, let alone relay a longing! I prayed—like most prayers, mine seemed unanswered. I closed my eyes, expecting to recall her address. I had looked at it with such dumb reveries that I hadn't even read it. I went on writing to her, explaining to her the intricacies of my longing for her, and the intricacy was that I had lost all hope but not the desire. I was in the First Circle of Hell.

The following summer I got the round-trip fare from my grandmother in Cleveland to visit the United States. I had written to her in English, and she had heard from our relatives how obsessed with English I had become—how I had read English books all my waking hours and listened to the *Voice of America* when asleep. So she wanted to help me learn English.

In Cleveland there were no pedestrians outside the bus terminal, and many cars on the road, in each car only one person. A man in a three-piece suit stepped out of a black car and said, "Would you like a blow job?"

"No, thank you. I am on a tourist visa." What a nice country, I thought. You step off the plane, and people offer you employment.

I rang the bell outside the wooden house, my grandmother's address. Slow steps drummed on a wooden staircase. Squirrels ran atop fences, gray, unlike the red European squirrels. After a silence, the door opened, and there she was, exclaiming in a mixture of Slovenian and Croatian: "Ah, my! You. All the way from Yugoslavia, all by yourself. My little grandson, but look at you, you are so big now."

The living room was bright, sunlight reflecting from the linoleum floor and a white round refrigerator, solid as a tank.

"But wait, it's nine o'clock, we are missing the news!" Her hands trembling with the passion of an addict, she turned the radio knob. I was nearly trembling myself with curiosity, because this was the first time I would hear the American radio. The announcer's voice was a convincing resonant masculine voice as was becoming to the news of the most powerful empire on earth. Watergate. I thought Nixon took a boat and passed through some gate. Impeachment. What is the peach doing in the word?

Books on World War II covered Grandmother's bookshelf. She loved to remember her partisan days out loud—scraping worms out of soldiers' wounds, shaking hands with Tito. I didn't listen; I had heard enough about World War II in Yugoslavia— now I wanted America.

Every day I biked to Public Square, trying to strike up conversations with absolutely anybody so I could improve my English. I wondered where the real America was. Wherever I step is not America was my axiom. Wherever I went, I took the Balkans along, and could not see over the mountains. Each night for ten nights I had the same dream: I am back in my hometown, in front of the cinema where young vagabonds spend summer days. My friends ask me, Why are you here? I reply, I must have stepped onto the wrong plane. Instead of in Cleveland, I landed in Zagreb!

A policeman gave me a free front-row baseball ticket when I asked him for directions. I hadn't known cops could be friendly. In the stadium, I stared at the field, leaving the front row because I wanted to be above the field. The radiant green was so soothing that it did not disturb me that apparently nothing was happening on the field. After half an hour of watching a guy tightening his ass, sticking out a large thick stick, and others now and then run a bit, I was tired of the warm-up, and asked people around me when the game would begin. "Begin? It's been going on for an hour," said a fat man in green trousers and sized me up and down

as if I had just escaped from an asylum for the criminally insane.
Finally, the man with the bat swung it, and I feared that he'd blow
away the head of his squatting compatriot. The bat struck the
ball, the whole audience screamed with horror, so that for a second I feared that the squatter's head must be flying. I didn't see
him squatting any more. Tacky organ music shrieked, and the
large billboard flashed: Go! Go!

Petroleum darkness loomed beyond the green fields, Lake
Erie. I begged a man to explain the rules of baseball to me. He
chewed the hamburger and stepped away from me. During the
break people bought green and red popsicles and screamed. I
wondered how such an empty-street city as Cleveland could produce so many hollering humans.

Outside the stadium I suddenly recognized a woman from
ten paces away—Deborah! I ran toward her with my arms out-
spread. The woman was startled. It was not Deborah. I didn't
excuse myself because I was so let down, and the woman walked
away, scandalized. I wished I were in Yugoslavia, hiking in the
mountains, and that the American dreams did not exist.

When I discovered that nearly everybody American was listed in
phone books, my heart leaped and my ribs danced—I'll trace
Deborah! With hands as trembling as my grandmother's when she
turned on the news, I opened the black phone book of Cleveland. Her name was not there. I was thrilled entering the glassy
Ohio Bell building. I'll find Deborah. I will hitchhike to New
Jersey; we will be happy!

In a room on the ground floor, I looked through all the New
Jersey books: not a single instance of her last name. My hopes
were riddled with doubt, and that only made me more desirous. I
flipped phone books one after another, one region after another,
looking for several permutations of her last name. Americans
moved a lot. She could have gotten married. Still, she could not
be the last Mohican of her family. I will find her!

I did not notice that everybody had left, at six. A guard

warned me, "Sir, we are closed," and he accompanied me to the door as if I wouldn't leave otherwise. "I am not a Sir," I said, "I am not even an Englishman." I felt as if I were being escorted into a jail; the jail was the outdoors—indoors with the phone books was liberty, liberty to continue looking for her.

After a sleepless night, I was at the steps of Ma Bell before it would open, freezing in the wind from Lake Erie. Black men unlocked the building and the doors began to revolve. Employees walked in, some smiling, others frowning. I wondered whether to pity them for not having such an extraordinary hope as I had— but maybe they had similar hopes?

I pored over the names of M——— from all over America, shivering as if I had remained exposed to the Erie winds. Who are all these people in the Book of Names, the Book of Life? I slowed down my search, to make it more thorough—I feared that my hope had an expiration point, the last phone book of the United States. From frenzy I had lapsed into nostalgic langor. I did not eat, I only drank Coca-Cola. I grew dizzy with headaches. In moments the room turned purple in front of me, then bright orange, green, and I had to lean on the table not to collapse on the floor, from the high chair. My hope drove me back to my senses and on with the search. With zest I opened books of Oklahoma, Pennsylvania . . . and after each book, a thrill of loss, a stabbing of cold metal passed through me as it had through the woman I remembered from the Vienna train station—as the last passengers without the beloved had trickled by, and the controller had hammered the iron wheels.

By noon I got as far as Virginia. Not much remained. In the afternoon, with the last book of Wyoming, I hesitated long before I dared open it.

It was not there. My hope was slain. Everything around me was of stone, polished stone, with sticky coffee stains over it.

Bricks

It is said that physicians are fortunate because their mistakes hide in the ground while their successes bask in the sunshine. Well, with Zivko Zidar and me, the converse is true—the ground hides him as my success.

Zivko came into my office one windy morning and stood in the doorway, pinching his blue worker's cap in his hands. He was of medium height, stockily built, and his hair was bright gray. "*Herr Doktor,* I would like to talk to you confidentially."

"Shoot."

"Here?"

"Why not? The law and the professional code of honor guarantee that everything you say here will remain here, strictly confidential."

"But . . . " He turned his head halfway toward my secretary. I told him to visit me at home after supper, at eight. I was used to the stealthy ways of VD.

"Thank you, thank you." He shook my hand energetically. The skin of his palm was cracked, dry, calloused.

"Don't rush your thanks. With physicians you have to wait until well after the treatment before you thank."

My doorbell rang at the appointed time, and I was, as usual, alone at home. I used to be married, but my wife had committed suicide—her note, addressed to nobody in particular, claimed that it was because of an affair—a totally insignificant one—I was having with a patient of mine, a nun. I'm sure it had nothing to do with me but with a chemical imbalance in her brain.

"Are you alone, *Herr Doktor?*"

"Like a scarecrow. What ails you?"

"I am as healthy as garlic."

"So, how can I help you?"

"I have a strange request—it calls for a bit of preparation."

Mistrustfully, I watched him as he unbuttoned his fake-fur overcoat and placed it on the shoulders of the armchair behind him. He leaned—his widow's peak formed a sharp V—and opened a worn-out leather bag. I hoped he was not pulling out a gun.

He took out a bottle of slivovitz. "Here, Doc, *der beste plum brandy* in Slavonia, and besser than the Slavonian you can't find. My old man lives to brew his shlivovitza. The Central Committee used to buy it from him."

We downed several shots, grunted to ease the pain in our throats, and chatted aimlessly, it seemed. I got to know that Zivko Zidar had worked as a laborer at Bayer Pharmaceuticals for almost twenty years. That's where he had acquired the habit of sticking German words into his Croatian.

He changed his tone after the fourth shot. "I am tired of working. I *bin zu alt* to start something *neu*. In this life you usually get the second chance, but not the fourth."

"Wait a minute, how old are you?"

"Forty-two. I know I look older and I am older. I have swallowed a lot of dust and worn out many soles."

"But you are a lad! Well, what do you think, how old am I? No need to answer. Sixty-four."

"Doctor, I don't want to kill myself."

"That's not unusual. You need morphine?"

"There's no drug to compare with slivovitz. What I would like is a certificate that I am dead. Can you make one out for me?"

"What would you do with it? Out of the question!"

"I'd give you a lot of *Geld* for it."

"It's as though you asked me to renounce my profession. No way."

I was convinced that he was out of his mind. I began to wonder how to get him as far away from me as possible.

"My request won't seem so crazy to you if you lend me your ears for a quarter of an hour."

I walked to the phone. It may be immoral for a physician to unhook his phone; someone in mortal danger could try to call. But I never know, the phone may be tapped, and my guest could say something political. My elbow brushed a framed picture of me in a military uniform hugging my German shepherd. The picture glass broke to pieces on the floor, and I didn't clean it up. My orange cat sniffed the glass particles. It struck me as stupid that I'd cut off my phone connection with the world to remain alone with a desperate man.

"The whole thing started early." He talked. "I dropped out of high school because I rushed to make my own money so I could ride motorcycles. I got a job at our barrel factory—on the export line for Bavarian beer—and the work gave me strength during the day and money at night, but it took my future away. I was shortsighted. In youth, your mind is at its peak, and yet it's at its most foolish. But I am not stupid. It's hard to believe. . . . "

"I believe you. But why do you want a death certificate?"

"I'll get to that. A friend of mine got me a job in Germany, at Bayer. I thought I'd stay for a year, until I bought a good car. Then I'd go to evening classes, get my high-school diploma, and enroll at a university to study medicine. I'd wanted to be a doctor, to get into people, into their marrows, the way my nephew does with his toys. Whenever he gets a toy he hides in a pigsty and tears it to pieces to see what makes it move. He doesn't have enough patience to dismantle the toy and put it back together.

His parents don't buy him toys anymore, but I do, just to see him flush with curiosity, and then to see him five minutes later, sullen and sorry.

"*Alles* in *Deutschland* was work. Even walking in the streets was work—signals and signs in a foreign language, rushing bodies, cars. You couldn't ask for directions because people despised you for not speaking German or English. You start work late and finish it late. After work, you have a couple of beers and fall asleep. The lifestyle got to me, so when I took my first vacation, I thought, This is it. I am not coming back.

"At home I drove around, treated everybody, and met a girl named Miriana. I clung to her as if she could save me from slavery. In Germany, I had had no time for whores, let alone honest girls. Where would I have met honest girls?

"Miriana and I had a big wedding. I woke up with a terrible hangover, married, penniless. *Keine Schule* no more. From now on, Push the tool, there's no school. Pull the wheelbarrow, ox, for the new pair of blue socks.

"Her family were like mice in a mousetrap with cheese, except the cheese was gone. Well, we could go back to my old man and be peasants, but you can never go back to the village—our people despise peasants. Also, Germany didn't look too *schlimm* from that distance. In a year, we'd spare enough money for a down payment on an apartment, and then maybe the Yugoslav economic miracle would start to work.

"I loved Miriana almost as much as myself, but I saw the yoke. I was reined to a cart, my wife sat on it, with a whip and gentle words and tears; Whip! over my skin, and soon there would be kids there, one on each side, whipping too, so I would pull uphill. Miriana wanted to stay in Brod for a year to finish her last year of high school while I labored *Ausland*. She needed a little room near the school and she needed this and that, all kinds of things, which I sent her from Germany. On *lange Wochenende* I took trains home. I was tired and happy.

"*Aber* the following year I couldn't come back to Yugoslavia for good because of the economic crisis. Miriana wanted to study economics in Zagreb. Every *Dummkopf* studies business or economics, what kind of work will you have? She wouldn't listen.

"Winters in Germany are dark and long, spring and fall, rainy and *grau*. I dreamed of a house on the Adriatic Coast near Zadar. It was expensive to buy a *Hausplatz* but I managed to do it in two years. I kissed the stones where my house would be, and lizards ran out from under them.

"In my free time I drew plans for the house and consulted an architect from Zagreb. He admired my ideas, and we cooperated, but it all cost. Whenever Miriana and I could, we went down to the building site, carried bricks, cleaned around, and then, with cement dust on us, jumped into the turquoise clear water, pulling each other, weightless like cosmonauts.

"In Germany, at night I wondered how she waited for me. Jealousy began to work in me, out of love. But how could it be out of love? Love is trust and jealousy is mistrust. I decided that we needed a child. You need to seal the marriage, give your wife something to do, so she wouldn't start fooling around while I pissed blood in the factory. Out of jealousy I devised my *Lebensplan*. I would step onto the terrace of my villa, wipe my forehead, breathe in the salty air with its cypress fragrance, embrace my thankful wife, and listen to my smart son ask me whether there is an end to the sea, and why the water is down and not up, and why the clouds move in the sky and not underground.

"My wife got pregnant. I baked an ox and several piglets and opened up a barrel of brandy. It was fall, and fruits were dropping onto cabbage and lettuce everywhere. A hundred people came to the feast, and they asked, Who's getting married? And I told them, my son. He is getting married to mathematics. Where is your son? Here, I pointed to Miriana's belly. How do you know it won't be a daughter? I know. I'll name him Nadan. But there's no such name—there's only Nenad. Yes, but Nenad means unhoped for, in a good sense, I guess, but my son is hoped for, Nadan. But that's like Nada, a female name for hope, they said. So, can't a man have hope? I asked.

"And it turned out to be a girl. *Sehr gut,* I thought. Is there anything more beautiful than a pretty little girl? She'll sit in my lap and I'll tell her fancy tales. I was happy, but the more I looked at her, the stranger she seemed. Even as a baby she was pretty. I am so rough, and neither is Miriana a beauty. We are both blond and blue-eyed, and the baby was a dark-eyed brunette. How's that possible?

"I went back to Germany. As I said, whenever there is no trust, there is no love. I imagined all sorts of things—that my wife, behind my back, behind the cliffs of the Alps . . . she probably wouldn't even know whose the bastard is. No, she isn't a bastard, she's a wonderful baby—too wonderful!

"With such thoughts I ran to the *Bahnhoff* to catch a night train. At *Daemmerung* I broke into my wife's apartment, and there she was, sleeping alone, hugging a pillow. I was ashamed. But still I went to the library and read about genetics, and *sicher,* two blue-eyed parents can't make *braune* eyes. I took the case to the court. I won the case, and I lost. As soon as I signed the divorce, I was sorry that I hadn't been *stark* enough to keep my doubts to myself. I understood my lonely wife. People even adopt children. At least one spouse was the real parent—beats adoption by 50 percent. But as soon as I remembered my slave drivers at the factory—all the insults—my eyes turned green.

"I lost my job. I'd left on my jealousy trip without a notice to my boss. I began to drink, and it was a lucky thing that my earnings had been buried in the foundations and walls. Drink and emotion now blurred my mind.

"The aspirin factory took me back after I'd proved that I had gone through a divorce. Divorce is a respectable thing in the West. I wanted to get married again and fill up my house with little screamers. But at a physical examination it turned out my sperm count was too low. So I had relationships. When I had no relationship, I visited whores. Financially, it was all the same. Whenever I came, I imagined how many bricks I spurted.

"When you aren't at the *Baustelle,* the construction workers rip you off. They say, "Why work for a *Yugo-Schwabba*—he's got lots, it won't hurt him if we take a sack of cement and a couple of wood planks. The house slowly got raised to the third floor, a roof was angled over it. But, I still needed *viele Fenster,* plumbing, heating, wiring, marble steps, tiles, mortar, stuccoing, *Farbe* . . . I couldn't see the light.

"One Christmas I came home. It was cold, windy, and I was forty, and I couldn't find a warm place for my bones. I had put some windows in one room, but they were gone. I stared at the walls, touched them, rough cold hollow bricks. Who am I working for? I ask myself. When I finish, I'll be fifty, done for. Eh, you ox, these walls will bury you. This isn't your home, this is your tomb.

"By the way, isn't it ironic that my last name is *Zidar (mason* in Croatian)? Maybe my name doomed me to get into the wrestling match with the rocks, walls.

"Back in Germany, the thought that the more I worked, the more I buried myself, pricked me like a swarm of wasps. My eyes were swollen. I could barely get up in the morning. I spat blood. Coffee was no help, bitter and upsetting. But I had to work. What else could I do? Be a bum nobody wants to talk to? But who wants to talk to me anyway—even if I lived there for a hundred years, no Germans would be my friends. You come out of the *U-Bahn* on the escalator, and stare at the black writing in dripping paint on the yellow walls way up there in the street, AUSLAENDER RAUS. Foreigners, get out.

"You can't fight against your hosts. They exploit you, but that's all right. I like exploitation—it means there's a salary, somebody thinks you are useful. To Germans lately you seem to be something smuggled in, a tool that's outgrown its use. Everywhere you have to watch your step, and work according to Saint

Mark's Gospel. In the Bible they don't give you Mark's last name, and there they do. *Deutsch. Saint Deutschmark.*

"By the way, Doctor, do you know that joke about Germans and Yugoslavs?"

"Which one?"

"Just imagine how it would be if the Germans had won the Second World War. *Ja,* we would be forced to work in Germany, while they sunbathed at the Adriatic Coast.

"That's just what has happened. Anyway, I did finally decide to come back to Yugoslavia for good. The Yugoslavia I had left twenty years before doesn't exist anymore. Old hospitality, kindness, talkativeness, generosity, that's all gone. Around Zadar people hate me as a usurper, a *Yugo-Schwabbe,* a Serb, though I am not, so where do I belong? You don't notice these things if you stay for a weekend, but after staying for months, you suffer. I watch my big house and say, Eh, my grave, where is my name? How many years before you take me in? And the idea suddenly pops up, If my house is my gravestone, let me make a gravestone.

"I rushed to Germany and was rehired. My life got a new meaning, My Tomb. I would sell the house and build a Mausoleum. I was no longer in a hurry. I realized the Germans were *wirklich gemütlich* and kind. My German became smooth, my grammar good. Nobody insulted me—the wisdom of the grave shone out of me.

"Every morning I woke up before the sunrise and whistled with the blue sparrows at the open window. I was rejuvenated. Everything was now so good that I suspected I could still start from scratch. Even my sperm count might go up if I ate enough caviar. But I knew better. I loved the things around me only because I had hated them. I was free from them, I could leave any moment, I was leaving. Closing my *Augen,* I could see my destination, HEREIN LIES IN PEACE ZIVKO ZIDAR.

"I continued to *arbeit* for a couple of years. I got a promotion—became a supervisor. I sold my house and bought a *Platz* on the edge of the Slavonski Brod cemetery. My old man's house would be thirty meters away from the tomb, over the railroad tracks, Munich to Athens. I kneeled to kiss the soil and the ants that walked it. I dreamed the plans for my tomb, like that chemist had dreamed snakes swallowing each other's tails. I saw the tomb from above, below, inside, outside. The walls shifted in my mind, changed shapes, stretched out, rose, slid into the ground, they combined into pyramids, towers rising and sinking, and finally, the idea of sinking took over. I settled the tomb below the *Grund,* at least twenty meters deep, with a cap above. It would be energy efficient—in the summer, cool, in the winter, warm.

"I've made indentations in the tomb floor to fit positions of my body, like an embryo, like a dead man on the back, like an elbowing Roman eating grapes, reclining like a dental patient, kneeling with a support for my belly like a drowned swimmer. I have a library there—religion, history, philosophy—and a Grundig stereo system with thousands of religious music tapes. In my afterlife, I will have *genug Zeit* to think, and . . . "

I couldn't keep my attention on him throughout his recital. His plans reminded me of how as a boy I had visited my grandfather in his village one summer. Grandmother, Father, an uncle, and two aunts showed me Grandfather in an open casket in the dark, with candles at the four corners, white powder on Grandfather's gray face, and told me he had died of too much drink. Then they carried him out in the casket and put him in a hole underground, sang chants, wept, gave speeches. They had all worn black. Father axed the bottom of a varnished cross into a sharp spear, and stuck it into the mound on the grave, amid bunches of flowers. I didn't know that Grandfather had built a fall-out shelter with large cans of supplies. I'd wept for him for two days, and on the third, as I'd been twisting chicken necks backwards to see how death works, he staggered out of the tomb, his chin stubbly, and I believed he'd been raised from the dead. He then read to me about Biblical resurrections. For a whole year I was the greatest believer around, reading nothing but the Bible, praying for hours on end on my knees. But the following summer there had been no cross and my grandfather had left the shelter open. I'd walked in, seen the opened and rusted cans, and decided nobody would ever again make a fool out of me.

Now I laughed to myself at the memory.

"You may laugh," Zivko said, "but I'm on the right path."

"And on what grounds do you believe there's afterlife?" I asked.

"There is too much suffering here that there shouldn't be a better life afterwards."

"That's like saying that because my rotten tooth gives me too much pain, once it falls out, a better one will grow in its place, which will give me pleasure!"

"But we do go through two sets of teeth. Why not two lives?"

"The second set is more painful. By that analogy, if there is afterlife, there's only hell and no heaven."

"Oh, you simply don't remember the childhood pains. The first set probably hurt more."

"So, when you die, you think another you will grow, like the second tooth, but in whose mouth? In the mouth of God? And what will God bite with you as his tooth?"

Zivko laughed and two silver teeth, dead teeth, faced me like little tombstones. "We always hope and we are always disappointed—we think we hope for something that could be found here, but *wirklich* we hope for something deeper. We feel there's something better. Afterlife."

"You feel it. How can a feeling be that informative? Hot? Cold? Tingling? Tart? Feelings are sensations, not thoughts, not information about something far out, but about something right here, something that touches your taste buds, your skin, your retina, your eardrums. Feelings don't answer metaphysical questions."

He looked at me with pity as if I were sick and there was no cure for me. "You are a physician, of course you're gonna think physical. But, you see, the Bible too tells there's *Leben* after *Tod*."

"The Bible says all sorts of things. How about this, 'I said in mine heart concerning the estate of the sons of men, that God

might manifest them, and that they might see that they themselves are beasts. For that which befalleth the sons of men befalleth beasts; even one thing befalleth them: as the one dieth, so
dieth the other; yea, they have all one breath; so that a man hath
no preeminence above a beast: for all is vanity.' Ecclesiastes. See?"

It took him a while to digest that, along with another shot of
plum brandy, which rallied his spirits. "On the German TV I saw
Life after Life. People float when they . . . "

"Spare me that hallucinogenic bullshit. When you are falling
asleep, you hallucinate. Of course you are going to hallucinate
when you are dying—death is a tempestuous biochemical event.
Your center for balance is affected, your inner clock misfires . . . "

I was about to punch on, but he looked groggy, his head in his
palms, his creases rising even into the smooth bays aside his sil-
verized widow's peak. He looked like a poor Jack Nicholson,
without enough money to dye his hair, if such a picture could be
imagined. We kept silent for several long minutes, long as if the
conversation had died, and the death of it changed our time per-
ception. The minutes seemed like hours, and I was reminded how
a thousand years is like one day, and one day like a thousand years
to God.

He broke the silence. "Doctor, yes, you did hit a sore spot.
Yes, I don't know that there is life after death. Yes. That is why I
am here. I need a preparation. Give me a *Zertifikat* so I can go my
way, get myself and everybody else used to the idea of my death.
And I'll be waiting for the eternity."

"Why not among the people?"

"You die alone. Groups can't teach you anything about death.
If there's *Leben* in *Ewigkeit*, I don't want to meet it in a decrepit
body, locked in a coffin."

"You are naive. Bodies rot fast."

"Damn you, you aren't gonna spoil my plan." He stood up
and hovered above me, waving his big arms in rage. "I need my
space! Give me my papers!"

"It's not that simple. Anyway, what are you after—a life insurance scam?"

"Don't you tell me it's not simple. You know that our people die like mice, and nobody questions any deaths. One relative and one doctor, or just one doctor, is enough to certify."

"I am afraid you are right."

"How much?"

"It'll be on the house. Well, give me a dozen liters of that plum brandy."

"Don't be that cheap. I could sign you up for one-third of my life insurance policy."

"I knew it." I threw up my arms in despair. Once a Yugoslav, always a crook.

"I'll give you one-half, three hundred thousand *Deutschmarks* spread over fifteen years, if you promise that you'll ship me the newest findings in parapsychology, the newest medical findings on the soul, the newest religious thinking. I'll show you the slot."

"A doctor can't get his patient's life insurance. That's absurd. I'll be jailed."

"Doc, don't be naive. Who's gonna worry? The cops? They are too busy stealing. The Germans? They are too regular, it beats their imagination."

"And what about your father?"

"He'll testify that I am dead even if my chest moves like the chest of a dead actor in a movie. He wants to get there too. When I am abroad, he hangs around in my tomb and when I come home, he pretends to live in his little house, doing yard work, chopping the wood. In the tomb I find his white hairs caught in the radio antenna, the dial's shifted to the folk-song channel, the place reeks of tobacco and brandy, and his muddy footprints are on the Iraqi carpet. But once I get there, I'll lock up the tomb, I'll never get out, and he'll join me only when he's dead, in a separate little room. Doctor, there's space even for you there, one stylish room, medium size, with a sauna. I kind of like you. What do you say?"

It was late, and the old clock in my corridor banged eleven, a brassy, yellow sound. We agreed upon the time and place.

As planned, I scribbled out a certificate once I got to his father's home a week later. His father ran out screaming for the priest in his broken voice while I injected a sleeping drug into Zivko's buttocks. The priest walked around the body, swinging his cup of incense, sang off-key, crossed himself, and spat his phlegm into the pail of ashes next to the stove—all routine. The old man and I placed Zivko in the coffin we had bought at the neighborhood undertaker's, and the mortician showed up only to nail the lid. He was so drunk that he missed the nails several times, and crushed his thumbnail, screaming like a whipped child. So I myself nailed Zivko in. Of course, I hadn't forgot to enclose in the coffin a hammer, chisel, pliers—small tools a mason would need.

The procession was medium: a local brass band, senior citizens, a priest, nuns, school comrades. Four men lowered the coffin into the tomb on two rasping ropes, and let the heavy stone fall over the entrance with a bang that resounded and echoed deep in the ground for a long time, shaking us all above.

Now and then on my evening walks with my mongrel dog, I stop by the heavy tomb and light a candle. The tomb looks like an abstract partisan monument, the type that was in fashion twenty years ago, with black marble wings, pentagonal, smooth, reflecting moonlight. ZIVKO ZIDAR is grooved, with 16.x.1948 for his birthday, and 23.x.1990 for his death-day. His color picture, inlaid in stone, egg-shaped, gold-rimmed, gives me his startled stare from above his thin mustache and lips pursed in ambitious self-denial. My dog growls at the picture, tears away the leash from my hands, and runs home. The insides of the letters away from the main inscription gleam out quotations of wisdom in Latin, Cyrillic, Greek, Hebrew, and German Gothic—one script per side of the pentagon. Two pots sit below his name like trophies, and sometimes I place white tulips there, but most often a slice of roast mutton with crackling skin, something for the owls.

I walk back on the path through the freezing mud, scrape my

muddy soles over the gravel and the stainless steel of the rails, and I go on to his father's moss-covered mud house. Late in the evening the lights are out. I sneak into the backyard, and a dog yawns and comes out of a bread-baking brick oven, and he doesn't bark. He smells my shoes and yawns even wider in loneliness. I tug at his hanging ears, promising I'll bring along my mutt next time. I open a lid inside the brick oven and insert the *New England Journal of Medicine, Deutsche Wissenchaft,* and the *Ecumenical ESP Quarterly,* and listen to the way the journals slide.

Above an empty chicken coop, with years-old frozen chicken shit trapping pigeon feathers on the splintery wood, I check the electric meter. Two wires branch off from the house toward the Mausoleum, sinking. The meter disk rotates swiftly with a little hiss. The red stretch comes back every second, and I know that the student of death still clings to life, trying to cheat death on the border of the cemetery, beneath the tombstone.

A Drop of Cognac

A decade ago, visiting my widowed cousin-in-law Ishtvan in Nizograd, Croatia, I was determined not to drink much, only perhaps two drinks, the optimum amount for the heart and mood. We placed on the table a bottle of cognac and a pack of cigarettes. We used to be Baptists, and this way of conversing, doing what we had been taught was wrong, gave an edge to our conversation perhaps unfamiliar to those who were not brought up in repressive churches.

"Just look around," said Ishtvan. "See how large and comfortable my house is? Did I build it? No, I only put the finishing touches to it. My father laid the foundations, raised it, put a roof over it; he built it by his own strength. We forget how much our fathers accomplished. We are proud, we have better opportunities, we are better educated; but look, what have we done?"

I replied nothing, quietly resenting that he should place me in his category, though I was more than a decade younger than he. So, he expects I will accomplish nothing, I thought, and feared he might be right.

"Each of us carries his father in him," Ishtvan went on. "Mine I feel right here more and more," he pointed to his chest. "Now I am as old as he was when I was two years old. I am very similar to him; I feel that he is in my blood, in my motion; wherever I move, there is my father moving. When I have an intuition, it's my father speaking; sometimes it's unsettling. I am never free."

"How about your mother?"

"Well, her too. Even my grandmother. I am a walking cemetery of my family! Hahahaha!" He took another sip of cognac; the label read, *aut Caesar, aut nihil.* We knocked our pitifully small glasses, so small that you could rationalize to yourself that it was no more than a couple of drops you were drinking. Some of the brandy flew up and sprinkled us, like sacramental water.

"To your health!" we both said.

"I'll never forget the things my father taught me," he said, "things I have to remember over and over again. You see, some people are too proud, think too much of themselves. For example, your older brother. Granted, he is a doctor, but that does not mean that he could not return visits and phone calls. I have called him so many times, and guess how many times he has called me?"

I didn't like being put on the spot, as if I should be responsible for my brother. The number must be beyond, or rather below, any expectation; he would gladly see me incredulous. If I said "zero," I would take away some of his rhetorical pleasure. So, insincerely, I guessed, "Once a year."

"Well, my Yozzo! Not a sin-gle time! Anyway, let me tell you what my father taught me about pride. He took me into a wheat field, and said, 'Now, son, choose the stalk of wheat with the most grains on it!' I looked around and plucked the tallest I could see. My father smiled, said, 'Look, son,' and separated a multitude of tall stalks and among them found one, low, bent, and plucked that one. 'Let us count the grains!' His stalk carried at least twice as many grains as mine. 'See,' he said, 'the ones you cannot see because of the tall ones are the most laden ones. They are the best. Remember that! If you look for the best, don't look among those in the first rows, the proud ones.'

"I recalled his telling me the wheat parable only a week ago.

Oh, I don't mean to say anything against your brother, I don't know why I brought him up, I must be getting drunk. Well, to your health!

"Our fathers outstripped us in everything, and we think that we are more unique. They thought more deeply than we do, and what I think now, he had already thought out for me.

"Yes, I am a walking cemetery of my family and you know, I feel your cousin, Tanya, too, in my blood. Oh how she suffered! You know lupus eretrocitis?"

"Yes, I guess so, the degenerative disease of the red blood cells."

"One organ after another is reduced to its minimal functioning, decomposes, and there is hardly anything of you left; you wonder how you can still be alive, a tingling body of pain. Tanya held through it all heroically.

"And you know what the 'Reverend' Iliya Lukich told me?" Ishtvan went to the cupboard, brought out two regular milk glasses, poured some cognac into them, and sucked out nearly the whole contents of his glass in a big gulp. "He used to tell me, you know, before she was taken ill, that I should mend my ways, return to the fold, repent, lest I should be visited upon with the iniquity of my deeds—that's how he used to express himself. He claimed he had visions about me; God told him a disaster would befall me, unless . . . You know how he was, always some visions and bullying."

"Yes, I know, once I broke my left arm, and in the youth group he said that God was warning the whole group against the sin of self-gratification! I told him that I was right-handed, so the warning was misplaced."

"Well, when he learned about Tanya's illness, he came to me fuming with triumph, and said, 'See, what did I tell you! It has come true. You haven't repented, and God is punishing you through her! She will die, and you will have to live with it! She will die because of YOU!'

"You know, her disease horrified me. The house looked doomed. When things are so bleak, you are liable to believe almost anything. Your mind cannot work then. It had better not work! How else can you face reality? I tried to repudiate what Iliya said—oh, he's just a joker, things just happen, that's all there is to it. But in vain did I try. Each day as she withered away, and you know that she had been beautiful, my heart shrank. The more she withered, the more wretched I was. I drank savagely then, and fought in the bars, just to relieve myself. Oh, not to relieve myself, quite the contrary, to degrade myself, it's true, I am the sinner, it's all because of me!

"It was worse when I was sober. I could not harm myself. I was winning all my fights, against all odds, and people were scared of me."

"Yes, I heard that you beat three policemen, piled them on top of each other outside the Happy Cellar. Did you really do it!"

"Oh, yes!" His voice, low and slow and falling apart under the burden of memories, now became resonant. I used to box seriously. For a year I was a pro in Argentina. I had the skill and the strength. And since then you should see how they respect me, the cops!"

He grew silent and it was already becoming dark outside. As we did not turn on the lights, I could no longer see his features, and his face was merely a heavy silhouette. The sky was dark blue, and it was bound to grow darker.

"You know, one of the worst things about growing older is that your strength leaves you. As your powers diminish, so does your self-reliance. I used to think when I was your age that I could do anything. Now I doubt everything."

His voice became low and slow. "What anguish that was when she was dying! She was in this room. I took out the bed after her death and burned it. I wonder why I continue to live in this house. I guess I like the memory of her. And where could I go anyway?"

I could not reply to that.

"Every day when I came home from work I saw her here, right where you are sitting, or in the white hospital. Her hair fell out, her eyebrows did too, she was pale yellow. Her eyes were red, without luster, her face contorted, there was something saintly in her face; sometimes a glow would return and she would whisper to me how happy she was that she would see God, how she loved me, how to have courage. I am happy she had so much faith! I had none.

"Then she would have another relapse, her eyes would be swollen, and her face shriveled up, her body too, she could not even whisper. I watched her for hours and shivered with horror and disgust. Yet I could not move my eyes away from her. I longed for the dark to come, just as it is coming now, and when it did, I wished to turn on the lights. But then I was afraid of what I would see of her. How much dread I experienced! I never thought it possible. And that is all because of your sins! I continued repeating to myself. All because of your blasphemies, debauchery. I am a murderer."

"But," I said and my voice was feeble because of not having said anything for a while—I cleared my throat—"Why should she suffer for what you did? You know, if I killed somebody, my brothers would not have to answer for that in the court, just me alone. Don't you think God's justice would be the same, provided He existed? If you sinned, you'd suffer for it, not she."

Here he took a deep smoke, and so did I. In the dark I saw only the small red circle of his cigarette as he inhaled, and then it receded into a dull ash-filtered glow.

"Well, we rarely suffer for what we have done, it is usually for what others have done, and they rarely suffer for what they have done, but for what we have done! That's the whole idea of Christianity! You don't get punished for your own sin, somebody else does. She was a Christ for me . . . but there is no salvation here.

"When Iliya told me she suffered because of me, I believed it. You have no idea what savagery conscience is capable of! If I could be in hell then, I thought, it would console me! The squirming of my flesh in the fire would set things right; being tortured to the utmost and still kept alive so I could be tortured more, forever and ever, I would be relieved! What a wonderful place hell must be. But the most painful thing about hell is that it does not exist! That's what tortured me—that I could not be tortured, that I walked about brimming with health and strength, smelling the southern flowery winds in the spring, and listening to swallows return from the Mediterranean!

"I still cannot understand where the illness came from. It's a rare disease."

"Maybe a genetic accident," I said. "An inner Chernobyl."

"Accident?" he looked at me quizzically and ironically.

"Anyway," he went on, "You know how Iliya went around, preaching against sins, laying his hands on the sick, bragging how God cured the people through him. And lo and behold, you know what happened?"

"His wife got sick."

"Yes, almost as soon as Tanya had died, Iliya's wife, Vera, contracted the same disease, lupus! And with her the progress of the disease was in the beginning as rapid as with Tanya, but before she would die, she hovered in that agony for four years! Iliya prayed over her, he constantly laid his hands on her, he had visions of her being healed, he prayed his prayers in all the churches around, but nothing. She died a month ago. She died a much longer and worse death than Tanya.

"Half a year ago I went to him, to return his visit, and said to him, 'You boastful saint, remember what you told me when Tanya was ill, that she was dying because of my sins? And now, what do you say now, for whose sins is your wife dying?'"

There was a glee of victory gleaming out of my ex-cousin-in-law. "Ha, what do you say? Almost enough to return to the faith of our fathers!"

He turned on the light. Blinking, I tried to pour a shot of cognac, but only one amber drop slid out.

Darkened Vision

Pavle, attracted to women who wore glasses, married Zora when she still could see. Through her glasses, her irises looked magnified, removed, and, even when dry, brilliantly tearful. Not that the glasses had been the key factor in his attraction to her, but they had enhanced her; she had looked dreamy and sensuous. Her dim vision had perhaps enhanced him as well; who knows whether she would have married him if she could have seen him in focus. Looking through her blue irises to the crystals of green and black, he dreamed. Her look grew dreamier and dreamier and steadier and steadier until it became clear that she was blind. He bought her a pair of black glasses as if preparing her for the eclipse of the sun.

Wherever he went, the black glasses hovered in his mind, and the eyes behind the glasses loomed accusingly as if he had blinded her. It is not always true that the blind feel the seeing more than the seeing feel the blind, at least it wasn't in his case. He developed a sixth sense for her. Cutting wood miles away from her, he saw her sitting on the wooden steps in the sun, moving her ears and expanding her nostrils.

She sat on her steps, her ears moving like a hawk's wings in landing. She could hear Pavle's vehicle on its way home from a mile away, he was sure.

At home, she monitored his every motion, suspecting he would leave. When he opened the door, she asked, "And where now so late at night?" Most often she said nothing, and he felt the question all the more, "And where now so late at night?"

Late at night, out of their house came snoring sounding like a saw cutting a knotty log of oak. Pavle was hiding in his snore from his wife's flesh. As he slept he felt her ears moving unhappily, and he would wake up and toss and turn in bed until he fell asleep again or lust took possession of him. He touched her and she embraced him like an octopus. To him it seemed she felt more than he ever could. A smile of knowledge floated around her lips, forming two spiraled dimples. He shook, as if to shrug off his skin like a snake in the spring. Her limbs turned into electric eels. He shivered like a prey whose strength was being conducted away. His revulsion ignited his marrow and returned to him his strength doubly. In heavy weightlessness, as if in water, they twisted around each other. Sensing the commotion of slimy marine wonders in the ocean underneath, he tried to swim to the surface, away from the maelstrom swallowing him into the underworld.

The carnal storms between them were rare. The oceanic horror stayed with him, concentrated in the image of the iris-less whites bulging beneath her black glasses. The mutilating empty eyes watched him as his helper, a crimson peasant, lifted logs onto the platform of Pavle's vehicle, and as Pavle pushed the logs onto a vertical motor-propelled disk saw.

Pavle worked accurately and rhythmically as though regretting that not more skill was involved so that he could be proud of his handiwork. There was something encouragingly simple in the repetition of motions in work—the sensation of becoming mechanized and infallible. There was also something discouragingly simple, which bored him and prevented him from becoming a machine. As he pushed a log, the high-pitched sound of the disk saw grew lower and lower until it reached the midpoint of the wood—it was not clear which moaned more, the steel or the wood—and then higher and higher, to buzz freely when the wood slid off. His helper poured water over the saw, as if baptizing the steel, lest it overheat. During breaks, Pavle and his helper poured slivovitz over their throats, lest they overheat. As the helper tossed a mouthful of brandy from one cheek to another, his face grew redder, his irises bluer, and his eyeballs whiter. He swore against the government. The government had collectivized his land, reducing him to bare hands no one but Pavle would hire. Old people sat in chairs and, under the pretext of entertainment, watched the work being done; now during the break they were ready to joke, but Pavle's mood quieted them. Pavle charged his services uniformly. Old and poor people he charged so little that he made no profit. He charged them like a judge, who, despite the evidence that you committed the crime, pronounced a mild sentence on the account of your extenuating passions.

Having finished the work in one yard, Pavle moved to another backyard, and yet another. He was in the paradoxical position of being thankful that there was more wood to be split asunder and of waiting to be finally over with it.

After work he drove home slowly. He did not brush sawdust off his clothes. It stuck to his sweaty forehead. As he passed the house of a brother of his, he did not turn his head. His nephews and nieces stopped playing and stared at him in awe, whispering. Pavle had left the church, and for him who renounced Christ, it would be seven times more difficult to be saved than it would be for a nonbeliever.

Pavle, aware of his wife waiting for him, feared her bleak loneliness. Hearing the engine, she went into the kitchen and put several dry pieces of wood into the stove to warm the meal she had prepared by touch and smell.

Zora did have a social life—she chatted with her neighbors. Her sister-in-law walked her to and from the church, talking to her.

After sermons Zora held her chin up as if surveying a vast

space. She puzzled over the voices, discerning vague family re-semblances. She nodded her head and leaned it against her right palm. The sounds gave her clues of the past when she had dreamed of the future. Now she dreamed of the present, through the past, recognizing the voices she had known twenty years before, and construing a picture the way someone gone to Aus-tralia daydreams about the people in the Old Country, across two oceans in either direction. Foreign friendliness murmured around her, clothes rustled, bones crackled in handshakes, lips smacked cheeks. *God-bless-you*'s reached her ear, startling her whenever she realized they were for her.

Palms touched her right hand; the fingers embraced it like many small arms, gently. She shivered from the touch and loved the hands that reached out to her, out of the ghost world now made corporal. Sometimes she knew the hands and not the voice, and sometimes she knew the voice, but not the hands, and some-times she knew the hands and the voice, but not the lips that moistened her dry cheek. When the lips and fingers parted from her, she stood in the pew, like a stone that the river passes.

Soon no one would address her anymore—the voices mur-mured dissolving into the slow muddy-brown river. She had tried to imagine how the people looked, what colors they wore, and in her mind flowed only the old brown watercolors.

She created a world from a few sensory clues. The clues were torn, unnumbered pages of one ceaseless novel about a country that had exiled her without explanation. The wind tossed the pages away, so that she worried whether she could recapture the plot.

Every day after dinner, Pavle walked—slowly, moderately, as though he deemed reaching his destination not much preferable to being at any particular point in the walk. He was neither fat nor slim, and dressed neither poorly nor richly. This moderation gave him a gentlemanly air. If he had not had much success, well, he could repair that—each step well done and each precise unstrained gesture of his hands created an aura of dignity, not of enthusiasm or tragedy such as illusions spur. He seemingly walked neither in the path of Hedonism nor of Stoicism, but between pleasure and pain, unperturbed. His light brown hair, combed back, receded in the front, but he made no attempt to hide the recession.

In Pavle's nostalgic manner you could suspect that he savored forbearance, the way he drank wine that was neither too sweet nor too sour, yet sour enough to excite his Adam's apple to leap.

No matter how drunk he was, he did not swerve from his straight path. And the black glasses haunted him and asked, "And where now so late at night?" even before sunset.

One Sunday evening Pavle took a walk under orange clouds. His countenance bore a self-absorbed expression, though his self absorbed him least of all.

He walked somewhat impatiently, as if wishing that the street blocks were shorter, over the bridge into the park's alleys of clipped tree crowns and fountain snakes squirting water through their eyes. He breathed in the cool air and smelled moist amber leaves. When he came out into the clearing for the rails, coal steam and smoke hovered and the rails clanked, though the train was out of sight.

He entered a beech grove, dark though the tips of the trees glowed with the sun. He drank cold water from a spring and let it flow over his arms to cool his blood. He climbed a steep hill into the oak grove to a Jewish cemetery overgrown with bushes. Pavle took a brief rest, leaning against a tilting tombstone. The cool air moved noiselessly, making the flushed treetops quiver before they sank into darkness. When he reached the top of the hill, the sunshine had left even the high evergreens and withdrawn into the clouds. He walked onto a gravel path, where a dog began his fervent cold war against him, from behind a wooden fence. The narrow space below the planks could accommodate only a closed muzzle. The dog had a dilemma: to bark without showing his teeth or to show his teeth and be quiet. He alternated, and occasionally found a hole through which to do both.

A car passed by and raised a cloud of brown dust. Pavle held his breath till the dust settled. The veins on his forehead protruded crookedly.

An insomniac rooster shrieked somewhere in the neighborhood, and his shrieks echoed from the vineyard hills on both sides of the road that split into a broad one flanked with houses and a narrow one entangled in vines. At the forking stood a cross with a porcelain Jesus. The thorns of his crown were so large that he looked like a contrite defrocked Statue of Liberty.

Pavle came to the small whitewashed house where his mistress Katitza lived. The door opened as if by itself, and no one came out. Soon after his entering, a lantern was lit. The town was suffering one of its usual blackouts, sinking into the previous century from which it had never quite emerged. Around the orange flicker of the lantern golden rays formed a halo.

Guitar sounds pulsed from the house, dispersed by the winds over the dark vineyards. Pavle's voice, deep and unsonorous, carried melancholy melodies from Croatian Zagorye, "Wine, wine . . . you are my porcupine; Rhein, Rhein, why can't you decline," and so on in that vein and in other veins to be filled with wine.

The following morning, instead of Pavle walking to the park in his leisurely Sunday manner, a voice went from mouth to mouth, through the ears of many. It traveled somehow as slowly as he had walked. Pavle had died making love to Katitza.

Dying in his orgasm—while Katitza had passed out from alcohol—he clasped her tightly in his embrace. By the time she woke up, he was dead, and cold, and well advanced in his rigor mortis. She could not get out of his grip. She screamed. At dawn late drunks swerved by the house on the way home and listening to her got erections and admired her orgasmic passion and envied Pavle's skill and prowess.

At sunrise, when the screaming had not ceased, people who had gone to bed early, happy, sober, and wise noticed there was something unearthly and unsettling in the shrieks. When they broke through the door, they saw a green woman with bulging eyes clasped by a yellow corpse. The icy corpse and its feverish prisoner were taken, naked, to the People's Hospital. Only when the doctors had cut his tendons could his embrace be unclasped.

When two male nurses brought Pavle on a stretcher into his home, they found Zora seated at the table, tirelessly waiting. She walked to the corpse and finger-tipped it. His hands were wrapped in thick layers of cloth, like boxing gloves.

For all Zora knew, the night had killed Pavle. While her neighbors went out to buy a casket, she washed and oiled his body. Her neighbors helped her bend his arms backward, enough to slide him into his shirt, and then the arms sprang back and the hands met in unison as if for prayer. In the varnished fir casket, supine, he looked like a dead dignitary of the church contemplating the vastness of God's grace.

She placed four candles around him, one toward each corner of our square earth. It was so blazingly hot outside that the heat seeped in through the bricks. Zora's calico tomcat sniffed the corpse, crying like a sick baby. Waving his tail about, he knocked down a candle. The tablecloth caught fire and the flames licked the casket greedily and obscenely. Zora grabbed a pail of water from the chair and watered the fire. The flames went out and the wood resin hissed in steam. Zora blew out the remaining candles. The heat continued to radiate through the walls, entering the corpse, which swelled like a leavened loaf and pressed against the squeaking wood.

The mortician couldn't close the casket. To his suggestion that he pierce a hole in the corpse so the air and water could leak out, Zora declined, and the mortician then nailed laths of wood he found in Pavle's workshop atop the casket to increase its depth. He hammered on the lid; some nails peered through the wood outward, others inward, and only a few sank straight into the wood.

At the funeral, when the brass band took a break, half a dozen paces away from the hearse one could hear the crackling of casket wood. The corpse continued to bloat. A putrid smell spread through the cracks and permeated the steamy heat. Frightened by the stench and the creaking, the horses foamed at the mouth. The coachman barely restrained them from taking off in a gallop like dogs with tin cans tied to their tails.

In front of the hearse walked only women; behind, the relatives, and after them only men. Zora walked with her son and daughter holding her by her white-gloved arms; beneath her dark glasses flowed tears past her red nose.

At the grave pit Pavle's relatives, dressed in black and white, solemnly stared at the casket, from which came crackles and farts.

When the casket began to sink into the ground, Zora's lips muttered so fervently that it seemed they twitched; she prayed. The ropes rasped the wood and the casket dropped into the ground with a thud. Her son and daughter nudged her to drop the first fistful of soil into the pit, but she pushed them away and shrieked a high-pitched shriek, like a doe being slaughtered by wolves. The crowd gasped and blood scurried away from their faces. As if she had heard the goose-bumped crowd's blood rushing in sympathetic terror, she shouted shrilly to them: "Up till now I prayed to God to bring him back to life. I believed He would. He won't! He won't! I can't believe any longer!"

For days and months after the funeral Zora grieved with complete dedication as only a blind person could. She walked to his grave each day and put down tulips and carnations. The gravel in front of the grave cut into her knees. She caressed his silvery name on the varnished cross, dug with her fingers into the soil, and moved her ears as if she could hear his vehicle from blocks away, within the hollow ground. On rainy days she came to the grave just the same and listened to the frogs leap.

In the streets, Pavle's assistant limped, leaning on his bumpy cane. He stooped now more than when he had last worked with Pavle; his eyes were bluer, his face redder. When Zora walked past him, she swished her rod like a machete. The old peasant stood against the wall of his mildewed home, and the mortar sand behind his gaping boots trickled as though in an egg timer. Her broad nostrils sniffed the peasant's alcoholic aura. Saying nothing, she walked past him, but on one occasion, she said, "Why are you so quiet? Are you afraid of me?"

He invited her for tea laced with plum brandy and they talked about Pavle. He kept enumerating the good Pavle had done, how he had cut wood for free for various widows.

"That was not necessarily good," she said.

Whenever she walked by his house, he invited her in for tea. When he visited her, she baked loaves of bread for him. His rejuvenated look gave rise to the rumor that he had become Zora's lover.

She continued going to the church, where she waited for the sermon on Lazarus. She whispered prayers for Pavle. Nobody dared to tell her that Pavle perhaps didn't deserve so many prayers and so much grief.

One Christmas Eve, she remained in the pews after the service. With her cane she walked to the Christmas tree, sniffed its green needles, and touched its iron base where the mutilated trunk rested on the wooden floor. The veins of her fingers felt the missing roots and stuck to the resin that oozed as a heavy and frozen mixture of blood and sweat. She lit a match and dropped it. A flame burst out. The tree crackled and roared, its lingual shapes multiplied in size. She took off her glasses and smiled. The flames climbed the curtains, rushed down the carpeted aisle and entered the beams.

The church was a huge flame by dawn, a tongue of the earth licking the heavens. The flame spread to the neighboring bus garage, and the oily iron and tires joined the flame.

In the rubble of the collapsed church her skeleton coiled in the corner; she had died like blinded Samson among the Philistines, who had brought down the pillars with thousands of the enemy. After her death the old peasant continued to limp in front of his house, his hair completely white, his blue irises ringed with the haze of cataracts. Leaning against his bumpy stick now and then he lifted the brown hat off his head even when no one was passing by.

Dresden

Upon hearing on the phone that his mother suffered from the last stages of malignant lung cancer, Klaus walked out onto his small balcony, leaned on the parapet in the narrow space between precarious aspidistras, and lit a cigarette as though his lungs should hurt in sympathy with his mother's. When he turned around to walk back, he saw his neighbor, Ulrike, sunbathing blissfully naked. He thought he should not look at her, but then, she enjoyed being free, and so why shouldn't he enjoy being free and looking at her? But how can I think like that now? he wondered.

Back in his apartment, Klaus thought about his mother plucking feathers off steaming doves before making a stew of them, her tall forehead frowning, eyebrows arched like a crow's wings. After the war, in the famine in Dresden, Klaus's maimed father, a Lutheran minister, had crouched in his damaged church steeple and caught pigeons with his bare hands. The servant of God had strangled doves to feed his family. Absently, Klaus stared at his wife Renate, who was reading a blue tour guide on Greece and saying, "Let's go to the islands this summer!"

"The Yugoslav Adriatic is all we could afford, at best," Klaus said.

"But there's not much history there!"

"Daddy, why can't you see stars during the day?" shouted their five-year-old son, Albert.

"Who needs history?" he said absentmindedly. He thought about how he could not talk to her about his parents, especially about his father, and he wondered how many Russians his father had killed and whether he had burned Byelorussians trapped in wooden village churches. Had he had a chance to desert?

"You are a lot of fun today, aren't you?" Renate said, putting a pair of shoes on Albert, who still complained about the stars.

"I'll go and pay our electric bill," Renate said. "By the way, have you made up your mind whether you'd like to accompany me to Vienna?" She would lead her *Gymnasium* on an educational tour. When he said nothing in reply, she left.

He lit a cigarette and walked over to the terrace. Ulrike was gone, and a white pigeon—perhaps a real dove—sat on her parapet, shaking its tail, drizzling white crap on the wall. "*Na ja*," Klaus muttered and wondered whether to rush and see his mother: but death made him feel inadequate and theatrical, self-conscious, as though he should walk on a stage and face the severest jury in the world, God, Devil, and demons. So he did not go.

A week later, in the house of his parents, Klaus poured scalding water over a fresh bag of Earl Grey tea and added milk. He had liked tea the English way ever since he had begun to study English literature. He kept the cup in his hands to warm them. His frugal father, the Reverend Rudolf Traurig, refused to turn on the heat despite the cold rainy morning. He sat on the opposite side of the table, like a chess player, and coldly stared at Klaus's tremulous hands. Klaus put down the gilt porcelain cup and withdrew his hands to his knees beneath the table. The Reverend lit an aromatic pipe, and it was not clear whether he was sighing or drawing in the smoke. The father and the son seemed to have nothing to say although they had not seen each other in two years; being able to keep aloof and dignified intrigued them almost as much as did the death of the mother and wife, who lay in the next room in an unclosed coffin.

"Johannes should be here shortly." The Reverend finally broke the ticking silence.

"I know." Klaus thought about how his father had always preferred Johannes, his younger brother, who had learned the multiplication tables by listening to Klaus trying to memorize aloud. Once, when their father had asked Klaus, "What's nine times eight?" and Klaus could not answer, a thin voice from beneath the table said, "Seventy-two!" The father had picked up Johannes and tossed him on his healthy knee, repeating, "Now *that's* a smart son!" It struck Klaus as silly that he should remember that, as though that mattered. Well, maybe it did matter, he thought. If they had not put me down, maybe I would have had more self-confidence, and I'd be a doctor rather than a literature student—soon, a doctor of literature! Is literature sick that it too needs doctors?

The heavily varnished grandfather clock in the dark recesses of the room, beyond a fake Persian carpet, struck eleven, echoing heavily like a steeple clock. Klaus stood up and paced. His father sitting—his stick leaning against the table with a black hat over it, his artificial leg stretched out, the other spread wide, and his elbow sticking up as the hand clasped the knee in an imperial posture as though he were Bismarck or something—irritated him. This man, Klaus thought—staring down at the bald circle on his father's head, the pink skin with a gentle fuzz as though new hair was about to grow—promised to teach me how to fish in the Elbe. At dawn he took me to the grassy bank of the river on his shaky bicycle, and the river was so blue from chemicals that hundreds of dead-fish silver bellies glittered in the stingy rising sun. He wanted to teach me how to swim, but I didn't want to go into the dirty water. This is the man who took me for a long hike in the Thuringian Forest, limping, gasping, and telling me he could hike all the way to Austria. Mists drifted above the meadows and below treetops like ghosts. Gazing at treetops, I thought I saw angels in dark skirts walking in the clouds. When the sun came out, we sat on a smelly fir log smoking from the sun. He rubbed my wet feet, crumpled and purple, with his cracked dry hands. We hiked down a mossy slope, thick moss and pine needles absorbing our steps so that deer continued to graze peacefully. He taught me how to find mushrooms among layers of rotting foliage, and how to scratch a mushroom skin, to see whether lively colors appeared to show poison. After all, my father tried, didn't he? Klaus almost felt sympathy for him.

The memories came from East Germany, from before the Iron Curtain went up and before the family fled to the West with a couple of heavy paper suitcases, painted brown so that they would look like leather, in an old Volkswagen, to Frankfurt, West Germany.

Johannes now walked in wearing a black suit, smelling of cologne. He took off his scarf and quietly opened the door of the living room to be with his dead mother for a while and soon came out to join in the silence. Although Johannes had no university education, he did much better than Klaus. Because of his gift of gab, he was a star salesman of Grundig sound systems, and lately he had been working as a marketing manager. He had made so much money that he had bought a duplex near the heart of Frankfurt.

It was the time for the funeral. Klaus walked into the living room, reluctantly, and faced his mother's high forehead—it was yellow as though she were a wax figure. He kissed the forehead, fought the tears, and wondered why he'd managed to conquer them: not a tear fell from his eyes. In a way it was a defeat because he should cry out loud to let all this tension go, but he knew it wouldn't work, the tears would be an illusion. Johannes and the mortician closed the casket—the smell of chemicals and putridness spread out, hitting Klaus's nostrils (despite his smoking habit, he was struck by the violence of the smell)—and pulled down the clasps. The funeral, the sermon on the side of the grave, the small gathering—all refracted brilliantly through Klaus's wet eyes, as though the world had melted into leaden lava flowing down from a mountain: whatever you were doing when the lava caught you, you would do for the rest of time, as a sculpture. He would always be standing at the graveyard. He shivered, attempting to shake off the pathetic image.

After the funeral the father and the two sons sat at a round table, like card players, and drank *Weinbrandt*. The father, who had looked terribly ashen during the funeral, now joked and laughed and remembered. "Would you believe me, the time I felt best in my entire life was the siege of Stalingrad—strong, scared, and brave. And I never told you, did I, that I was not just a plain soldier, but an officer!"

"*Kwatsch*!" said Klaus.

"I was a young minister, at the peak of my powers, happy that I was not behind the pulpit, moralizing about the war. I was part of the war!"

"How could you feel like that after a forced conscription?"

"Let me be honest with you. I was first in the volunteer line in Dresden when the war with the Soviet Union started! I was there at three in the morning! I thought it was my duty to stop Communism—the sinister atheist force that would make heathens of us all."

"But didn't you know that Nazis wanted to push out Christianity for some original natural, Germanic religion, if they could find one?"

"Scholars will always distort things."

Klaus gulped *Weinbrandt,* which burned his throat. He had thought his father had been a victim of circumstances, but he was actually the circumstance that victimized people. It now occurred to Klaus that his mother must have gotten cancer from living with this hard man, who went to war to kill for principles. He remembered one night when his father had shrieked because his mother had put a cup of coffee on the Bible, leaving a brown circle on the white cover. He had struck her on the mouth, and her nose had bled, but she had kept calm. She had not run out, nor had she

wept, and his father's wrath had worsened; he had shaken un-
controllably, as though with epilepsy. In the corner Johannes and
Klaus had trembled and hugged each other. Klaus had wished to
be a little bigger, to grab an ax and split his father's skull. Now he
had the same desire, looking at his father's bald spot. Klaus smoked
a cigarette, inhaling deep until it hurt him. He had no ax, but he
had words. He spoke deliberately: "Herr Rudolf Traurig, now
that I know that you *enjoyed* being a Nazi officer, I will never
speak a word to you again as long as we live!"

"What's come over you!" Johannes said. "How can you say
such a thing? He could not have thought differently at the time!"

"What, you too?" The old minister trembled and grabbed his
stick, either to support himself or to attack Klaus, who stood calm,
with the certitude of hatred, his arms crossed, one hand up, another down, like a collapsible swastika. The old man tossed the
stick in the middle of the room, on the fake Persian carpet, and
one end of the stick leaped, as though a Magus had commanded
it to become a snake. Klaus stood like a pharaoh, unimpressed, for
his father was no Aaron, his father had no people to lead out of
Egypt, he had only stranded his people in Egypt.

Klaus had already begun to put his vow of silence into practice; he looked for a cigarette, searching his pockets. He walked
out to buy a pack.

Johannes ran after him. "You can't do that to him! He has a
bad heart, you'll put him in his grave."

"That's where he belongs, I am sorry to say. I did not choose
him as my father. I don't have to accept the biological accident."

"It's no accident, it's destiny."

At the corner kiosk, there were no cigarettes. Klaus kicked a
clean yellow garbage box. He remembered how an American
friend of his had confused a German garbage box for a mailbox;
she had mailed many postcards and found out later that nobody
had received them.

On the way home, he drove by his department to pick up the
registration forms for the next semester. On the wall in the cor-

ridor he saw an ad for Ph.D. studies in the United States, at the University of Pennsylvania.

When the sun came out the next day, he walked out on the terrace—Renate and Alfred weren't back from Vienna yet—and a southern wind stroked his nostrils through his mustache and tickled his neck through his Marxian beard. And there she was— Ulrike; her fair body seemed to blush, like a maiden caught doing something unfair. Since I am married, I should not look at her, on principle. Principle! What's a prince doing in the word? Maybe principles have to do with being obedient to a prince, and what is a prince but a despot; *despotos* in Greek does mean *prince*. Why should I volunteer to be subjected to despotism? He laughed, satisfied with his impromptu etymology, which he suspected was false, but so what? He lit a cigarette, and gently blew smoke out of his mouth.

"Don't you need some sunscreen?" He asked.

"Not a bad idea." Ulrike did not cover her breasts.

"I have some, do you want to borrow it?"

"Sure thing."

"Should I toss it to you?"

"I am bad at catching. Why don't you bring it over?

And he did. She turned her back to him and asked him to put some lotion on the hard-to-reach spot. He continued rubbing her shoulders and the round sides of her body; he crouched, nearly sitting on her buttocks, straining his legs so that he would not press her too hard. She turned around and her breasts spread opulently. As he creamed her belly, pressing toward her navel, her breasts swayed and nipples rose. Out of breath, he buried his face in her bosom, while she played with his hair, gently, with her nails; shivers ran down the side of his neck into his tight shoulders.

"You have a baby-bald spot here, did you know that?" she said.

They had sex indoors, while a parakeet frolicked flying in and out of its open cage, screaming as though in celebration of a tropical holiday. In the mirror, Klaus saw himself straining, fresh, muscular, sharp. Seeing the couple in the mirror make love gave a voyeuristic enhancement to his lovemaking.

Before this, Klaus had slept only with his wife.

Klaus once lost his sock in Ulrike's bedroom, and, digging through the sheets, he could not find it. Another time, he left the seat up after urinating. Ulrike's husband, a big man who liked to drink at the sharp-shooter's club, asked Ulrike, "Has a man been in here today?"

"No."

He showed her the lifted seat. "A man was here!"

"No, I lifted it to clean it."

"How come there is a dark hair here on the edge, look! You have no dark hairs, neither do I! What the hell's going on!"

Klaus, who was teaching sniffling Alfred how to play chess, heard the quarrel through the window. Renate commented: "Those two don't have a happy marriage, do they? I am so glad we don't quarrel like that."

"Why can the knight jump over pieces and the bishop can't?" Alfred asked.

"Because the bishop has only God on his side, and the knight has a horse. The horse is much better than God."

"Jesus, don't teach him your cynicism," Renate said.

"I am teaching him a natural religion."

"No, you are teaching him atheism."

"I am only joking, for heaven's sake!" Klaus swept the pieces off the board with a violent backhand. Alfred ran and hid behind the oil furnace, and Klaus groaned, trying to calm himself.

"Is wife abuse the new rage in our neighborhood?" Renate locked herself in the bedroom.

At their next stealthy meeting, Ulrike told Klaus that her husband had threatened to kill her and her lover.

"Did you betray my name?"

"*Betray,* what a funny expression. If anybody was betrayed, it's him. He tried to force me to tell him who was here. But he's on to us, and we better call it quits."

They made love to music—"Love Me Two Times, One for Today, and One for Tomorrow." That time Klaus forgot his cigarettes, filterless Chestertons—he was the only one to smoke that brand in the apartment complex. Ulrike's husband, visiting him once to borrow jumper cables, had commented that Chestertons were too strong—so probably he would make the connection.

And he did. He banged on Klaus's door, and Klaus did not stir, pretending that nobody was home. Renate was out, teaching, and Alfred was in kindergarten.

That morning Klaus had received a letter of acceptance from Philadelphia, and that afternoon, after the banging on the door, he drove off to the airport, *weg* from the mess.

Several years later, Klaus earned a Ph.D. and divorced his wife. Once every two summers his son Alfred visited him in Philadelphia.

Klaus never read German, avoided Germans, cringed when he overheard German in the streets, and altogether did his best to become an American. He read American newspapers and books, watched baseball on TV, and wrote in English, but he could not get rid of his accent. He talked like Kissinger.

Klaus married a Chicana, Ramona, half his age, when he was forty-four. She taught Spanish at a local high school and played the flamenco guitar. He wore white sneakers, jeans, and a white shirt, which contrasted with his graying black beard. When lecturing in the auditorium flamboyantly, he often wondered whether he had inherited his father's talent for rhetoric, and winced at the association.

Klaus kept rewriting the last third of his book on the history of tobacco and had no success selling his work, for which he blamed his wife, who could not line edit attentively because the writing bored her. Irritated with the whole business—though he was a professor of English some nuances still escaped him, and now and then he got the prepositions wrong—he shouted at her

then that she was stupid. She told him that he was a senile professor who even forgot to make love to his wife. "Professor, you have
forgotten your umbrella at the school again. The girls there must
make it sunny for you!" In the middle of an argument with his
wife, Klaus received a call from his brother Johannes, who told him
that their father had suffered a massive heart attack and wished to
see his sons and grandchildren before he died. "Your son's on his
way to visit you—isn't he?—so could you bring him along?"

"What does he think, that he is Jacob or something?" Klaus
said.

"You've been horribly hard on him, not talking to him for
twelve years!"

"No, I can't talk to him, I've taken a vow not to."

"You don't have to talk—just be there so that he can see you.
For once, don't be selfish!"

For once. Klaus hated that, especially from his younger
brother. What a brat! I don't have to take that crap from him.

What hurt Klaus was the ease with which Johannes seemed to
accomplish everything. Not that Klaus would want to forgive, but
this ease in his brother struck him as—almost enviably—slick and
thoughtless. The will was probably written in his name! Johannes
was a millionaire, and Klaus could not finish a simple history
book. Perhaps the place of his childhood was to blame. Dresden,
where blocks of charcoal buildings, ruined churches, burned cas-
tles, and plain rubble stayed untouched like a kind of open wound.
Now, in the middle of the conversation, he recalled a ruined castle
where he'd played Robin Hood with the boys from the neighborhood. One older boy, to punish him for opening a mousetrap and
letting ten mice run free, had tried to push his penis into Klaus's
behind, but the large penis was limp, limp and cold like a dead fish
in the Elbe, and Klaus didn't understand what kind of punishment
it was since nothing had happened.

His brother's voice brought all the charcoal memories to him
in a flash. "No, I will not talk to *your* father, ever."

"That's just a vow, a word, nobody's word is that important."

"If nobody's word is that important, why do you want mine?" Klaus hung up, and walked around his sunny apartment, erect, proud of his soldierly walk. In the army he had been one of the best runners in his whole division; he was second, he ran one hundred meters in slightly above eleven seconds. Though he was now forty-eight, he had not gained weight—not owing to exercise but to two packs a day, "a terrible stinking habit," which his wife hated.

She had just come out of the shower, naked and singing."Who made you so mad?" she asked.

"Oh, don't worry." He watched a VCR tape, *The Music Box,* a movie with Jessica Lange and Klaus Brandauer. Jessica reminded him of Ulrike, his neighbor in Frankfurt, and Brandauer, uncannily of his father, the same grisly, tormented, quasi-sensitive face. At first it seemed that Brandauer was acting a loving father, unjustly accused of having been a Nazi. Yes, he thought, that's a topic that should be explored because some soldiers did get stuck against their will in the Nazi troops. But the father turned out to be a staunch Nazi, a disappointing and usual twist in a movie— just like in my life, Klaus thought, and drank beer from a black-and-gold can—colorwise, two-thirds of a German flag. When he noticed that, he crushed the can in his fist, foam bubbling and bursting on his fingers.

Filing her nails so that they would be optimal for the guitar strings, Ramona said, "Have you ever thought of joining Alcoholics Anonymous or Adult Children of Alcoholics?"

Why aren't there Adult Children of Nazis Anonymous? he wondered. There must be millions of them. He recalled a summer day with a double rainbow in the north when a bee had stung him below his right eye. His eye had been swollen over, eclipsed, and his mother had put a cold piece of cloth soaked in chamomile tea over it. She had held him in her arms on the swing and had sung him a poem by Schiller while he cried, until he had realized that the eye did not hurt. His father's voice had broken his enjoyment: "You should call a doctor!"

Memories from Klaus's childhood surged and gave him no

peace. He could not concentrate on his work, and did not respond when his name was called during faculty meetings. He
received notice that he would not get tenure. That same week his
wife left him and said she would sue him for the house that they
had just bought.

His son Alfred showed up and wanted to climb Mount
McKinley in Alaska. Alfred, now taller and more muscular than
Klaus, was a skinhead: regular shaved head, tattoos, black leather,
the works. He said that the damned foreigners from the East and
the South flooded Germany, that there were only 6 percent blue-
eyed people in the world, that the blue eyes would disappear if
the world did not do something about it.

"Foreigners! Aren't you a foreigner too? Aren't I a foreigner?
Wherever you travel, there are Germans. In fact, you can't travel
anywhere without running into the damned Germans. I bet there
are more Germans abroad than foreigners in Germany. That's all
bullshit, my son!"

"You are an old-fart Communist, that's what you are," his son
came back. "How can you be that much behind the times, don't
you see that Communism has died? You buy into this conspiracy
against Germany, that the world is our fault. *Arschloche!* I will never
talk to you again, never!" Alfred spat into Klaus's face. "*You* aren't
my father. Where were you in my childhood?"

"You are damned right." Klaus picked up a baseball bat that
he kept leaning against the door frame in case burglars tried to
break in, and brought it down with all his strength on his son's
shoulder. Bones crackled loudly and his son shrieked. Klaus opened
the door, grabbed his son by the neck, and shoved him down the
steps, grinding his teeth, enjoying the rumbling and the smashing
of the pissed aluminum garbage cans. Then he locked the door.
Twice. He was surprised at his swift action, shocked by his son,
stunned by his impulse.

Out of breath, gasping with an attack of asthma, he took a
look at himself in the mirror in the bathroom. Back at him
peered a grisly guy with small blue eyes deeply set, a big forehead,

a strong nose, a small chin covered in a gray beard, and a balding head. What struck him most was that his face was ashen gray. Ashes to ashes. *Arschloche to Arschloche.* The skin around his eyes was purple and brown, creased, a dry cracking soil of an infertile, doomed country. I am a wizened—but not wise—dried-up old man!

Even his eyebrows were gray. He scrutinized himself without mercy. Back at him looked a nervous, deserted man, a recluse.

For hours he gazed at himself in the mirror, wheezing, and was pulled out of the stupor by the sudden ringing of the phone. He picked up his red phone, and Johannes's voice was in his ear, as though it were a part of him.

The Reverend Rudolf Traurig had died with Klaus's name on his lips: he said *Klaus* and *forgiveness,* and it was not clear whether he forgave Klaus or wanted Klaus to forgive him, or whether he was just thinking out loud about the two.

Turkish Coffee

Through clouds of coal and diesel-oil smoke, at the train station in Zagreb, I boarded a blue tram that sparked and rang all the way to the Circle of the Victims of Fascism. The tram clanked around an old minaret-less mosque that the Yugoslav government had turned into a museum. Coming from a provincial town four hours east of Zagreb, I visited the city once a month, to see as many movies as possible. More than the movies, though, I enjoyed Uncle Ivo, who lived in a basement a block away from the Circle.

He smoked unfiltered Drina cigarettes, drank Turkish coffee from a bronze pot all morning long, and jested. His laugh lines cut past his aquiline nose into his double chin. For breakfast he had four eggs, sunny-side up, like yellow eyeballs. He soaked his bread in these eyes, and, as he chewed, his own eyes vanished in his face. His Bosnian wife, Angela, smiled and braided her black hair. She cut me a slice of white bread on which she spread thick pâté.

Ivo was kind, and he did not preach and forbid like the rest of our family. As a boy, in the last world war, he had walked fifty miles to tell his sister—my mother—that her husband was alive—for a year she had not known it. He drove a green truck full of wine and brandy on the most accident-afflicted road in Europe, the Highway of Brotherhood and Unity, from Zagreb to Serbia and Macedonia. In forty years he must have shipped more drunkenness through the federation than anyone else. Unlike my father's teetotal family, he was a *bon vivant*. We called him *Veseljak*, Jolly Man.

Once, after watching four movies during the afternoon and the evening, I returned to Ivo's apartment before midnight, unembarrassed at my lateness. I was recovering from the glaring images of *The Seventh Seal* (Death, clad in a black robe, turns around in response to the question "What is there after life?" and says, with a blank gaze amidst a sallow skin, "Nothing"). In the kitchen, shrouded in sheets of blue tobacco smoke, Ivo was playing cards with his buddies who wore white T-shirts, their belts comfortably loosened. Glasses of slivovitz, yellow-green like petrol, tremulously approached the edge of the table with each board-whack. In the orange light of the living room, I blinked at Ivo's daughter Maya, whose curly blond hair streamed over her math book. Some hair that had fallen into her ink pot drew thin blue lines over alphas and omegas. I envied her, living in the city of movies and concerts, although the gray city was haunted by lost wars and its cobbled corridors exuded dank gloom. I envied her even more for having such a permissive father.

Several years later Ivo's family moved to the Square of Flowers, near the Badel liquor factory. Maya made fragile model airplanes from balsa, and suspended them from the ceiling. She wanted to become a pilot. Ivo laughed at her ambition, as he laughed at everything. He retold me dozens of Tito jokes ("Soon after Tito's leg was amputated, a cable from hell came to the hospital, and it said, 'Please send the rest urgently!'"), a dozen Croat wine-country jokes, and a hundred Bosnian jokes by Serb truckers; the jokes appeared cheery at the time.

Maya's application to the school of aviation was denied—no woman in Yugoslavia had become a pilot before—with the explanation that her nerves were weak. She complained of sex discrimination, and when I returned from the United States to visit, she wanted us to talk in English. She became a secretary at the liquor factory, and at thirty-three, still lived with her parents, and hadn't yet been on an airplane. She blinked frequently, smoked, and her teeth were coffeed out. One morning she jumped from the sixth-floor balcony and crashed to the pavement of the Square of Flowers.

A year after her suicide, my wife Jeanette and I visited Zagreb. Angela offered us tepid mud—Turkish coffee—with a carton of spoiled milk. Most of the cheese, bread, and grapes in the refrigerator were green with mold. The windows closed, the air in the room did not move. Through smoke, Ivo asked me what I'd become in the States. I delayed answering. Thousands of wrinkles cutting his thickened and ashen skin distracted me. The creases did not run in harmonious parallels and rays, but clashed with each other. His black-green eyes looked like two flies twitching in a spiderweb; the spider must have been drunk, zigzagging and falling. Ivo said, "Nothing, what else would you become?" Cigarettes burned to his yellow fingers, their unshaken ashes falling to the table. Cigarette butts, sucked to a brown stain, jammed glasses, cups, and cans. I asked him whether he knew any new jokes. No, and he'd forgotten the old ones. Angela, breathing with asthma, told us that he had retired, since he could no longer truck through the Balkan federation. Croatia was cut up and too small for good trucking. He had an ulcer, and one night he had fallen over the kitchen threshold and nearly bled to death so quietly that he had not woken her. She had found him unconscious in the morning. Now he was back from the hospital, spiting the doctor's orders against coffee and tobacco. "*Na ja,*" he said.

When he inhaled smoke, his diminished eyes had some life in them—tobacco light—but his skin was dead. How could you live in a dead skin, a corpse's skin? I knew he would soon die. Even our hug was empty.

The man who had seemed the greatest optimist and comedian in my youth was, like many humorists, a depressed cynic. That's probably what he'd been all along. He'd seen one mad Croatia and two intoxicated Yugoslavias collapse (the Kingdom in 1941, and the Socialist Federation in 1990), and he had drunk and talked with thousands of people in the Balkan federation. He expected nothing good to come out of the Balkans, and that included me. I was nothing. His family was nothing. He was nothing.

Honey in the Carcase

Ivan Medvedich was washing his silvery mustache after eating a slice of bread with honey when a whistle cut through the air, deepened in frequency, and sank into an explosion that shook the house so that a bar of soap slid from the mirror ledge into the sink.

"Lord have mercy!" his wife Estera said. "What was that?"

"The *chetniks*, what else."

Soon, another whistle, and another explosion.

"Run for cover!" Estera shouted.

"What cover? This is the safest place in the house." Ivan had built the house alone—actually, with a little help from his oldest son, Daniel, who had groaned more than he had worked. It had taken Ivan twenty years of careful labor to finish the house, but it lacked a cellar, perhaps because snakes had nested and floods had crept in the cellar of his childhood home. *God is my fortress and my strength* was his motto. But now, in addition to God, a cellar would help. He turned off the lights and prayed, and after his last *Amen,* no bombs fell for the rest of the night.

The following morning Estera walked to the bakery, early, because after six o'clock the dark whole-wheat bread disappeared, and only milky white, soft, cakelike bread, as expensive as sin, remained. The old baker said nothing, handing her a two-kilo loaf as usual. When Estera left, she heard a dog's howl and a high-pitched whistle. A bomb fell in a ditch ten yards away from her, exploding. Shrapnel flew over her head, shattered the bakery attic windows, and riddled the nearby housetops, which now looked like lepers' foreheads. She walked home hurriedly.

If the bomb had fallen outside the ditch, the shrapnel would have flown low and struck her. She and Ivan concluded that God had saved her. Still, as Estera peeled onions that day, her neck twitched, jerking her head to one side. Estera had given birth to five sons. The youngest, whom she'd had at the age of forty-six, had died several months before because the wall between the chambers of his heart had collapsed. Ivan was playing the violin. Tears, from the onion fumes, glazed her eyes. She grieved so that salty water flowed as though her swollen eyes, like balloons, needed to drop sand to gain in altitude. Tears slid down her cheeks like little eyes, mirroring knives and violins.

Ivan walked out to the rabbit cage. The rabbits' split lips quickly drew grass into their mouths. He gripped a white one by its long ears. He had often petted the rabbit, so the rabbit was not scared, not even as Ivan's fist went down and hit its neck. The rabbit twitched and went limp. Ivan walked into the house and lay the rabbit on the table to cool. "You skin it this time," he said.

That day he could not eat rabbit for the first time in his life. He ate more bread with honey, old honey that had crystalized into white grains.

At dusk, more whistles and about a dozen blasts sounded, all in the neighborhood. It went on like that for a week. A crater loomed in their street between two shattered houses. When Ivan cautioned Estera not to go early in the morning to buy bread, she said, "I am used to bombs."

He said nothing to that, but hummed a tune, sounding like a buzz of bees, and bees were on his mind. It was time to collect honey in his apiary, ten miles east, in a meadow of wildflowers near an acacia grove. He drove his old pickup, put on a beekeeper's hat and gloves, and opened the hives. His bees were so ardent that they had made honeycombs even outside the frames. He placed framed honeycombs in a barrel separator. Turning the wheel, he listened to honey fall out of the hexagonal wax trenches and hit the metal wall, sticking to it and dripping. He did not mind bee stings—he'd gotten more than a dozen that day—because he believed they benefited his heart.

He harvested alone. His sons used to help him, dancing around the honey separator like Joseph's brothers around the grains of Egypt. But now one of his sons was in Australia; another, Daniel, his first-born, worked as a doctor; the third one, Jakov, worked as a carpenter in Germany; and the youngest, Branko, stayed at home, studying for his entrance exams at the school of agricultural engineering.

When Ivan returned home with three barrels of honey and saw his son Daniel, he rolled up his sleeve because Daniel always took his blood pressure—especially since Ivan's heart attack. Ivan still suffered from angina pectoris but could not get a retirement settlement because his boss hated him and, he suspected, wanted him to die at the factory.

Daniel talked about how in the village where he practiced medicine, *chetniks* went door-to-door, beating up old Croatian men, as though these men had been *ustashas*. "The *chetniks* with skulls and crossbones painted on their black caps drove people out of their homes, stole TV sets, burned haystacks. They cut off three old men's testicles and forced them to eat them. One bled to death, the others I stitched up as best I could."

"You should leave the village," said Ivan, "because of your young wife and child."

Daniel waved his hand as though to chase away a slow and fat fly. Before his parents and brother could react, he was out, in his wobbly Citroën. This was the first time in five years that Daniel had visited without taking his father's blood pressure. Ivan rolled down his sleeve and turned on the radio.

The announcer said that Vinkovci was eerily quiet. *Eerily*

quiet was a cliché in a newscaster's voice, but not so through the window when Estera opened it. There was no machine-gun fire, no cars, not even birds singing; only a woman's wailing far away.

"Estie," Ivan said, "we must take care of the honey. You know what the Montenegrin poet says, 'A glass of honey asks for a glass of spleen, together they are easiest to drink.'"

"What kind of poetry is it if it doesn't even rhyme? Besides, give me no Montenegrin junk when you know that Monte-negrin *chetniks* are bombing us."

Ivan let the honey sit in the barrels for several days, and then he scooped the creamy foamy top. He was certain that this was ambrosia, the drink of Greek gods. He and Estera poured honey all evening long into glass bottles. Ivan looked back at the filled larder shelves and said, "It's good, isn't it?"

Just then a bomb fell at the edge of their garden so that the floorboards shook and squeaked and the tiles on the roof quivered and slid, like loose teeth grinding. But the honey stayed calm in the bottles. Soon another bomb fell. Ivan and Estera stayed in the larder, the safest room in the house because it had no windows.

The next day, federal MiG jets flew low, sharding people's windows, but no window burst on Medvedich's house. At night, light from houses on fire flickered through the shades that could not be quite shut; the red light on the wall seemed to be painting a message. The following morning, despite continuous mortar explosions, Estera wrapped a scarf under her chin and walked out.

"Where are you going, old woman?" Ivan asked.

"To buy bread."

"I think you shouldn't."

She walked out, apparently proud of her courage.

Half an hour later, when she was not back, he stood on the threshold and chewed a honeycomb with fresh honey; chewing the wax calmed him better than chewing tobacco could. The phone rang; it was the baker. On the bakery steps, mortar shrap-nel had struck and wounded Estera.

Ivan picked up Estera—unconscious, her abdomen torn—

and an ambulance took them to the hospital. A doctor took a quick X ray and found that shrapnel had penetrated her liver. He dug in with his scalpel and gloved fingers, saying, "Too bad that we're out of anesthetics." As he fished for the metal, Estera came to and swooned again. Just as the doctor tossed the bit of iron in the garbage bin, mortar hit the hospital, setting the roof on fire. The electricity went out. The doctor sewed up the wound while Ivan held up a flashlight. They carried Estera to the basement, where the stench of crap and vomit hung heavily.

For several days Estera lay half dead, green in the face, unable to sleep, too weak to be awake. Ivan spent many hours with her but more at home lest brigands should break in, steal, and burn the house. He prayed but lost the meanings of his words in reveries and forgot to say his *Amens*. *Words without thoughts to heaven do not go.*

He missed his bees, now abandoned behind the advancing enemy lines. As he drank his ambrosia, he decided that the next morning he'd drive into the eastern fields—even through gunfire—to his apiary.

The following dawn a bomb fell in front of his house, shattering the windows and digging holes in the stuccoed bricks. The gate collapsed. Another bomb fell in the backyard, and demolished his pickup. The shrapnel pierced the house windows. His son, trembling on the floor, was not injured.

A pharaoh did not weep when Persians slew his sons and raped his daughters because his sorrow was too deep for tears, but he did weep when after it all his ex-minister came by in rags and begged for silver. Just so, Ivan had not wept when his wife bled in dirty hospitals, when his house had been nearly demolished, and when the truck he had saved for, for fifteen years, burst into pieces and shrivelled in fire. But that he could not go out into the fields and take care of his bees, that made the cup overflow. He wept in his armchair, in his wooden shoes, nearly motionless, will-less.

That noon, four Croatian soldiers walked in and asked for Branko. He was in the bathroom, but Ivan said he'd gone to the library. He was surprised to hear himself lie, but then he remembered that Abraham had lied saying that his sister was his wife to save her from a marriage in a foreign land. That Branko should be a soldier struck him as absurd. Ivan had raised him to turn the other cheek. For years other boys had beaten him and broken his nose, yet he would not fight back even when Ivan told him to. When Ivan complained to the school principal, the principal laughed. Ivan had given Branko a beekeeper's mask to save his face, and had walked him home while boys threw stones and shouted, "Baptists, Claptists." Branko, who had grown up as a theological experiment, spent his days developing landscape photographs in a shed, so that his eyes stayed watery and bloodshot.

Estera began to improve and her son Daniel took her to Osijek, where he now worked in a hospital and lived with Branko but Ivan would not leave his house, as though it was his skin. On his block there were fewer than a dozen people left, and in the city of forty thousand, perhaps three thousand had remained. Neither phone nor electricity worked anymore. He lived on water from a hand pump in his yard and on honey.

He used to be a corpulent, double-chinned man, but in a month in which it no longer mattered to him whether he was alive or dead, he became a thin man with sharp, pentagonal jaws, overgrown in a Moses-like beard. Perhaps he would not have eaten honey either if it had not reminded him of his bees. He ate honey in their remembrance, a sacrament to the little striped and winged tigresses.

One crisp morning Ivan felt tremendously alert. He wondered whether he was about to die, since before death one could seize a moment of lucidity to summon one's family and deliver blessings—that lucidity was a sine qua non in a Biblical death, and he, a father of several sons, would of course have a Biblical death. Or had his diet cleared his coronary arteries? The following day, since he still felt lucid, he concluded that honey had healed his heart and saved his life.

He biked to visit his brother David in their father's house in Andriasevci ten miles away. He negotiated his way among starved shaggy cattle that roamed masterless. Horses rotted in dried-up sunflower fields. Blind dogs stumbled into trees. Cats with red eyes purred so loudly that he could hear them even as he rode over cracking branches. Heads of wheat bent in the fields like contrite sinners; nobody harvested them.

David and Ivan hugged and kissed as brothers. After they had slurped rose-hip tea, David said, "I have presents for you: one coffin for Estera and one for you. Come, take a look!"

"What? But Estera is alive. And I am all right."

"Of course. But in case you get killed, you won't be dumped in a mass grave if you have a coffin with your name."

Next morning Ivan decided to go back to Vinkovci. Not that he had not thought about death enough, or seen it enough—but that his younger brother, who used to spend most of his time making tambourines and singing, should see the world as a plantation of coffins, incensed him against the invading armies. He rode through the groaning countryside.

From the edge of the village a black German shepherd followed him all the way home. There he wagged his tail and licked Ivan's shoe. Ivan gave him an old slice of bread and honey.

Ivan stood on his threshold and stared at the cloudy horizon and dark blue clouds. The stink of putrid animals, borne on an unusually warm wind, hit his nostrils. Smoke and gangrene.

And when the rains began, a ghost crept along the surface of the earth, not as an image, white and gray, but as the stench of wet smoke and pus. The muddy soul of the Pannonian valley sought fire to solidify into bricks a tower of Babel, in which all languages would merge into one, Serbian. *Govori Srpski da te ceo svet razume.* Speak Serbian so the whole world can understand you, the Serb folk saying went.

He rode his bike to a foundry converted into a bomb factory

and volunteered to make bombs for the underarmed Croatian soldiers. At the end of his shift, he always found the German shepherd, waiting for him.

One dawn MiG jets bombed the factory, mostly missing and hitting people's houses nearby, but they did damage it enough to close it down. Ivan could take it no more, so he dragged a cart east, through Mirkovci. Now and then he stopped and scratched his dog's fur. He ran into a checkpoint made of stacked beer cases in the middle of the road. A *chetnik* asked him, "Where the hell are you going?"

"I need to take back my bees from the fields."

"Bees?" The *chetnik* pulled out a knife. "Your ID?"

"I have none."

"I'm gonna tattoo you so we can recognize you next time." He pushed his knife against Ivan's face. The dog growled, ready to pounce. A *chetnik* grabbed his comrade's arm. "Don't be crazy. Don't you see he's crazy. Let him get his bees." And turning to Ivan, he winked, and said, "God protects the crazy ones. I like that, bees. Bees!" When Ivan was at a fair distance, they shot at the German shepherd but missed. That he had managed to pass surprised him. Perhaps the brigands had understood his beard as an emblem of Serbdom.

Ivan waxed the entrances to ten beehives and stacked them on his cart. When he passed by the *chetnik*s, they again shot at his dog, and this time they killed him. Ivan turned over soil on the side of the road with a shovel and buried his friend.

It took him five trips—and a dozen kilos of honey as the "road tax" to the brigands—to take back all his beehives. He built a brick wall around the hives. He melted sugar for his friends so they would survive the winter. Since he had seen a sign that the winter would be a long one, Polish geese migrating south, he filled the cracks in the hives with frame wax.

For hours he listened to the congregation of bees. They were his revelation: *For the invisible things of him from the creation of the world are clearly seen, being understood by the things that are made, even his eternal power and Godhead.* Yes, the invisible Godhead and his plan are revealed in bees. Bees fulfill the Old Testament through the perfection of their laws and the New Testament, through the perfection of their love for the queen bee, for whom every bee is willing to die. Ivan thought that even if he had never read the Bible, from studying his bees he'd concluded that God existed. After thinking so, he'd bring the bees several pounds of honey, apologizing for having taken it in the summer. He admired the heaven on earth, the earth in heaven.

His son Daniel visited and told him that Estera, although anemic, had nearly fully recovered. When asked to join her in Osijek, Ivan said, "Somebody has to stay here and protect the church and the bees."

The shack where his son had developed photographs had served as a chapel ever since Ivan had excommunicated himself from the Baptist church. Like-minded Baptist and Pentecostals, for whom their churches had not been pious enough, used to worship in the shack with Ivan and his family, until they discovered that they were not like-minded. Nobody came now, but still it continued to be God's space.

Ivan played the violin in his chapel and studied scripture. He was disappointed that scripture mentioned bees only a few times and lions many times. It consoled him that in one verse bees got the better of the lion: *There was a swarm of bees and honey in the carcase of the lion.*

One passage intrigued Ivan: *And it shall come to pass in that day, that the Lord shall hiss for the fly that is in the uttermost part of the rivers of Egypt, and for the bee that is on the land of Assyria.*

He whistled and hissed to call out his bees, and none came out. Then he made a flute from a wet willow branch, with a low note, and found a hiss that indeed excited the bees so that they came out and crisscrossed the sky, forming a mighty net. When they came back, they tossed out their drones, and they kept tossing them for days. A peculiar fratricide—that aspect of bees theologically troubled Ivan. Some kind of wrath of God built into the natural order of things? In front of the beehives fat drones with stunted wings curled atop each other and shrank; the ditch filled up with drones. On a sunny day so many crows flew over Ivan's head, to feast on the drones, that it grew dark.

After a prolonged bombardment, a band of *chetniks* came to Ivan's street. He was now the only person living on his block. When he saw them coming, he unplugged the beehive entrances and hissed on his flute. A bomb flew, with a low whistle, fell in the street, and did not go off. Bees from several beehives grew agitated and flew out into the street where several sweaty *chetniks*, having loaded his neighbor's furniture on a truck, turned their eyes to Ivan's house.

Thousands of bees covered each brigand, giving them the appearance of armored medieval knights. The brigands ran, helter-skelter, dropping their weapons. One of them staggered in circles and fell dead in front of Ivan's house. The corpse kept swelling even after the rigor mortis gripped it.

Hats and Veils

Vadim Abdich stood at a bus stop on Mythen-Quai outside the Lindt chocolate factory. He turned around, as though someone were behind him. Boats on the dark and colorless Zurich Lake tilted, their white sails swelling with the wind, and slid silently past fir trees on the shore. Fir trees, tranquil hooded giants, whose roots sipped from the lake unhurriedly, spread their dozens of hairy arms downward in an apparent welcome, as though they would embrace you once they stopped daydreaming.

Vadim smelled their daydreams—the windborne particles of water and fir oxygen, bursting in the hazy sunlight. He breathed in deep this musty fir aroma and remembered Bosnia's mountain pines above his red-tiled house. Serb soldiers had firebombed the forest and his house had burned in high, explosive flames. Sheets of fire, falling into the air from the liquid soil, had seemingly lifted him as he jumped through them. When he had come to, his left leg was on fire, and putting it out he had burned his hands. He had hopped on one leg to the local hospital while the other still sizzled. The wound had been a godsend—a passport to Switzerland. His family had already gone to Switzerland months before, but he, as a draftable man, had not been able to. Now, two years later, the leg was all right, although hairless and a little weaker than the other.

It was still sunny when it began to rain, yet there was no rainbow. If he had had a car he would not forget it, but, of course, he forgot the umbrella. At least he was done with work. If he worked overtime Saturdays, in half a year he would manage to save 5,000 francs for a used car, and he wouldn't have to wait so much anymore.

He climbed on the blue city bus and stood among seated children and the elderly with yellow hearing aids and fine walking sticks. A man his age—about forty—stepped in at the next stop, grimacing and talking to himself. Only if you suffered from a medical or criminal condition would you ride the bus, Vadim thought. Otherwise, you'd have a valid driver's license, with all the appropriate stamps. Here all things, even eggs, were inspected and stamped.

He had the impression that people's eyes—like snail's feelers—touched his back and crept sluggishly among his gray neck hairs. He strained to stand straight, pulled his head back, and pursed his full lips—the bristles of his mustache pricked his lower lip—so that, if he had worn an olive-colored cap with an infant porcelain starfish—he'd have resembled a partisan sculpture in the square of his native town. Before the stop—as the bus buzzed in a lower gear past a flooded soccer field—his stomach rumbled, and he moved stiffly, aware of his thin body, and burped. He said *"Entscheidung"* to the children who stood next to the door and would not move for him, for a second, long enough to make him feel his disrespectablity. When he stepped off, the children giggled, and he realized that he'd said the word for *decision* rather than for *excuse*. Stripes of rain hit the pavement, with drops bouncing and bursting.

At home his daughter Sonya sang *"Stille Nacht."* Her brown eyes glimmered, and her voice rose high, clear, into an alien, northern charm, reminiscent of a window frosted with stars and hexagons. Marko—who watched *Tom and Jerry* in French, his belly on the floor, and feet in new red sneakers in the air—shouted "Silence!" in English.

"*Ludnica,*" Vadim said in Serbo-Croatian, meaning *madhouse.* He smiled at Olga, his wife, whose black hair streaked with white was twisted in a bun. She did not look back at him, but went on figuring out the bills, whispering numbers.

"*Kolko fali?*" he said ("How much do we need?").

"*Stille!*" Olga said. She insisted that they speak German at home, so the kids would do well at school. The only language that their kids did not speak very well was Serbo-Croatian, or, as Vadim preferred to call it now, Bosnian. Bosnian they could always speak—and rarely did—with their father. So although Sonya was ten and Marko seven, their Bosnian was younger, frozen at the level at which it had been when they left Bosnia, three years before; actually, if it continued this way, their Bosnian would become a baby language. When Marko was a fourteen-month-old toddler, he'd say *bana* for *banana.* Then he managed to say *banana,* and noticing that his adding another *na* pleased his parents, he added many more—for a month afterward, he said *banananananananana.* Maybe that's how Marko would speak Bosnian again.

"Daddy, will you buy me a violin?" Sonya asked.

"Why a violin?"

"All my friends play the violin."

"So all the more reason why you should play the cello. That's the most lovingly sad sound."

"I don't need sad sounds."

"How do you know?"

"*Merde,*" Marko shouted.

"I want the violin!" Sonya said.

"Why not the piano?" Vadim asked. "You could do it alone, even after you lose your friends."

"Jeez, Vadim you do sound like a madman," said Olga. "No musical instruments. Music means lessons, and that means bills. Anyway, we need to renew our visas this month. It's a kind of harassment. They want to make sure that we don't stay."

"America or Canada—that's where we should settle," Vadim

said. "There almost everybody's an immigrant—or an immigrant's child, or grandchild, or whatever—so you can't be a foreigner."

"What's the point of dreaming?" said Olga. "We need to make the best of our situation here."

Sonya continued to sing "*Stille Nacht, schoene Nacht*" in a snowy voice, an octave higher than before. Her green vein swelled on her forehead, cutting a line from her parted hair like a wind-beaten path in a meadow down into her nose, between her thin black eyebrows, which looked, against her pale face, like two faraway crows gliding on a warm wind above two remote and glimmering ponds. As Vadim listened to her and gazed at her face, he felt happy and proud. After all, come what may, he had a wonderful family, and beneath the bickering there was playfulness and harmony.

"I'm going out to mail the bills and take a stroll." Olga wrapped a green veil around her head.

"Since when do you wear a veil?" Vadim said.

"We are Muslims, nobody lets us forget that, so let us be Muslims," she said. "And I like the idea of a veil, especially here; it's a statement that I don't mind the anonymity, I don't need eye contact with strangers, I'm not lonely."

"Nonsense, a veil draws attention to you."

"Mom, can I have a cat?" Marko shouted. "Why can't I have a cat?"

Olga said to Vadim, "You wear sunglasses, that's a veil without any identity!"

"But a veil makes you too foreign here."

"Nonsense. It's good to have a visible identity. You can actually fit in better that way, people here respect that. You be you, and I me."

"That doesn't sound particularly Islamic to me. You read too many Swiss magazines."

The doorbell rang. Vadim went to the door and looked through the optic hole, at a woman in a veil, who through the round lens appeared rotund and remote.

"That's my friend Fatima!" Olga opened the door and a gaunt woman exchanged kisses with her, and the two of them went out.

As Vadim baby-sat, he brooded. He could not get used to the Muslim identity, which to him seemed superfluous, something imposed from the outside, although, of course, his ancestors were Muslim. He'd never been religious, he'd been raised a Marxist atheist, as was nearly everybody else his age in the former Yugoslavia, and so what was all this sudden religiosity about? He could not change identities—just as he could not be a Communist before, now he could not be a Muslim, or a Swiss. He was no good at identities. Or at making new friends. Lucky thing that he had his family. His family were his friends.

Absentmindedly Vadim set up wooden chess pieces for a mate-in-three.

"Dad, you are a retard," Sonya said. "You should have a computer chess game, and not push chopped wood around like a peasant."

"A computer will hurt your eyes and your head. The wood won't!" He laughed. He was no peasant. In Drvar he'd been an artisan—he'd made hats and caps, but at the outset of the war, Serb soldiers had demolished his shop. They'd shattered all the shop windows downtown—it was a *Krystallnacht* of sorts.

"If you won't buy a computer, you are a peasant," Sonya said.

"So you'd like me to buy everything—the violin, the computer. What next, a horse?"

"The violin first," Sonya said. He said nothing, but placed his white knights—hand-carved horses—in a symmetrical position, removed by two horizontal L's from each other. The violin bow, he thought, is just a horse's tail, rubbed in resin, a fir secretion. Peasant elements. He imagined his daughter, grown, in a black-red-white folk costume, playing the fiddle at a peasant wedding, in a frenzied, quickening, Oriental rhythm.

Sonya sat in lotus position—there were American kids at her school, and she had probably learned to sit this way from them—and she did her homework, aloud. "Twenty minus x . . ." At least he had taught his kids good work habits. They'd do fine even in America or New Zealand. She sat, poised in her neon socks, like a modern Swiss child with her hair shiny from an expensive hair conditioner (nettle juice, eggs, aloe, coconut oil, and many other loudly advertised natural ingredients, a united nations of peasant produce). Vadim admired her modernity but it also vaguely bothered him.

Marko's sharp breathing and gasping interrupted Vadim's contemplation. Another asthma attack. In the rainy season, whenever Marko was frustrated or ignored, he had asthma attacks. Vadim placed a gray inhalator before Marko's face and tapped him on the back gently, the way he used to burp him as a baby. "I will get you a cat with three little kittens and a pair of mittens," Vadim said.

The following morning on the bus, Vadim looked at a young woman with blazingly beautiful coppery hair streaming from beneath her beret. As she talked to an old woman with braided white hair, her swelled lips languidly lisped. He gazed into the young woman's face with wistful yearning, although he wasn't sure what he yearned for. He was sure that he'd never talk to this woman and touch her lips. Age, nations, mores, religions, and her self-possession removed her from him, so that his physical proximity to her was illusory in the essential sense—that of being human neighbors. They were not neighbors. He continued to look at her, but her calm face acknowledged not in the slightest way that she might be aware of him. He thought how in Bosnian, when a man falls in love, the expression is, *Zagledo se*. He looked for a long while. Of course he would not fall in love—it would be preposterous, impossible, and that impossibility stunned him with melancholy. He missed his bus stop. To get back should be a five-minute walk, but with his tender leg that day, and a tingling loss of sensation, it took him ten minutes. He wished that he could have a cup of Turkish coffee and that he could dip his face into a Bosnian mountain brook and drink the aroma of oak-tree roots and moss, to sober him and strengthen him against his reveries. He still felt dizzy from a luminescent longing. Now he thought that veils made sense—a face could enrapture you more obsessively than a naked body would.

At the factory, as he passed a varnished booth, he said, "*Buon giorno!*" to the Italian porter, who frowned and marked down perhaps that Vadim was seven minutes late. And when Vadim got to his conveyer belt, he said "*Buenos dias!*" to his Spanish coworkers. He melted one white chocolate square on his sleepy tongue and chewed, until a nut wedged between his molars. His tongue pushed the nut, vainly trying to dislodge it. Other than this nut "shrapnel" and the sugary heat in the room, there was hardly any discomfort here. He tilted his white cap. Everybody was dressed in white, as though they were all doctors and nurses rather than chocolate *Gastarbeiter,* guest-workers.

He sat downstream from several robots. One wiry robot hand produced the lower level of a box, the other abruptly lowered a dozen chocolate cubes wrapped in gold foil, and the third one lowered and glued red-foil roses atop each one, all at once, with pneumatic pressure popping gently; past him, another robot capped the box with a crimson lid. Whenever Vadim noticed an irregularity (to err is robotlike)—a naked chocolate cube, or a tilted rose—he'd pull off the box, take out the irregular cube, and hand-place a good one, from a box at his side. God forbid that a customer should buy a box of cognac chocolates with one cube amiss. The customer would never buy Lindt again.

With all these red foils, when his eyes refused to move, he'd see thin red streaks, and above the streaks an image appeared: an ax stuck in a skull of a prostrate gray-haired man, with blood flowing down the steep granite-cobbled street and branching out into thin dusty streaks, which carried golden cigarette butts, like a file of red ants carrying dismembered bees, in the cracks among the cobbles. He couldn't push the image away from the back of his eyes, the brain, which, he thought, at least in his case, had become a mostly empty black space, a storage room of frozen images, which defrosted one by one (sometimes three or four at once) and dripped back into his eyes, into the scarlet light of his eyelids.

During the fifteen-minute midmorning break, the supervisor, a man with thin blue lips and a thick red neck squeezed by a blue tie, came to Vadim, and spoke in German slowly and loudly, the way you speak to the deaf or the stupid. Perhaps because of the excessive effort he put in his voice, he sprinkled saliva droplets over Vadim's forehead. Vadim, whose job it was to stare at the conveyor belt, stared now at the bursting droplets, each droplet visible, like dust in a stream of light. The supervisor said that Vadim had missed two defective boxes, and that he should not be late, because the conveyor belt could not be started until everybody was in his place. Robots could do the whole job. A laser scanner could notice any irregularities in the distribution of chocolate cubes and activate a robot hand to sideline the defective box. Spruengli-Lindt kept many people employed around conveyor belts—it was a form of charity. Otherwise, Vadim would be on exile welfare. That Vadim was allowed to work for his money was a favor to him. Human work is a luxury. One needs work, for mental hygiene.

"You are right," Vadim said. "*Entschuldigungung!*" He was aware that he'd added one *ung* too many, the way his young son used to do with *Banananana*. He resented the fact that he had to apologize abjectly—he was not sorry. He thought of adding that the bus was late—to lie, like a child with a schoolteacher—but thought better of it. The supervisor probably would take this statement as an insult to the Swiss system. And to explain that he was late because he'd gazed at a young woman's lips—that would sound ridiculous. He couldn't explain this to anybody; that an ephemeral visual effect threw him off balance was more disgraceful than adultery (which would be something substantial, physical, understandable); he had to veil this quietly impossible experience, let it cocoon itself like a silkworm, far away, in the Far East of his mind.

When the conveyor belt continued rolling by, to toast his work—because work cleans your mind—now and then Vadim placed a defective cognac chocolate on his tongue (although he was not supposed to eat chocolate during the shift), and there was nothing defective about that taste, which made him clear his throat; his throat could not take that much sweetness. The taste brought him back to his childhood, when he had climbed orchard trees, and chewed crimson cherries, sucked on their stones, and spat them out. The light of the strawberry slopes of Bosnia began to glow somewhere deep in his eyes; the hair of the woman from the bus leaked a magnificent radiance over his memories. And he was glad for it, because when he saw her afterglow, it kept away his memories of bloated bodies drifting down the Una River.

When he got home, he entered a microcosmic war. Sonya was pounding Marko's head with her walking shoes. He grabbed her hair and pulled it. They both shouted and cried.

Vadim pulled them apart. "How can you allow them to get so out of hand?" he yelled at Olga, who was crouching next to the sofa and pulling a hissing orange cat by its tail.

"I don't have thirteen hands," Olga said. "This cat's trying to eat Sonya's dove."

"Since when does she have a dove?"

"I'm nursing it—something bit its leg," Sonya said. "I found it in the hedges by the woods."

The bird fluttered in a cardboard box with small holes. One hole was larger than the rest; apparently the tomcat had torn it to take swipes at the dove.

Olga carried the cat by the scruff of his neck—the white film half-covering his eyes, his paws bent forward, hanging limp—to the window, and Marko ran after her and tugged at her green skirt. "Let me keep him!"

"No, you can't have him. We aren't allowed to keep pets in this building."

"Who'd know?" Vadim said. "Let him keep the cat for a day at least."

"Throw out the stinker!" Sonya yelled. "He'll kill my dove."

"Why?" Vadim said. "Just keep your bird in the bedroom, until it gets healthy, and let it go."

"They'll throw us out of the apartment, and then what?" Olga said.

"All right, I understand that, but let him keep the cat for an hour, to play a bit, feed it. He needs it."

Olga relented and swore under her breath, in Bosnian—the whole turmoil took place in Bosnian (there, thought Vadim, when you are pushed, you go to your mother tongue). Sonya locked herself with her dove in the bedroom, and shouted that her dad favored that bratty Marko. That's not a dove, Vadim thought, but just a pigeon, but let her call it a dove, as though a dove were something finer and better. Olga lowered the venetian blinds so no one would see the cat.

"What a country," Vadim said. "Can't keep a cat."

"Aha," Olga said. "You are the one to tell us about consideration. The whole house smells like booze just a minute after you get home. You'll get fired, we'll be evicted, and that's compassion for you?"

Vadim smiled distantly, like a blind man listening to an imaginary melody. He stroked the tomcat, who sprawled on the sofa, purred loudly, and licked Vadim's finger. Now and then the tom bit his fingertip gently and looked up to his eyes and put up a padded paw to his cheek. The tom slid the paw to Vadim's upper lip, and let the claws come out a little and comb his mustache. The cat's pupils, which had at first contracted into black clawlike exclamation points of alarm, relaxed into ellipses, becoming circles. The circles supplanted the translucent irises, but these irises shone all the more, around the gleaming blacks. The cat's eyes brought the serenity of night into a disappearing turbulent day.

And the turbulence, though diminished, went on. "You think you're doing your son a favor by letting him keep this stray?" Olga said. "He'll breathe the hairs in, his asthma will get worse."

Vadim smiled at the tomcat, convinced that they had reached an understanding. Vadim had heard Olga, but said nothing, and thought that since asthma was mostly a psychosomatic illness, Marko would get better, thanks to this feline psychologist.

But the following morning, the tomcat was gone. Olga claimed that he'd jumped out the window. This grieved Vadim quietly, and instead of going into a mosque with Olga and Marko—as he had promised he would, for the first time—Vadim went with Sonya to downtown Zurich, near Bahnhofstrasse. They would go to an old violin maker in Donaugasse, up the cobbled and narrow streets, with creamy houses with chocolate cross beams, and steep roofs, among goldsmith shops and art galleries. Vadim had sniffed around the place before, and now he'd buy the violin as an *Ied,* or end of Ramadan gift for Sonya.

They climbed onto the bus together. There were several elderly people; a dozen high-school students; a leathery adolescent with green hair and a ring piercing his lip; and two young women, with black lipstick, in mink coats and torn fishnet stockings. Vadim thought that for a change he didn't care about what the people on the bus thought. It seemed that he did not think much, and he wondered whether in fact nobody thought, but just daydreamed, as he did.

"Could we go sailing?" Sonya asked in German, looking at the bouncing sailboats among the choppy waves of the lake. He did not answer because he was busy with his reveries.

He remembered how when Sonya was thirteen months old, she had loved fish. Whenever she had seen a drawing of a fish, she'd silently opened and closed her mouth. When he had showed her a red starfish picture—and said, "Starfish!"—her finger had tried to trace the mouth, and not finding it, got confused, stopped on the picture of a submarine rock. She had put her tiny forefinger back in her fist, and stared at Vadim openmouthed, as though confronted with the concept of a lie for the first time. Later, on a moonless night with a breeze murmuring through pines, when he had pointed to the sky and said "Stars!" she had opened and closed her mouth happily, and turned to him to show him how well she was doing. She'd learned to accept all kinds of fishes, in their variety, even those that did not have mouths and that swam in the sky at night.

"*Sag mal,*" Sonya began again. Tell me . . .

"*Mozda kasnije,*" he said in Bosnian. "Maybe later, after I teach you how to ski. Would you like that?"

"Hush!" Sonya put her forefinger on her lips, and said in English, while blushing, "Somebody might hear you!"

As he stared at her red face uncomprehendingly, she whispered in Bosnian, apparently thinking that he was not capable of understanding other languages. "Keep quiet, people will hear you."

"So? That's what speech is for!" he said.

She turned her head away and bit her lips.

So that's it. She's ashamed of me. She's afraid of being identified as Bosnian. I'm a Bosnian peasant, and she's a Swiss lady. My child, my best friend, is a foreigner to me.

He was crushed.

They walked from the bus stop, past Fraumuensterkirche, on the way to the violin shop where he'd buy her a 2,000-franc violin. He pointed to the church with a motion of his head, as though he'd lost the gift of speech for good. He'd heard about Chagall's stained glass but hadn't seen it yet. She followed him, her gaze darting around, as though someone might see them. The sun's rays put blue, crimson, and gold flames into the glass. Beneath it all was a sheep, carrying the weight of the tall works, like a beast of burden, a donkey. Vadim stared at the lights, seeing the flaring pine flames he'd jumped through to get here.

When they walked out of the church, the sun glared at him from many cars, refracting into mirages of waterfalls. He decided not to buy a violin, to sacrifice for an imaginary family happiness comprised of fine artifacts so that his daughter would become more refined, foreign, and more ashamed of him. He'd buy a car, and, tomorrow, they'd all pack up and leave, go back to Bosnia, war or no war, flames or no flames. They'd be one family, one people, surrounded by cats and pigeons—and he'd make hats again: hats and veils. Well, maybe they would not go back, but at least he would have a car, a giant veiled hat, where he could nest, like a rabbit in a circus magician's sleeve.

Raw Paper

In a glass-door cupboard there are many big books in unpointed Hebrew—a friend of mine, a polyglot Hungarian Jew, archaeologist and chain-smoker, rented me his apartment in Budapest for the summer of '84—and I like touching them and smelling them because they are old. I like the darkened, fragile paper that I'm afraid to turn over because it might crumble. I also like new paper that still smells of wood, chain saws, and glue: I buy paper for the pleasure of sniffing it, from a nearby store, where it's made, raw, in large sheets, by two overweight red-faced men in blue work-clothes and dusty berets too small for their round heads. Anyway, I don't have much use for the paper—or for myself, for that matter. I mostly sleep, read, eat, sleep—closed in like that I could be anywhere, why Budapest? Still, I enjoy being idle here because I've heard that in Hungary if you are idle for more than three months, without seeking employment, you are liable to be imprisoned for "penal idleness."

I listen to an old varnished radio; a yellow cloth trembles over its speaker. There are too many operas for my taste, and too much talk, some inflected in a mannered way so I can tell they're reciting stories and poetry. I dislike the opera because of my unfair associations: colossal people with protruding bellies emit rapist screams, cultivatedly, at the helpless, well-dressed, stiff audience. I listen even to the opera in the wee hours, when Bach has vanished, when the Hungarian rock operas, imitations of *Hair* and *Jesus Christ Superstar*, are done too, and I fall asleep with the voluminous controlled screams. I fall awake to the high pitches. I waver between sleeping and snoring, feeling impotence and misery for not working, for not being a dignified human being, for not having the power to sing, for not playing music, and for suffering as it gets stuck into my ears, into the cochleae, increasing the pressure there and pushing it into my sleepless and wakeless headache.

This was my idea of liberty. I used to dream of getting to a place where I know no one, where I understand no one, where no one understands me, where I have no identity, where I don't have to be identified in any way, where I am not in files and dossiers, monitored by the ID tyrannies. I hate passports, driver's licenses, birth certificates, death certificates; yet my nightmare is to lose all of those, except the death certificate, which I still don't have. But maybe my birth certificate is enough—it proclaims the certainty that I will die; so really, I can economize by having the B.C. (birth certificate).

Now, in a dream, when a deep authoritative voice from the tremorous radio shakes me up, my first fear is, Where is my passport?

I roll out of bed, my hip crunching against the bed frame, barefoot, onto the dusty and oily floor, turn on the lights, and go to the top of the cupboard where I usually keep my wallet and my passport. Not there. Calmly, I look into one drawer, where I keep my important letters, then into another. I go through all the drawers, faster and faster. Nothing yet. I go to the bookshelf with the wind-up telephone. Not there. I flip my clothes on the floor over and over again, turn the pockets inside out. Below the bed. I walk along the long corridor into the kitchen. Among my dirty dishes, in the cupboard with crusts of bread, among the cups clinging against each other. I do not know whether to be terrified or thoughtful. I decide of course to become thoughtful, and become terrified instead. Wow! I am behind the Iron Curtain and I have no passport. How will I get out? How will I get into the United States? I have no papers whatsoever to prove who I am!

I walk to the bathroom, tripping over bricks and lead pipes. The bathroom is out of order; there is no running water; the floor is caved in here and there. The water pipes used to leak into the workshop below where plastic Marys and Jesuses are mass produced. The water dripped through the floor, making brown patterns on the yellow ceiling where you could, without wearing out your imagination, make out villainous faces, elephants, humans, and the Devil himself. First the wife of the owner of the shop came to protest when I didn't yet know what was going on, and I understood nothing of her shrill Hungarian. I thought she wanted me to leave the country, which she probably did. Then her husband would come to the apartment door before I woke up, banging. After him a state commission, three men and one woman (I understood no Hungarian and I believe they were a state commission because they were all dressed alike and they took notes), examined the bathroom, taking keen interest especially in the toilet that didn't flush. They shouted at me in Hungarian and I defended myself in the most militaristic language I could come up with, German, but as German is much better for offending than defending, they shouted at me even more; the neighbors peeped through the door, children stuck their tongues out at me.

The commissioners walked into the living room and stared at the dozen backpacks lined up against a bed. Before renting to me, my landlord had rented the apartment to an East German woman who had left the address with dozens of her compatriots, who came looking for her, usually around two in the morning, shyly knocking. If I didn't let them sleep in the apartment, since they had been allowed to take only a miserably small sum of money out of their country—which they needed for Zappa records—

they went over to the train station and slept on cement floors, huddled up as if in a mass grave, so that it was hard to walk through to the ticket counters without stepping on somebody's loose fingers or knees. The East German young men in the apartment used to roll cigarettes while their female compatriots walked topless to and from the bathroom; at night people gathered on the opposite side of the street to stare into the apartment. The Germans often lined up outside the bathroom; sometimes there were two or three girls in it at the same time, giggling merrily, while others were begging to enter the bastion of cleanliness. After being besieged for so long, no wonder the bastion gave in.

The commissioners, realizing there were East Germans there, threw up their arms in despair. I tried speaking Russian, thinking it an excellent defensive language, but I spoke so badly and timidly that they didn't understand me, or more likely, didn't care to understand me; and the Russian put them into an even worse mood. They shut off my water completely.

Today the neighbor probably won't bang because there hasn't been any water running in a week. I cannot flush the toilet. Yesterday my landlord—I used to call him my friend but as soon as I pay him rent and he checks on me, he's just a landlord—brought along the after-hours repairmen, but the repairmen claimed they could not find a replacement pipe anywhere in the town. Since the bathroom doesn't work, the invaders of the pale countenance have given up staying at my place. I go to restaurants not because I am hungry but to use the toilet.

I look for my passport in the bathroom, overturning the bricks. What would I do with it here, read it? Perhaps the bearded German mathematician stole my passport; he said he planned to leave for the West. Could he have taken it? On the black market a passport fetches more than four thousand dollars. But he left a week ago, and I had the passport yesterday, I had changed money.

I crawl from one corner of the apartment to another, open books, turn over my shoes. I look through all my pockets, below the beds again, with a sinking feeling of futility because I have done it all once or twice before. I look into the clefts between the mattress and the bed frames, although I have done that too. I open the oak-and-glass doors of the two long bookshelves, look between the books, thinking that perhaps in my absentmindedness I stored my documents in an inconspicuous place so that if someone should break into the apartment, he would not be able to steal my documents. Now I am prey to my own precautions. I close the bookshelves and wonder, Do I know my passport number? I had thought I did, but now I cannot recall it. Parallel with my fear of losing my ID papers is my fear that I've lost my memory, my real identity. So I sit and write down all the phone numbers I know by heart and my social security number. Big deal, social security number; you can make up any number; it makes no difference. Relax, at least you remember something, you haven't completely lost your mind. Eat! But I am not hungry. I look for money in my wallet and find about $500. It probably wasn't a burglar. On $500 I could live for three more months in Hungary, and what then? What time is it? I don't have a watch, but whenever someone had told me what time it was, I had cut a line between the sunlight and the shadow in the long window frame; the walls are nearly a yard thick and the window frames have enough space to register the light angles. The border between sunlight and shadow tells me it's two o'clock in the afternoon. I fry eggs, oil splattering and scorching my skin.

What can happen? I haven't committed any crime. I couldn't leave Hungary without a thorough investigation. I could call up the American consulate and let them secure a copy of my Green Card. But would they do that without my having any documents? I would have to have a witness . . . I soaked the dry bread in the yolk and chewed it.

On the other hand, if I went to the Yugoslav consulate to get a copy of my Yugoslav passport, I would have to go back to Yugoslavia, into the army. And who knows where that could all lead—I would lose my American Green Card, I would end up being a high-school teacher, and there goes my American dream; I might even fight in a stupid war, maybe against Bulgaria, Albania, maybe against students and peasants. But why am I not willing to let go of the American "opportunity?" I pace around the room, smoke cigarettes, one after another, and sometimes two at the same time, choking my lungs in the clouds of burned brown leaves, leaves of autumn, of fall, of my fall. Oh, no, not the fall of my dream. My stomach moans. Why is it complaining? I keep a pack of cigarettes on hand for my visitors; I like seeing people smoke, cough, hold up their cigarettes between their thumbs and forefingers or forefingers and middle fingers, light them, crush them in ashtrays—so much activity without cause, yet with consequence.

I remember an old Gypsy in my hometown who used to smoke through his ears and through his nostrils, four cigarettes stuck into him at the same time, smoking them all to impress us kids. I try to imitate him, and my sinuses are scorched, my eyes sting.

But what am I doing? I have lost my ID papers. Now I look below the carpet, through the drawers, even into the drawer that I know was completely empty twenty minutes ago, as if some miracle could have taken place in the meantime. God knows, and ophthalmologists also, that I am nearsighted. (Actually, I am not; a Texan eye doctor, when I wanted a new prescription because I had lost a pair of glasses, shrieked out at me: "Get out a here, you don't need the damn crutches!" Since then I can see well.) I look into the bookshelves, boring with my fingers among books although I had already done it—or what incongruous tense to use—I had had already done it. I have had—why not past-past perfect?—Why isn't there such a tense? I *had* had looked and I have it not.

Where the hell have the papers and the plastic cards disappeared to? I try to reconstruct what I had been doing in these last days. Did I have them in my wallet when I went swimming—that is, hanging around the pool? Didn't I leave my things at the front desk? Could the wet cashier have stolen my passport and my driver's license? No, coming back from the pool, I had had my plastic cards. When I had talked to a swimmer on the bus who didn't believe I was from the United States, I had showed her my Connecticut driver's license, and she had said it must be fake. Why? I had asked. Because you wear Hungarian shoes, she had said, pointing at my rubber-soled shoes, and laughed, expecting me to go as red as the crimson of the shoes. True, I had said, the shoes are Hungarian; I bought them because they were cheap. But I am not Hungarian. No, she had laughed. You are a Hungarian, a tricky one. She had spoken in Hungarian then, I had answered in English, and she had said, You are pretty good at it but not good enough. I study English and I can tell you have a Hungarian accent. So, I did have the driver's license then, and the passport? I think so—yes: I went to change money at the train station, was stuck in a long line of sparklingly dark-eyed Bulgarian high-school kids on a graduation trip, who gazed at the dark crimson of my passport and asked me if they could finger through it, admiring the stamps. They gave it back to me. And later? I took a walk around Budapest with an old hyper-alert tour guide, who showed me how he made money from Western tourists; he approached whoever looked confused and asked them to ask him for directions. Near the Hotel Ungaria, he had disappeared into the bathroom, and ten minutes later he wasn't back and I left. Did he steal my wallet? I wasn't sure I had had it on me. Was he ever very close to me physically? He had tapped me on the shoulder now and then, but my wallet had not been on my shoulder. All right, from the beginning. He said to me, You buy me a beer, and I'll give you an education. I bought him a beer, and he told me the etymology of *talent* from the Greek word *talanton*—that it meant *trade* and *languages* (I checked it later in the dictionary; he was wrong—*talanton* in Greek meant *balance;* in M. Italian, *talantum* meant *inclination of mind;* in Old French, *talent* meant *lust, desire,* that is, in a way, a loss of balance, the original meaning). I protested that I didn't want to be entertained like a dumb tourist in need of passing time, that he could get lost or have another beer for free, no *talanton.* He said, I'll teach you more. We walked out into the streets, and he said, Imagine, in '56, Russian tanks everywhere in the avenue and the square, the asphalt cracks, the bullets whistle and cry . . . I was there. Another story for the foreigners, I guess. He asked me how old I was, and told me to get married at once because after twenty-six it soon might be too late, and I would end up as miserable as he with nobody to care for him, with everybody wanting to get rid of his company just as I was wishing to get rid of it. If you live alone for a long time, you become a comedian and a whore, like me. Don't become like me! When he said that he grabbed my hand tightly. Well, I don't think he could have pick-pocketed me then. I remember though that night my pockets had bulged with cheap red-and-blue Hungarian money and other papers. I did have a hole in my pocket; now and then I felt my small address book sliding down my leg. The passport was much larger and wouldn't slide; and if it had, I would have surely felt it.

How about the neighbor's kid, the little plump Gypsy girl of about ten? She always walks in uninvited when it's hot and I leave the apartment door open for the air. She follows me around, looks at what I have bought, at the mess in my kitchen, my clothes, and my orange electric typewriter. She pokes the keys with her forefinger, and giggles when a letter bounces onto the paper, and runs away as though I might slap her. Then she comes back and presses several keys until they get stuck together, and she gets braver, lifts up the telephone receiver and wants to dial a number. Then her mother walks in, looks at me angrily, shouts at me something in Hungarian, and pulls her daughter by the ear out of the apartment. Later I feel sorry for the kid and give her stamps from the letters I receive from abroad. Next day she shows me a stamp and points to her palm to give her more; I tell her I have no mail, no stamps. She speaks Hungarian loudly and slowly as though I should now understand it. Then she runs in, overturns a pile of papers, and runs out. The wind from the draft blows the papers away. Could the wind have sucked the passport out into the crowded streets? No, the passport was too heavy for that. Could she have taken my passport, because it has good seals? Stamps? I doubt it.

I take out a bottle of vodka from the fridge, pertzovka, pepper vodka. I've lost liberty, I've lost the freedom to cross the borders. But I can still breathe the air; I can eat bread and eggs, and drink water. Well, for how long? I pace around the apartment and stare through the kitchen door into the small yard, walled on the northern side by a dilapidated synagogue, with blue Stars of David in top windows, about five or six of them, all intact, although the windows below them are broken and cobwebbed. I've often peeped in through the synagogue windows, glimpsing broken benches and scrolls scattered in the dark, but the plump Gypsy girl shouts at me and bars the way. I know she is a Gypsy because my landlord has told me so. Why does she feel it's her place? She's been growing around it, playing, and it's her secret playground.

I stare from the second floor through the metal parapet at the square yard below, where a fifteen- or sixteen-year-old boy with wetly combed hair is teaching the plump girl and another one how to dance. He is very professional about it, and he can dance skillfully. He sings, showing the rhythm, and his pupils react to it, dancing more broadly and continuously. His black shoes are loud on the cobbles.

The Gypsy woman who pulls her daughter's ears comes out on the terrace; next to my apartment the terrace covers two sides, mine, the west, and hers, the south, and the east is a blank whitewashed brick wall, the side of the building where the raw paper is made. The woman often sweeps the terrace, several times a day. If I had been brainwashed in Yugoslavia to think that Gypsies were dirty people, I was now certainly washed with the contrary belief. Whenever I pass beneath the terrace, she sweeps the dirty water from the terrace floor over me, and her kid giggles.

I walk to the southern end of the apartment, to my sundial window. It's about 4:30. The sunlit dust outlines the straight lines of sunlight and darkness, making three or four dimensions. I lean out the window and stare at a large crowd on the opposite side of the street in the shade of an old bullet-riddled sweater factory, from which the monotonous noise of textile machines comes; through the windows of the factory basement, I glimpse rows of women, no men, like galley slaves, sitting, with scarves on their heads, alongside long machines. Outside, on the broad pavement, there is a lively black-market trade. A large gathering of people pace, smoke cigarettes, crush cigarette butts on the pavement by turning their shoes left and right, and bargain and barter. Sweaters, digital watches, soccer balls of leather, panties, jeans, sunglasses, calculators, cassettes, hard-currency banknotes, and soft-currency banknotes, quickly change hands, amid loud exclamations, laughter, theatrical sorrow, whistles, and sneezing. At each street corner, there is a guard who whistles whenever the cops are near. On one corner, a man in a leather jacket whistles. The crowd hushes, and people walk like passersby. A man with a boy continues to examine a sweater, measuring it against the boy's chest. The man has large cotton balls in his ears, to guard against wind or an ear infection? Two cops leap out of a small blue-and-white *Lada* and grab the man by his elbows. He tears away and gesticulates. One cop examines the sweater, the other one takes out a notebook, brings his pencil tip to it, writes nothing, puts the notebook back in the square leather bag on his belt. The people are coming back, forming a circle, and murmuring. The cops grab the man by one hand and drag him to the car. The boy holds his father by the other hand and cries loudly, tears covering his face, snot hanging over his lips. The man cries and shouts, tears run down his face too; he swings his head toward the boy. I don't understand Hungarian, but he must be saying, I have to take care of my boy, I don't have a job, Fall is coming, He has no sweater, Don't take me to jail, He doesn't know his way home! The cops suddenly let the man go. They scurry into the car, their heads bent; the crowd boos them. The man kisses his boy, wipes his nose with a white handkerchief, and buys the sweater, probably at a very good price. People pat the boy on the head as he passes, slap the man on the shoulders.

I take a nap, the noises from the black-marketplace—my landlord has told me the local name for the marketplace is *Chicago*—make me dream that I sleep in the street and that the police come to interrogate me. An electric trolley accelerates, and in the dusk smoky electricity sparks from the wire nets above the streets. The trolley squeaks as it turns into the next street toward Keleti PU, the large train station of baroque appearance, in Hapsburg imperial yellow-orange color.

I wake up in the dark and wish to jot down the scene of the father and the son, having forgotten about my passport, and as I draw out one large sheet of paper with jagged edges from the thick pile of raw paper, my passport slides out, onto the oily maple floor.

JOSIP NOVAKOVICH moved from Croatia to the United States at the age of twenty. Novakovich has received numerous awards for his work, notably a fellowship from the National Endowment for the Arts, an Ingram Merrill award, a Vogelstein fellowship, and the Cohen/Ploughshares Award. His prose has appeared in the *New York Times Magazine*, *The Pushcart Prize XV* and *XIX*, *Paris Review*, *Antaeus*, the *Threepenny Review*, and elsewhere. He teaches writing at the University of Cincinnati.

This book was designed by Ann Artz.
It is set in Bembo type by Stanton Publication Services
and manufactured by Quebecor Printing-Fairfield
on acid-free paper.